NANCY DREW

girl detective

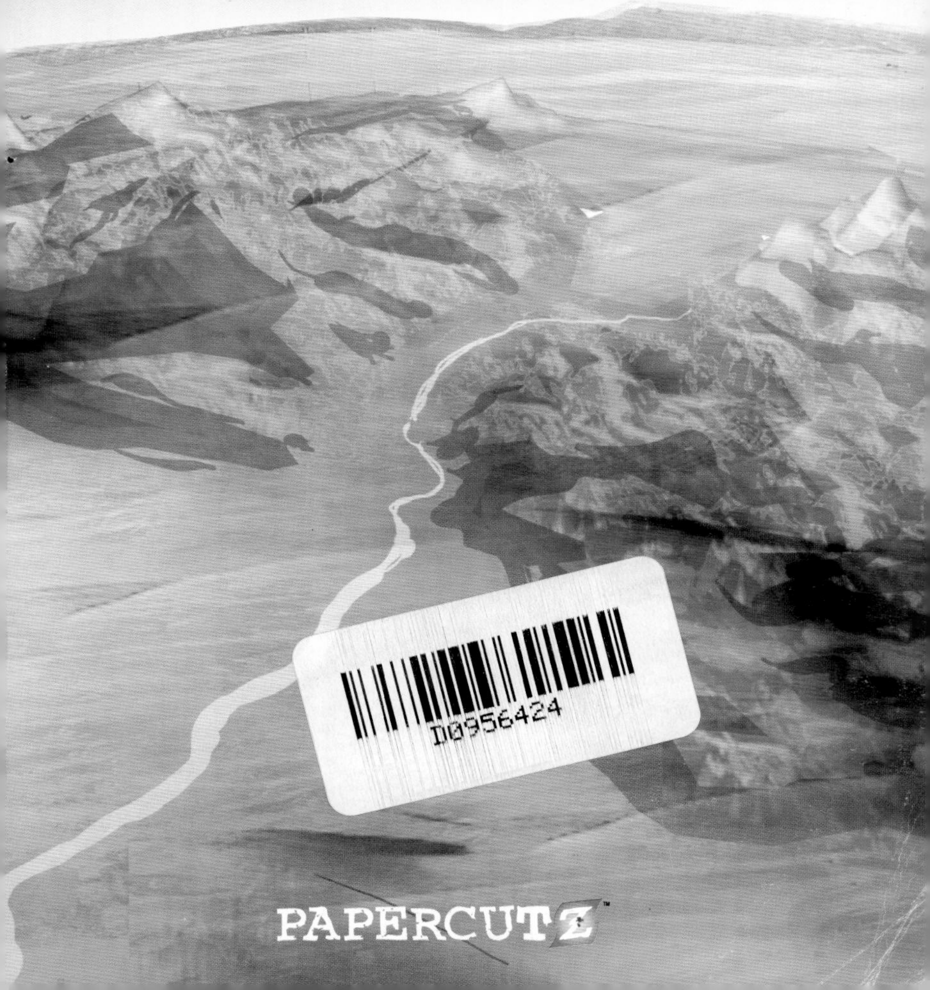

PAPERCUTZ

NANCY
DREW
girl detective ®

#11

Monkey Wrench Blues

STEFAN PETRUCHA & SARAH KINNEY • Writers
SHO MURASE • Artist
with 3D CG elements and color by CARLOS JOSE GUZMAN
Based on the series by
CAROLYN KEENE

PAPERCUTZ ™
New York

Monkey Wrench Blues
STEFAN PETRUCHA & SARAH KINNEY – Writers
SHO MURASE – Artist
with 3D CG elements and color by CARLOS JOSE GUZMAN
BRYAN SENKA – Letterer
JIM SALICRUP
Editor-in-Chief

ISBN 13: 978-1-59707-076-8 paperback edition
ISBN 10: 1-59707-076-9 paperback edition
ISBN 13: 978-1-59707-077-5 hardcover edition
ISBN 10: 1-59707-077-7 hardcover edition

Printed in China.
Distributed by Macmillan.

10 9 8 7 6 5 4 3 2

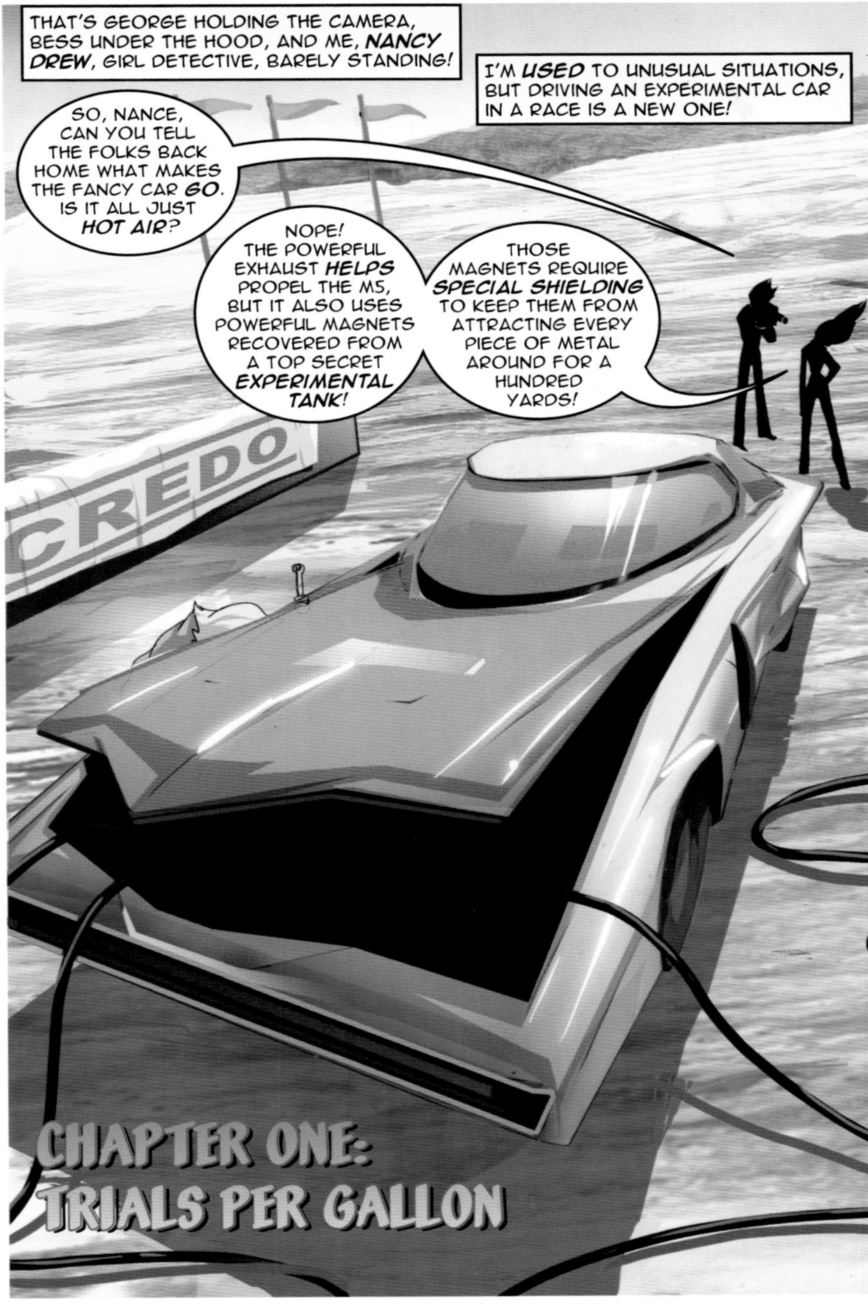
THAT'S GEORGE HOLDING THE CAMERA, BESS UNDER THE HOOD, AND ME, NANCY DREW, GIRL DETECTIVE, BARELY STANDING!
I'M USED TO UNUSUAL SITUATIONS, BUT DRIVING AN EXPERIMENTAL CAR IN A RACE IS A NEW ONE!
SO, NANCE, CAN YOU TELL THE FOLKS BACK HOME WHAT MAKES THE FANCY CAR GO. IS IT ALL JUST HOT AIR?
NOPE! THE POWERFUL EXHAUST HELPS PROPEL THE M5, BUT IT ALSO USES POWERFUL MAGNETS RECOVERED FROM A TOP SECRET EXPERIMENTAL TANK!
THOSE MAGNETS REQUIRE SPECIAL SHIELDING TO KEEP THEM FROM ATTRACTING EVERY PIECE OF METAL AROUND FOR A HUNDRED YARDS!
CREDO
CHAPTER ONE: TRIALS PER GALLON

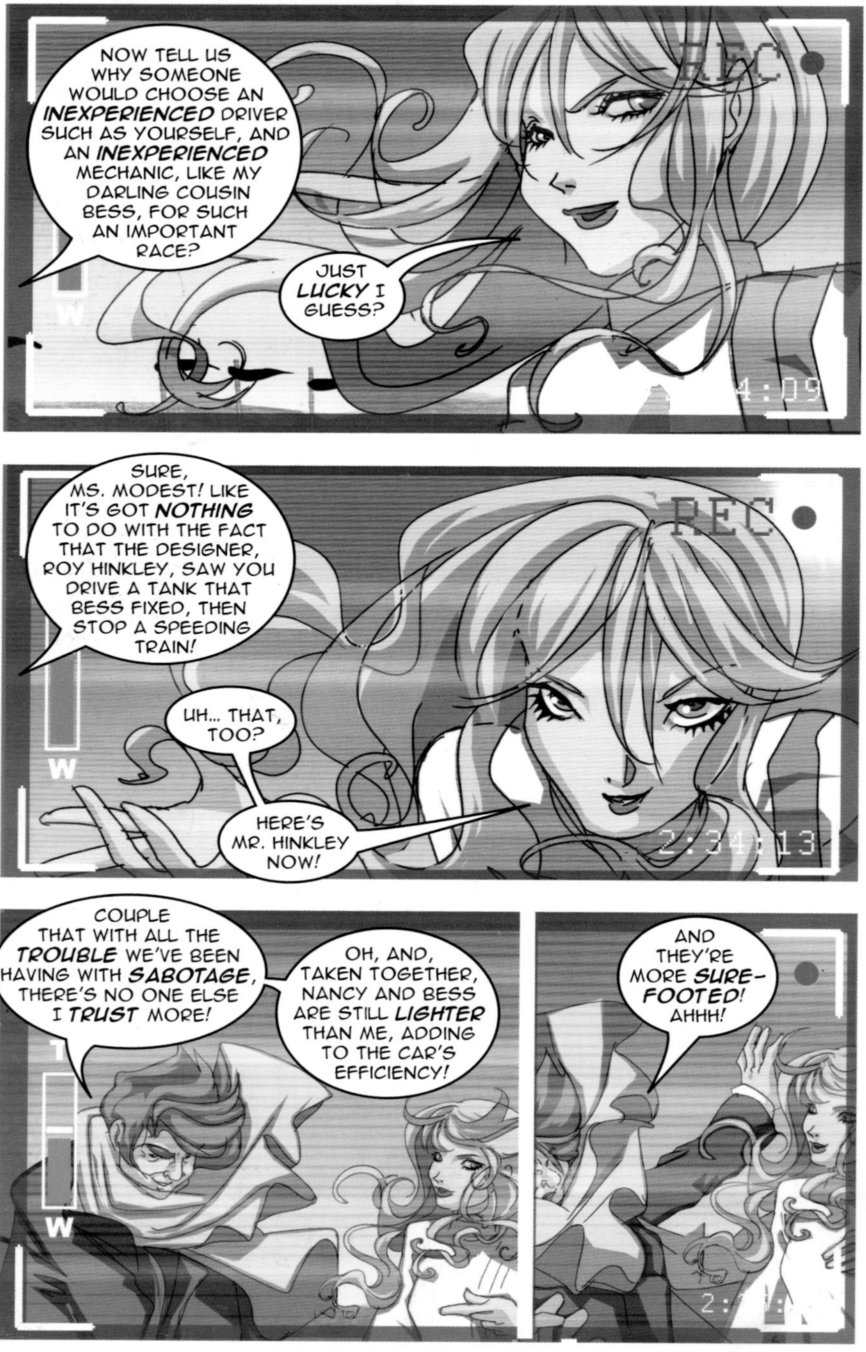
REC
NOW TELL US WHY SOMEONE WOULD CHOOSE AN INEXPERIENCED DRIVER SUCH AS YOURSELF, AND AN INEXPERIENCED MECHANIC, LIKE MY DARLING COUSIN BESS, FOR SUCH AN IMPORTANT RACE?
JUST LUCKY I GUESS?
REC
SURE, MS. MODEST! LIKE IT'S GOT NOTHING TO DO WITH THE FACT THAT THE DESIGNER, ROY HINKLEY, SAW YOU DRIVE A TANK THAT BESS FIXED, THEN STOP A SPEEDING TRAIN!
UH... THAT, TOO?
HERE'S MR. HINKLEY NOW!
COUPLE THAT WITH ALL THE TROUBLE WE'VE BEEN HAVING WITH SABOTAGE, THERE'S NO ONE ELSE I TRUST MORE!
OH, AND, TAKEN TOGETHER, NANCY AND BESS ARE STILL LIGHTER THAN ME, ADDING TO THE CAR'S EFFICIENCY!
AND THEY'RE MORE SURE-FOOTED! AHHH!

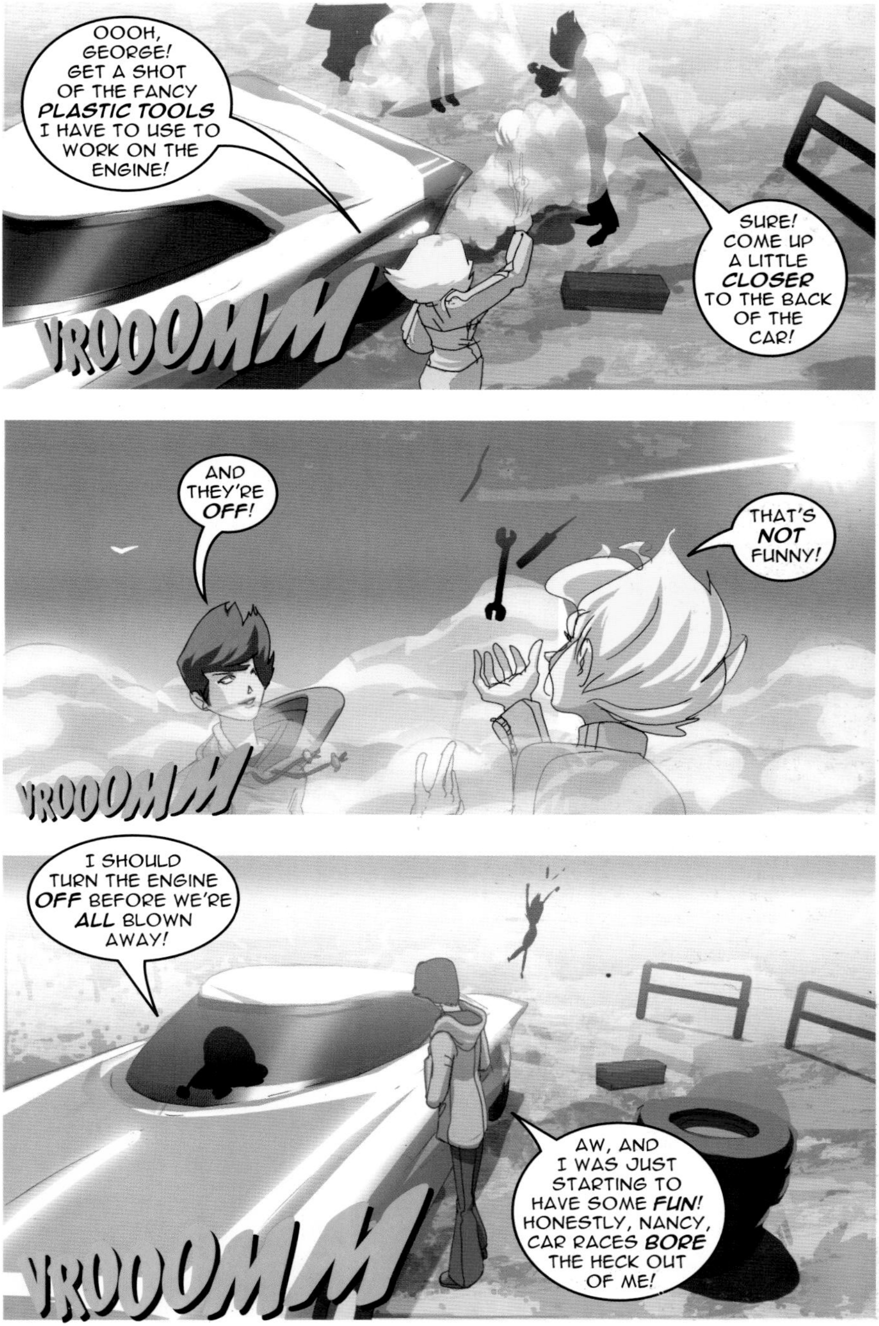
OOOH, GEORGE! GET A SHOT OF THE FANCY PLASTIC TOOLS I HAVE TO USE TO WORK ON THE ENGINE!
SURE! COME UP A LITTLE CLOSER TO THE BACK OF THE CAR!
VROOOMM
AND THEY'RE OFF!
THAT'S NOT FUNNY!
VROOOMM
I SHOULD TURN THE ENGINE OFF BEFORE WE'RE ALL BLOWN AWAY!
AW, AND I WAS JUST STARTING TO HAVE SOME FUN! HONESTLY, NANCY, CAR RACES BORE THE HECK OUT OF ME!
VROOOMM

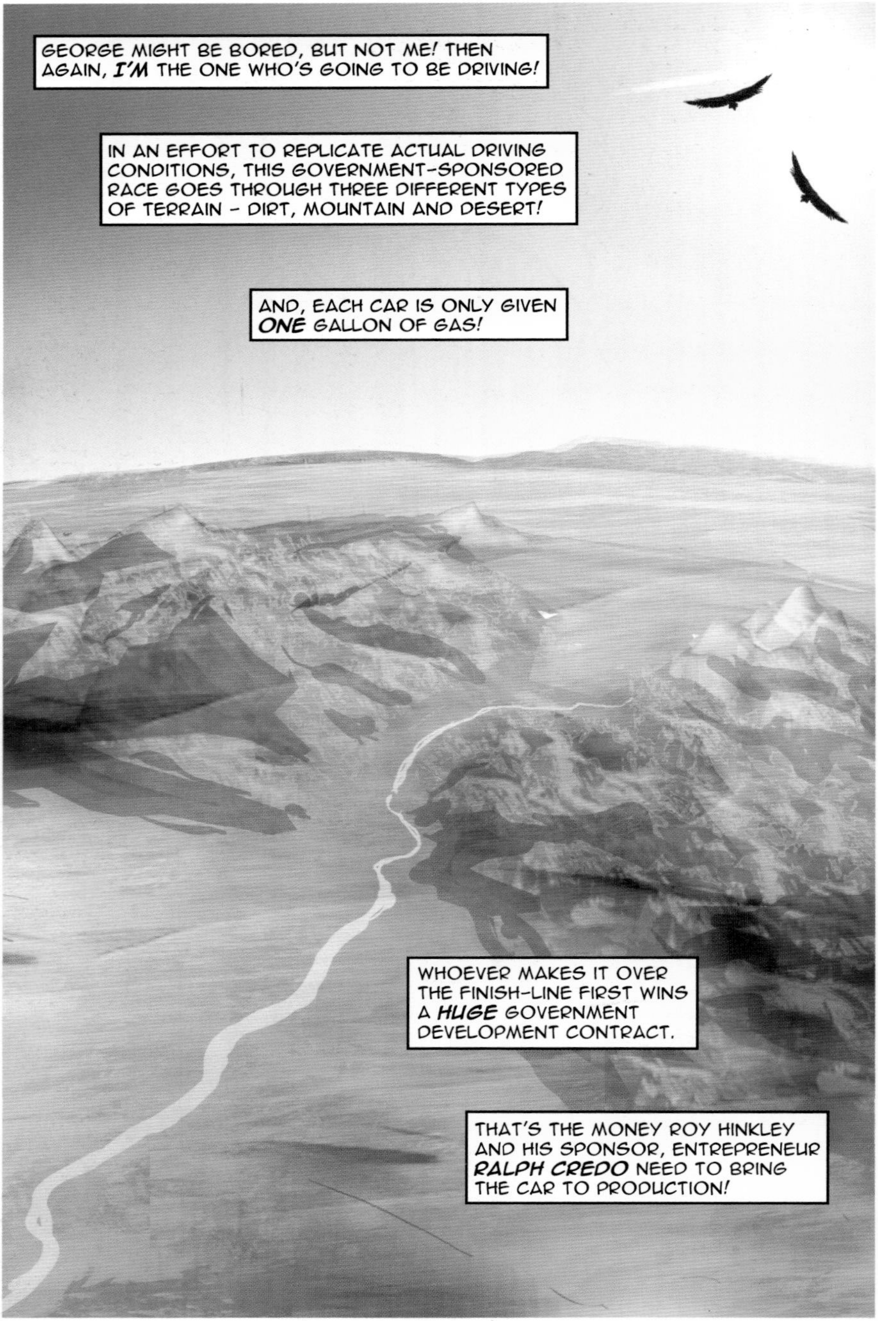
GEORGE MIGHT BE BORED, BUT NOT ME! THEN AGAIN, I'M THE ONE WHO'S GOING TO BE DRIVING!
IN AN EFFORT TO REPLICATE ACTUAL DRIVING CONDITIONS, THIS GOVERNMENT-SPONSORED RACE GOES THROUGH THREE DIFFERENT TYPES OF TERRAIN - DIRT, MOUNTAIN AND DESERT!
AND, EACH CAR IS ONLY GIVEN ONE GALLON OF GAS!
WHOEVER MAKES IT OVER THE FINISH-LINE FIRST WINS A HUGE GOVERNMENT DEVELOPMENT CONTRACT.
THAT'S THE MONEY ROY HINKLEY AND HIS SPONSOR, ENTREPRENEUR RALPH CREDO NEED TO BRING THE CAR TO PRODUCTION!

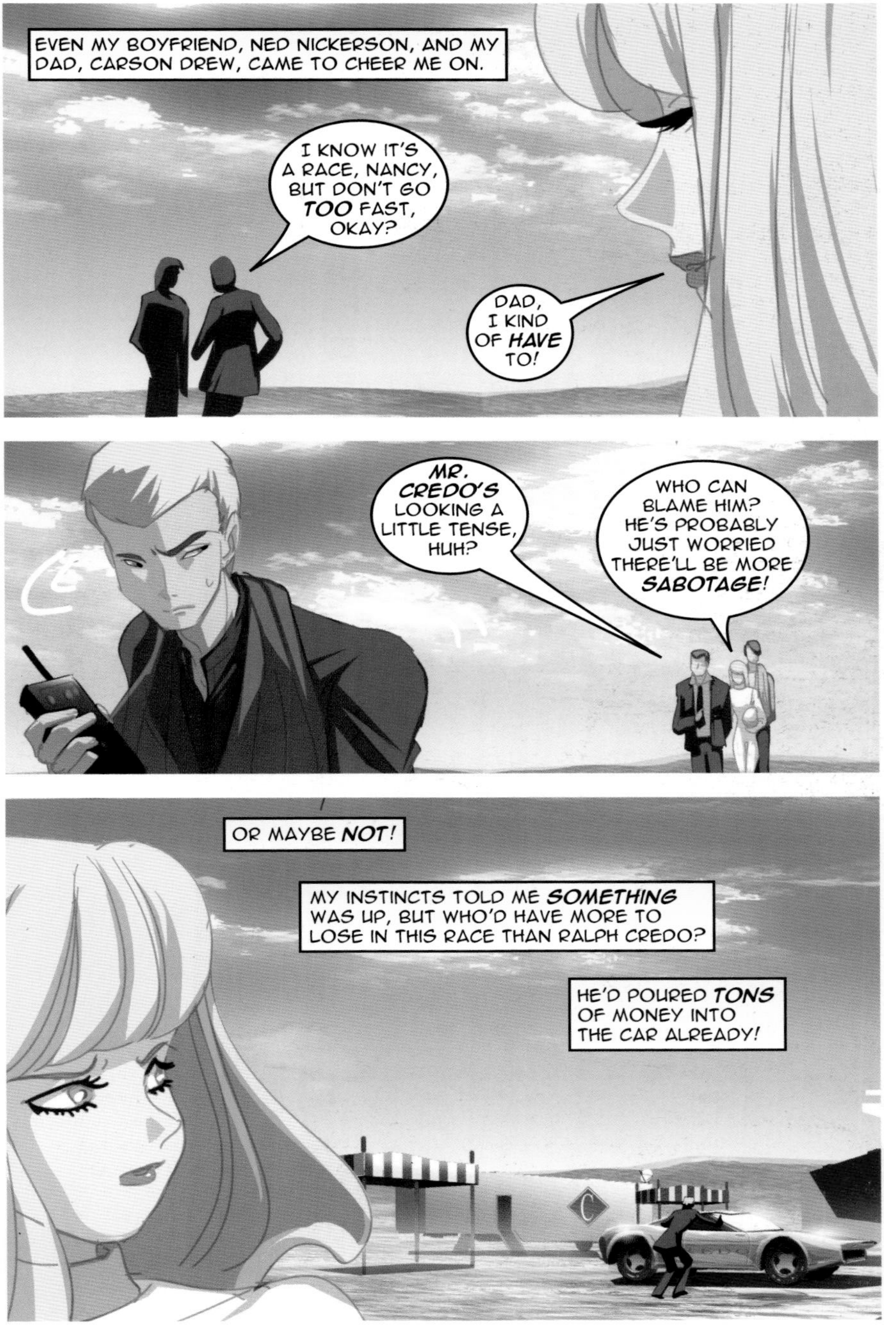
EVEN MY BOYFRIEND, NED NICKERSON, AND MY DAD, CARSON DREW, CAME TO CHEER ME ON.
I KNOW IT'S A RACE, NANCY, BUT DON'T GO **TOO** FAST, OKAY?
DAD, I KIND OF **HAVE** TO!
MR. CREDO'S LOOKING A LITTLE TENSE, HUH?
WHO CAN BLAME HIM? HE'S PROBABLY JUST WORRIED THERE'LL BE MORE **SABOTAGE**!
OR MAYBE **NOT**!
MY INSTINCTS TOLD ME **SOMETHING** WAS UP, BUT WHO'D HAVE MORE TO LOSE IN THIS RACE THAN RALPH CREDO?
HE'D POURED **TONS** OF MONEY INTO THE CAR ALREADY!

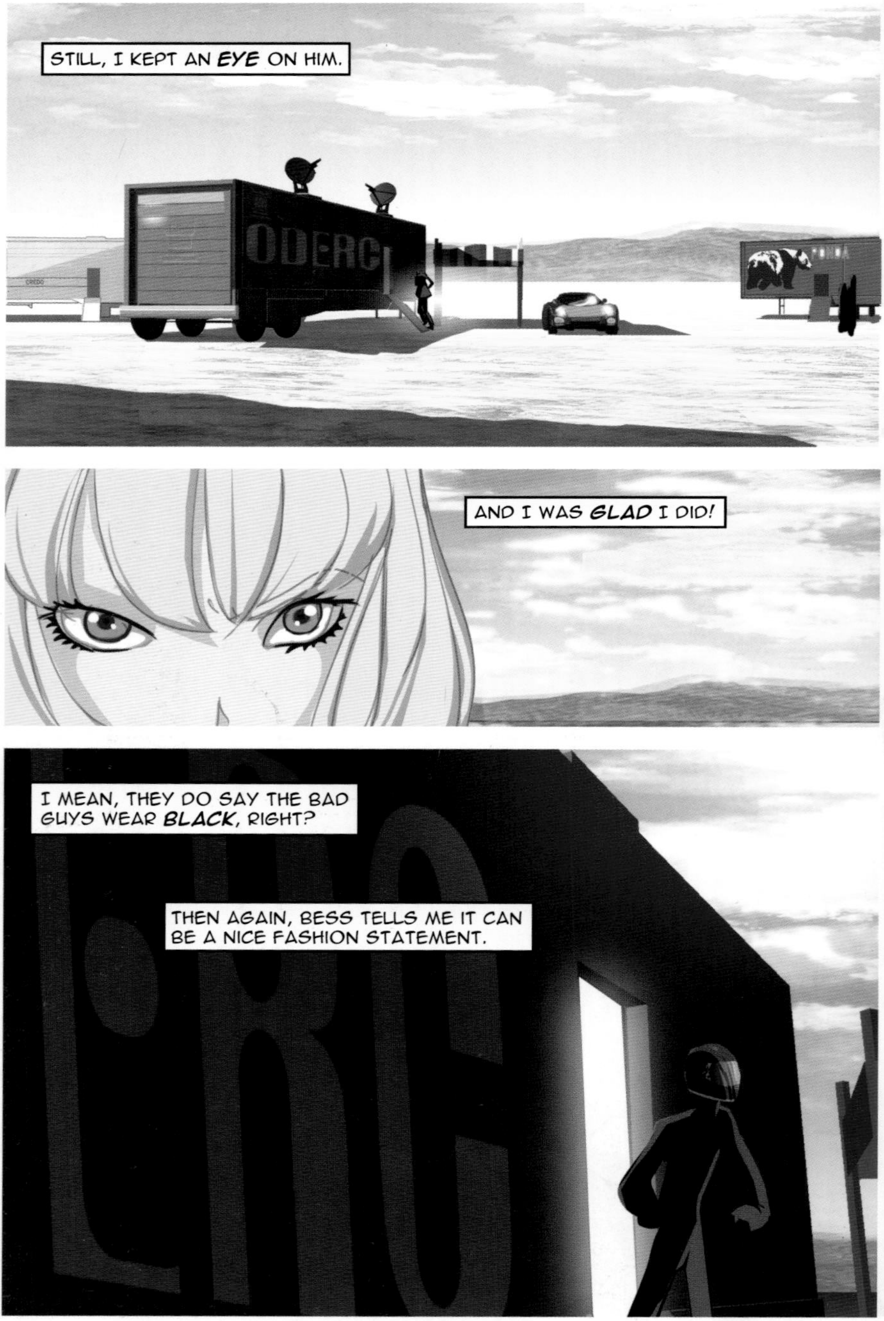
STILL, I KEPT AN ***EYE*** ON HIM.
ODERC
AND I WAS ***GLAD*** I DID!
I MEAN, THEY DO SAY THE BAD GUYS WEAR ***BLACK***, RIGHT?
THEN AGAIN, BESS TELLS ME IT CAN BE A NICE FASHION STATEMENT.

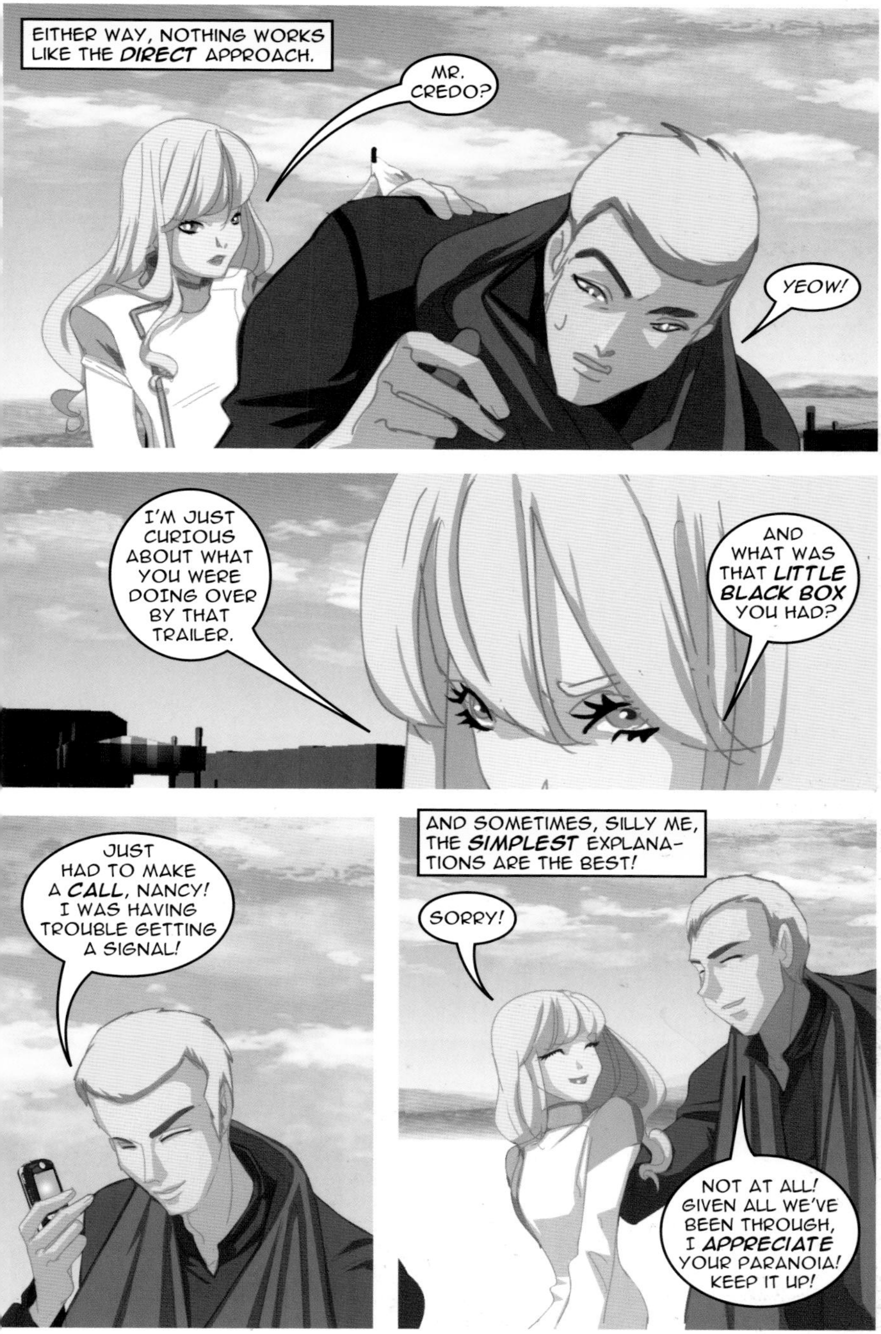

EITHER WAY, NOTHING WORKS LIKE THE *DIRECT* APPROACH.
MR. CREDO?
YEOW!
I'M JUST CURIOUS ABOUT WHAT YOU WERE DOING OVER BY THAT TRAILER.
AND WHAT WAS THAT *LITTLE BLACK BOX* YOU HAD?
JUST HAD TO MAKE A *CALL*, NANCY! I WAS HAVING TROUBLE GETTING A SIGNAL!
AND SOMETIMES, SILLY ME, THE *SIMPLEST* EXPLANATIONS ARE THE BEST!
SORRY!
NOT AT ALL! GIVEN ALL WE'VE BEEN THROUGH, I *APPRECIATE* YOUR PARANOIA! KEEP IT UP!

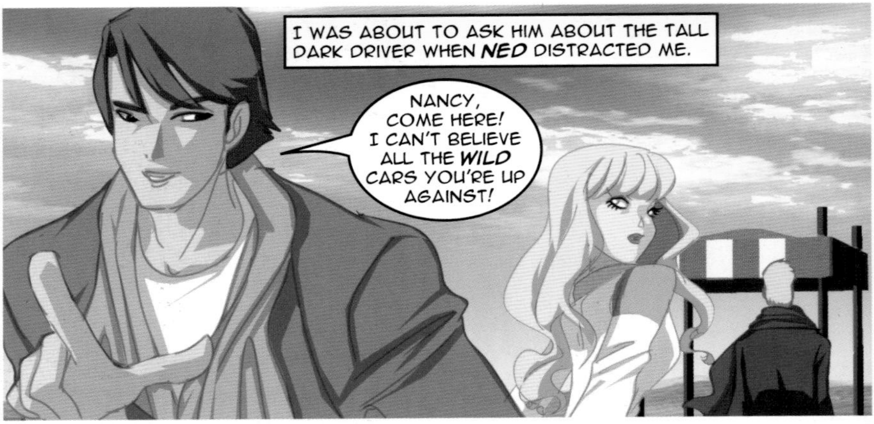
I WAS ABOUT TO ASK HIM ABOUT THE TALL DARK DRIVER WHEN NED DISTRACTED ME.
NANCY, COME HERE! I CAN'T BELIEVE ALL THE WILD CARS YOU'RE UP AGAINST!

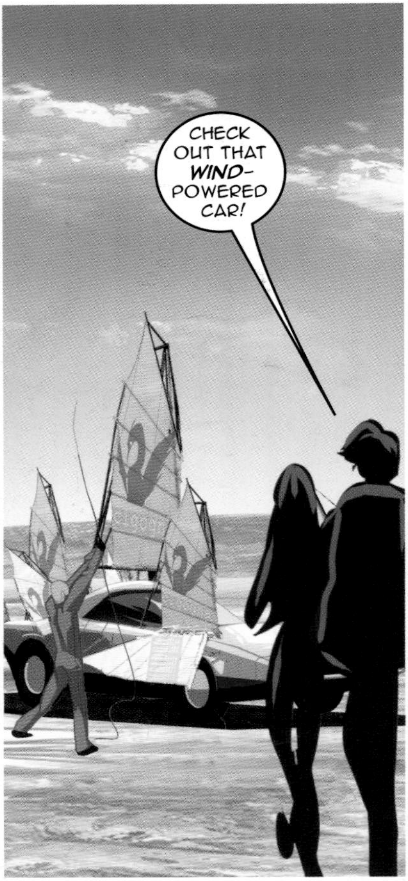
CHECK OUT THAT WIND-POWERED CAR!

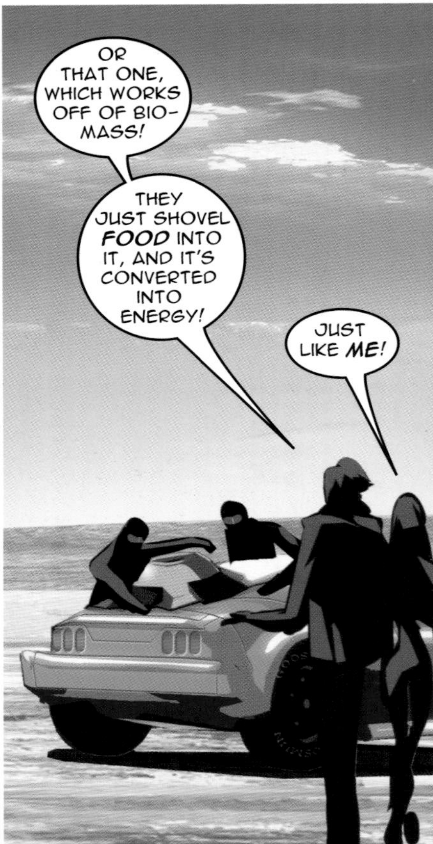
OR THAT ONE, WHICH WORKS OFF OF BIO-MASS!
THEY JUST SHOVEL FOOD INTO IT, AND IT'S CONVERTED INTO ENERGY!
JUST LIKE ME!

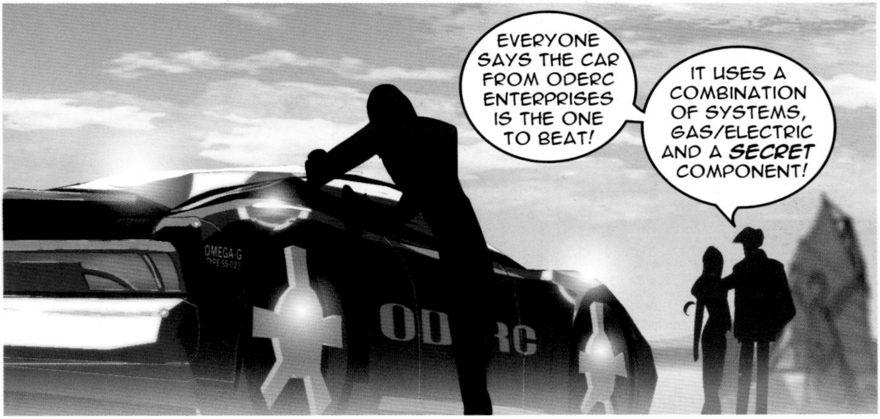
EVERYONE SAYS THE CAR FROM ODERC ENTERPRISES IS THE ONE TO BEAT!
IT USES A COMBINATION OF SYSTEMS, GAS/ELECTRIC AND A *SECRET* COMPONENT!
OMEGA-G

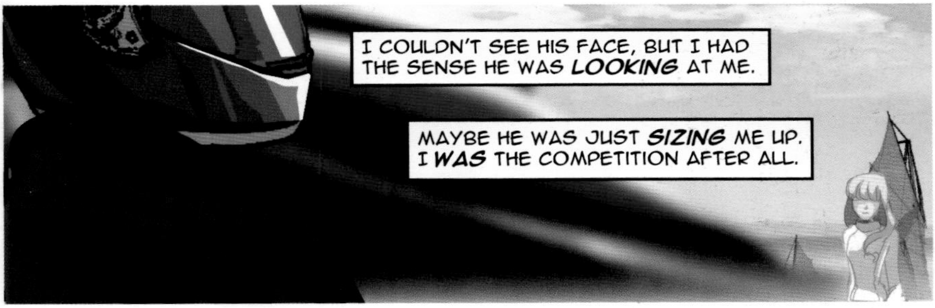
I COULDN'T SEE HIS FACE, BUT I HAD THE SENSE HE WAS *LOOKING* AT ME.
MAYBE HE WAS JUST *SIZING* ME UP. I *WAS* THE COMPETITION AFTER ALL.

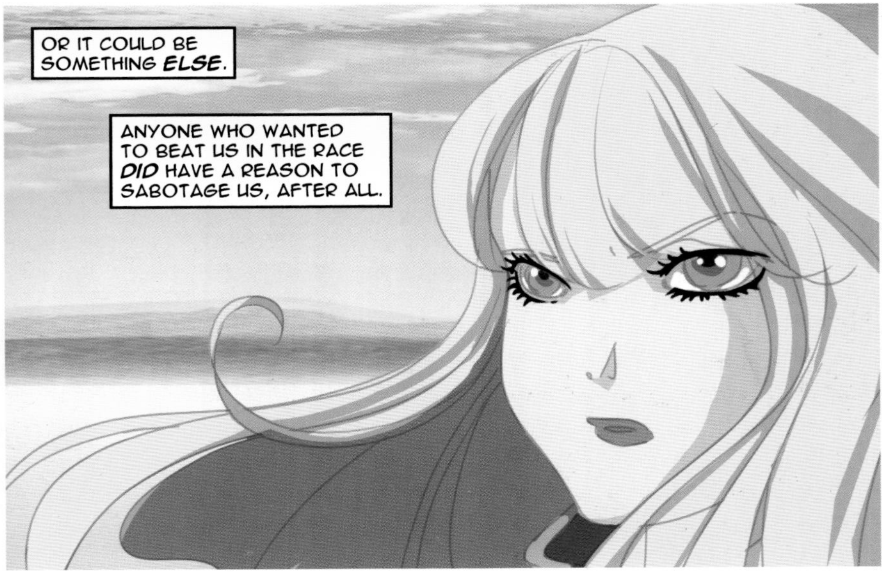
OR IT COULD BE SOMETHING *ELSE*.
ANYONE WHO WANTED TO BEAT US IN THE RACE *DID* HAVE A REASON TO SABOTAGE US, AFTER ALL.

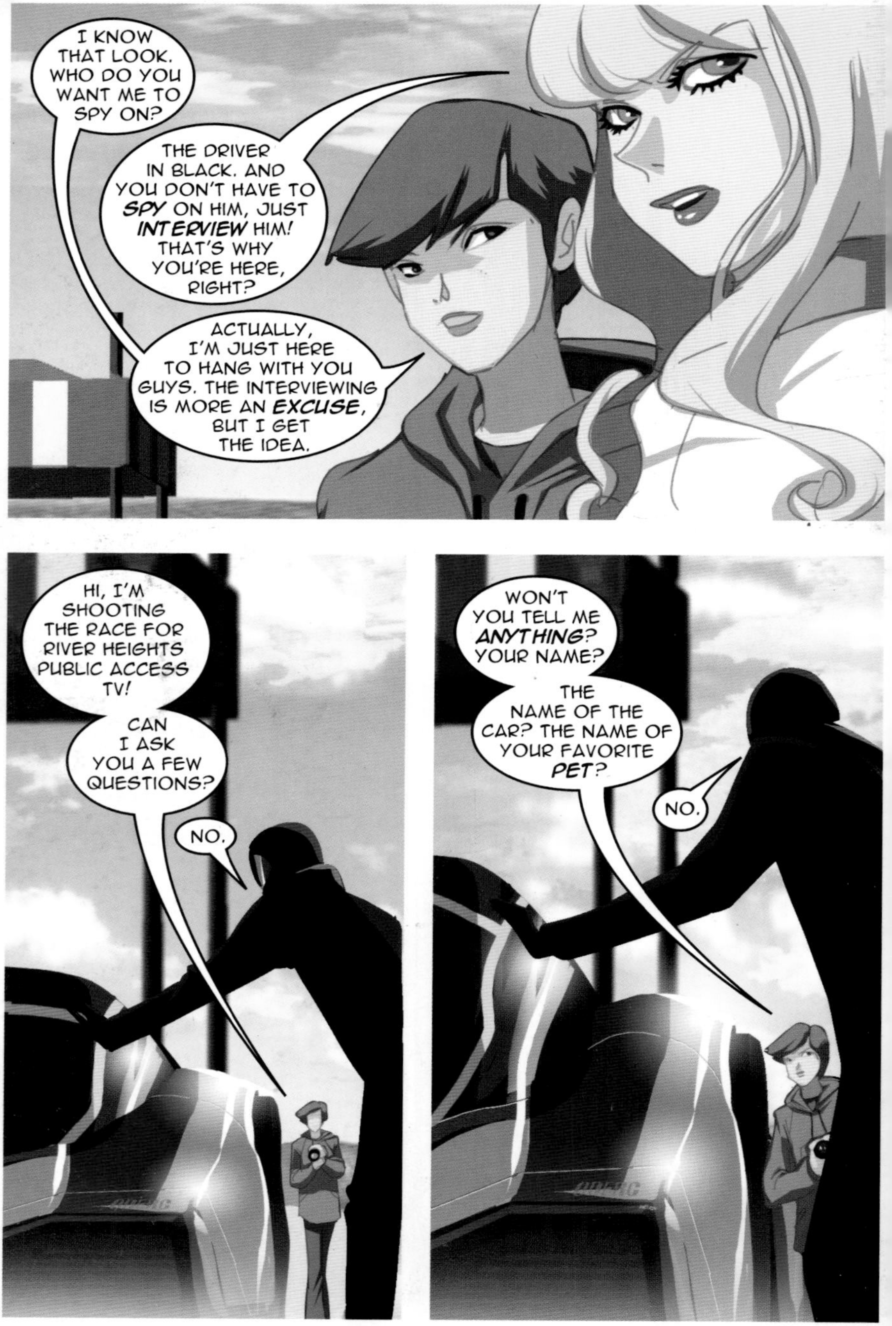
I KNOW THAT LOOK. WHO DO YOU WANT ME TO SPY ON?
THE DRIVER IN BLACK. AND YOU DON'T HAVE TO *SPY* ON HIM, JUST *INTERVIEW* HIM! THAT'S WHY YOU'RE HERE, RIGHT?
ACTUALLY, I'M JUST HERE TO HANG WITH YOU GUYS. THE INTERVIEWING IS MORE AN *EXCUSE*, BUT I GET THE IDEA.
HI, I'M SHOOTING THE RACE FOR RIVER HEIGHTS PUBLIC ACCESS TV!
CAN I ASK YOU A FEW QUESTIONS?
NO.
WON'T YOU TELL ME *ANYTHING*? YOUR NAME?
THE NAME OF THE CAR? THE NAME OF YOUR FAVORITE *PET*?
NO.

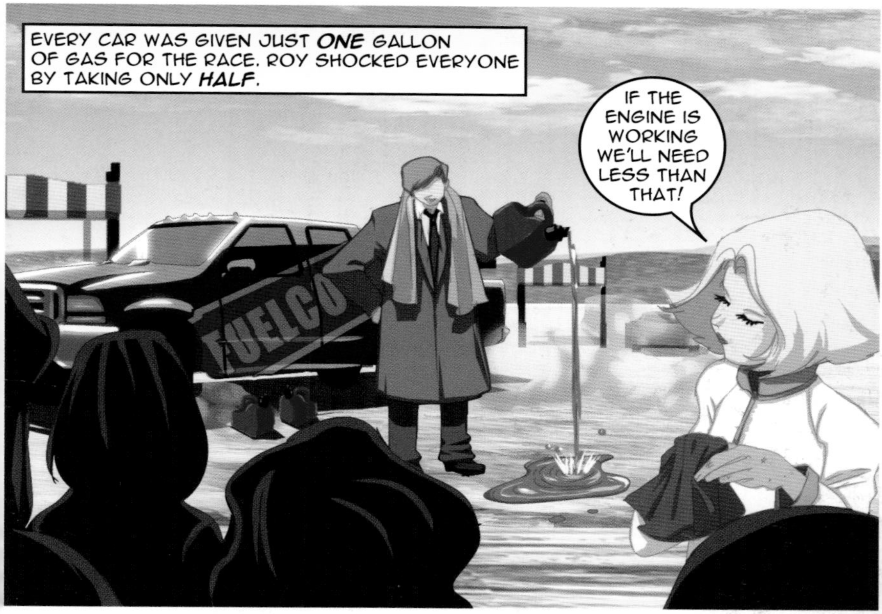
EVERY CAR WAS GIVEN JUST ONE GALLON OF GAS FOR THE RACE. ROY SHOCKED EVERYONE BY TAKING ONLY HALF.
IF THE ENGINE IS WORKING WE'LL NEED LESS THAN THAT!
FUELCO

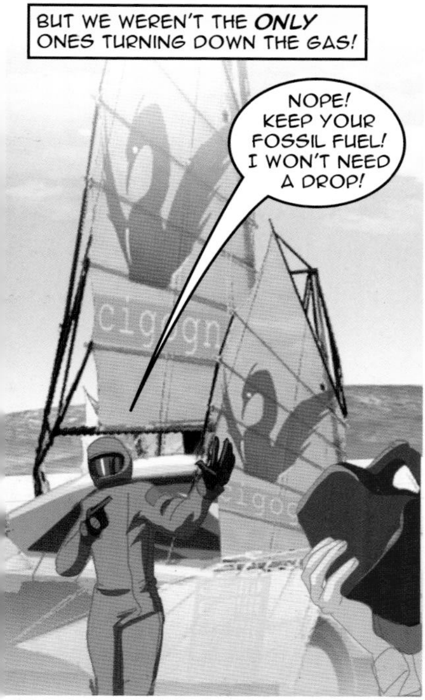
BUT WE WEREN'T THE ONLY ONES TURNING DOWN THE GAS!
NOPE! KEEP YOUR FOSSIL FUEL! I WON'T NEED A DROP!

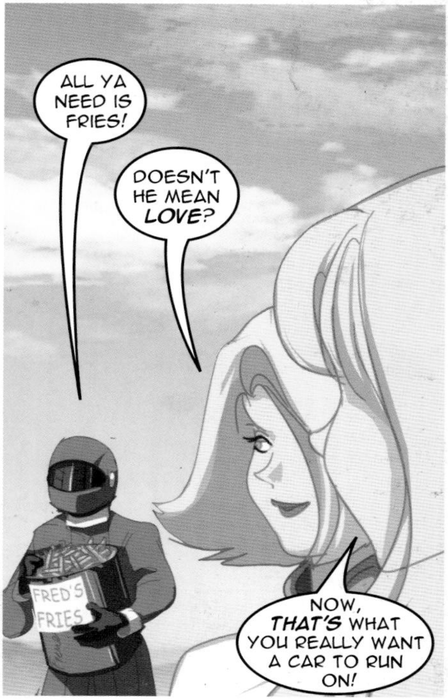
ALL YA NEED IS FRIES!
DOESN'T HE MEAN LOVE?
FRED'S FRIES
NOW, THAT'S WHAT YOU REALLY WANT A CAR TO RUN ON!

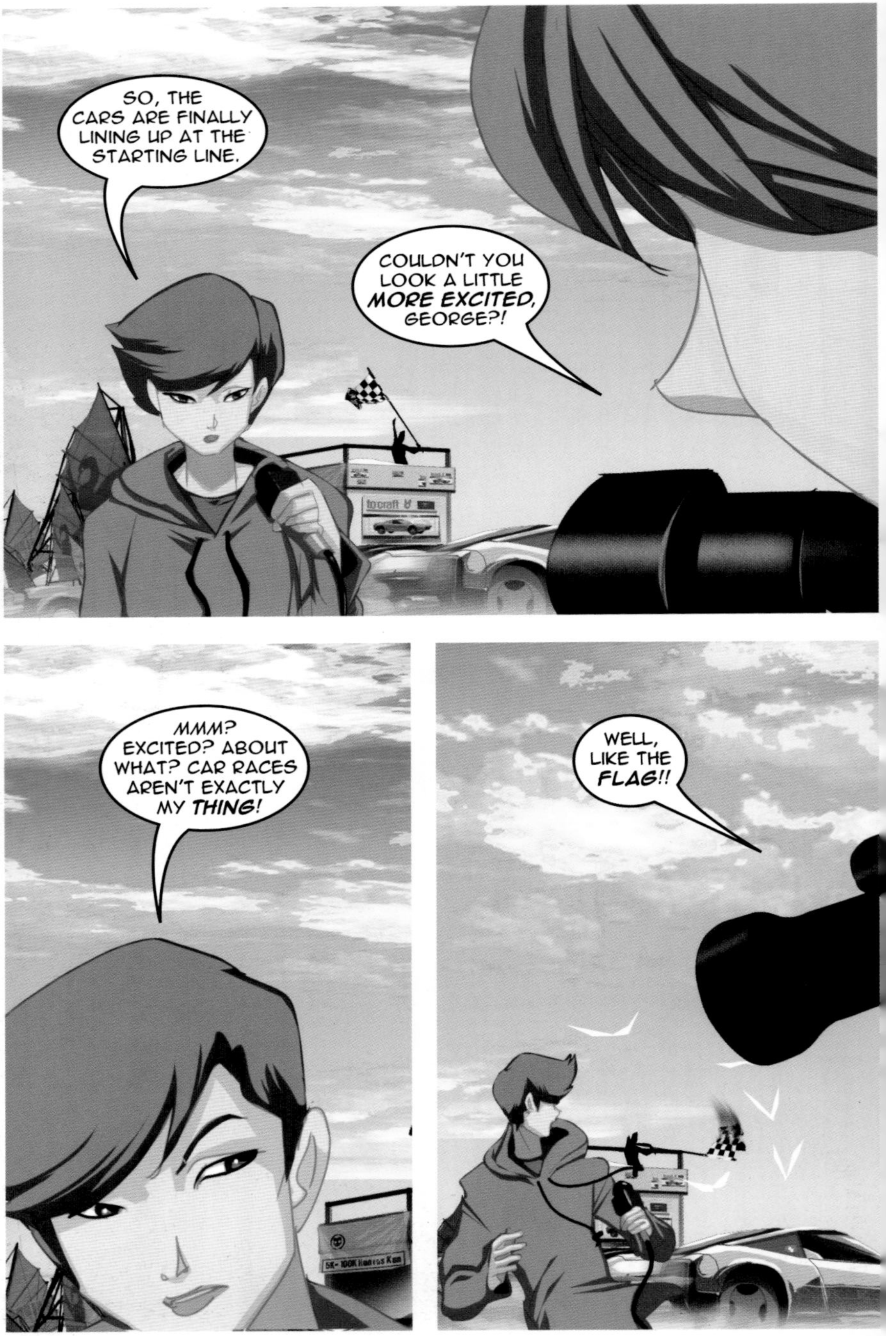
SO, THE CARS ARE FINALLY LINING UP AT THE STARTING LINE.
COULDN'T YOU LOOK A LITTLE *MORE EXCITED,* GEORGE?!
MMM? EXCITED? ABOUT WHAT? CAR RACES AREN'T EXACTLY MY *THING!*
WELL, LIKE THE *FLAG!!*

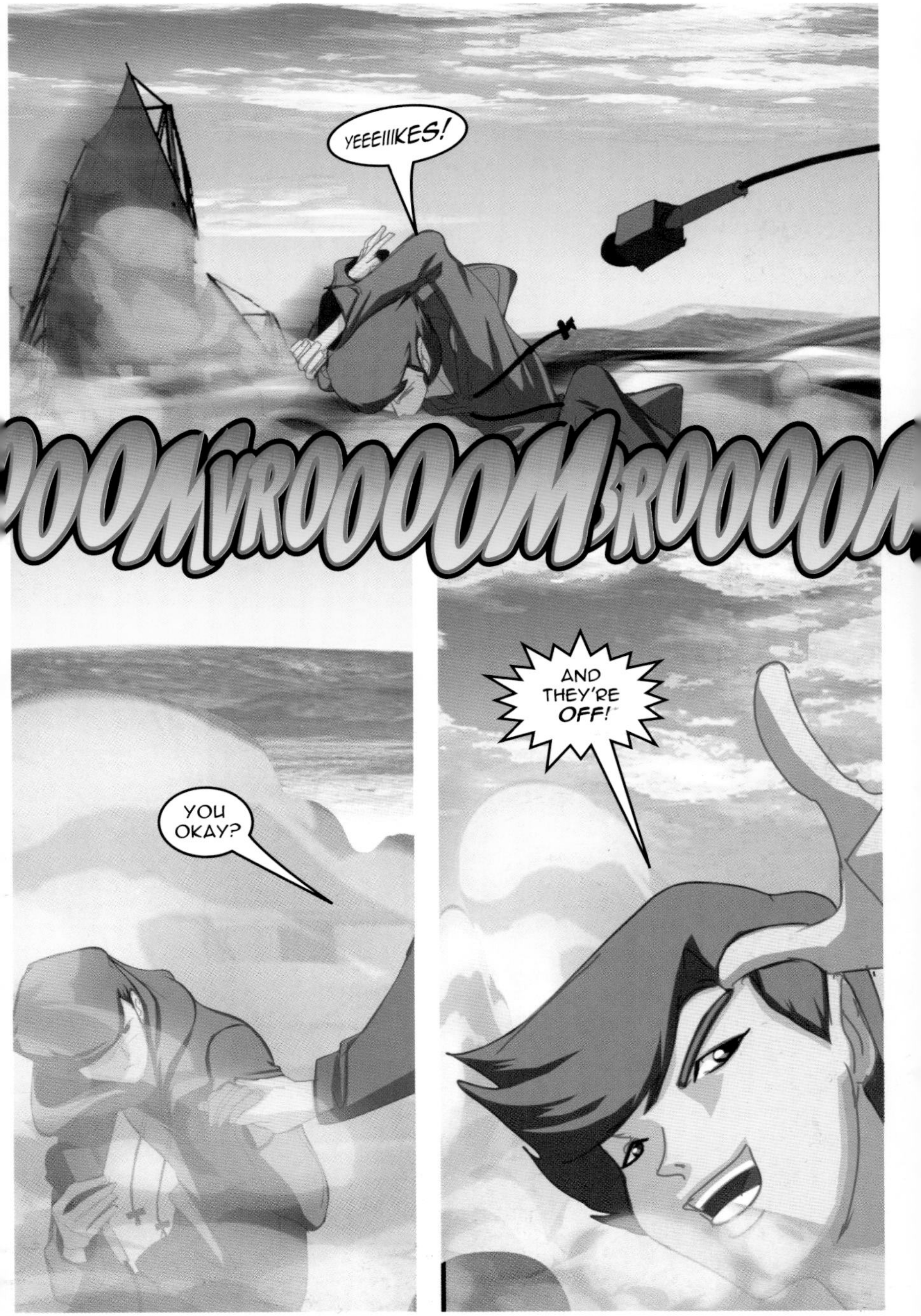

YEEEIIIKES!
VROOOOM VROOOOOM VROOOOM
YOU OKAY?
AND THEY'RE OFF!

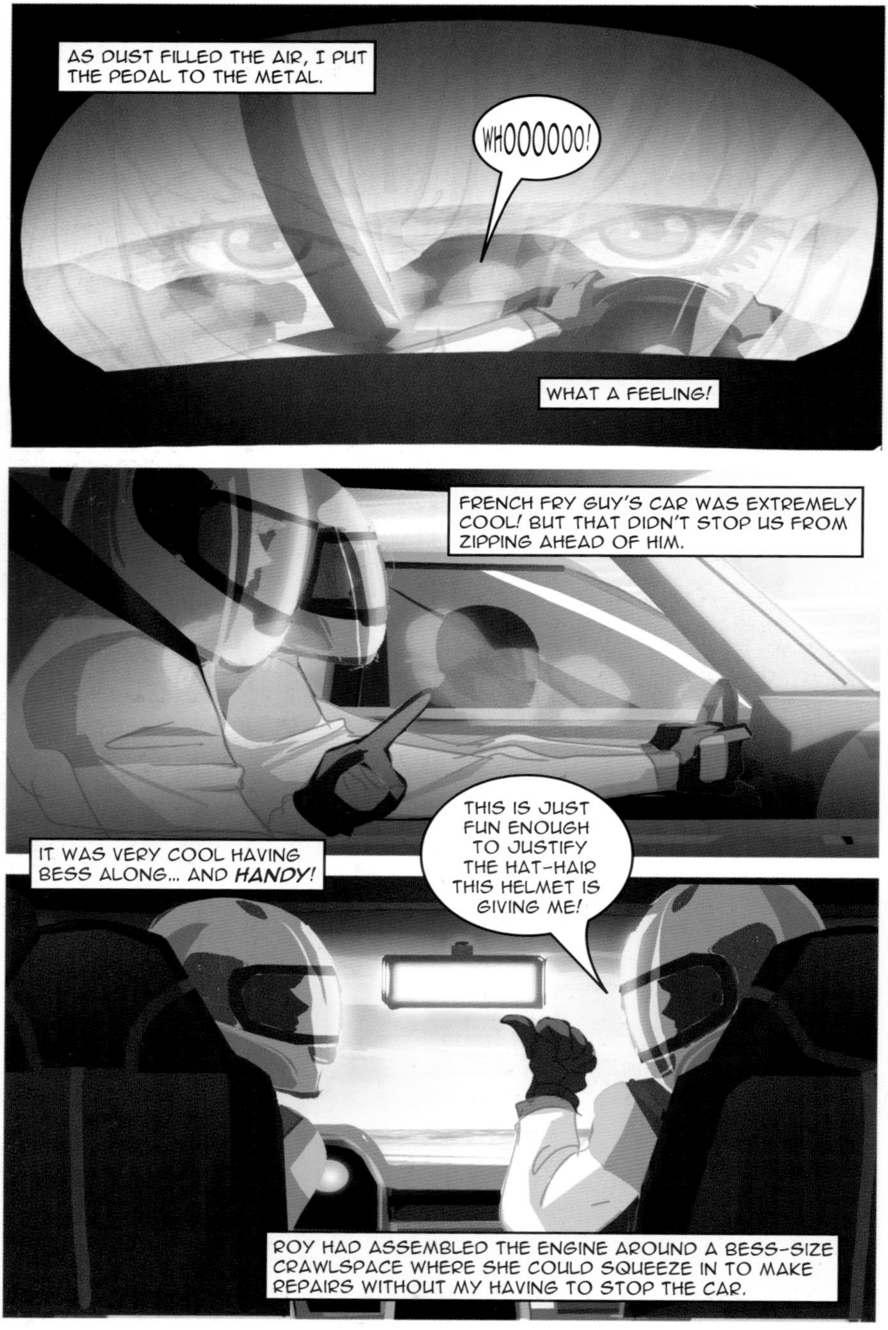
AS DUST FILLED THE AIR, I PUT THE PEDAL TO THE METAL.
WHOOOOOO!
WHAT A FEELING!
FRENCH FRY GUY'S CAR WAS EXTREMELY COOL! BUT THAT DIDN'T STOP US FROM ZIPPING AHEAD OF HIM.
IT WAS VERY COOL HAVING BESS ALONG... AND HANDY!
THIS IS JUST FUN ENOUGH TO JUSTIFY THE HAT-HAIR THIS HELMET IS GIVING ME!
ROY HAD ASSEMBLED THE ENGINE AROUND A BESS-SIZE CRAWLSPACE WHERE SHE COULD SQUEEZE IN TO MAKE REPAIRS WITHOUT MY HAVING TO STOP THE CAR.

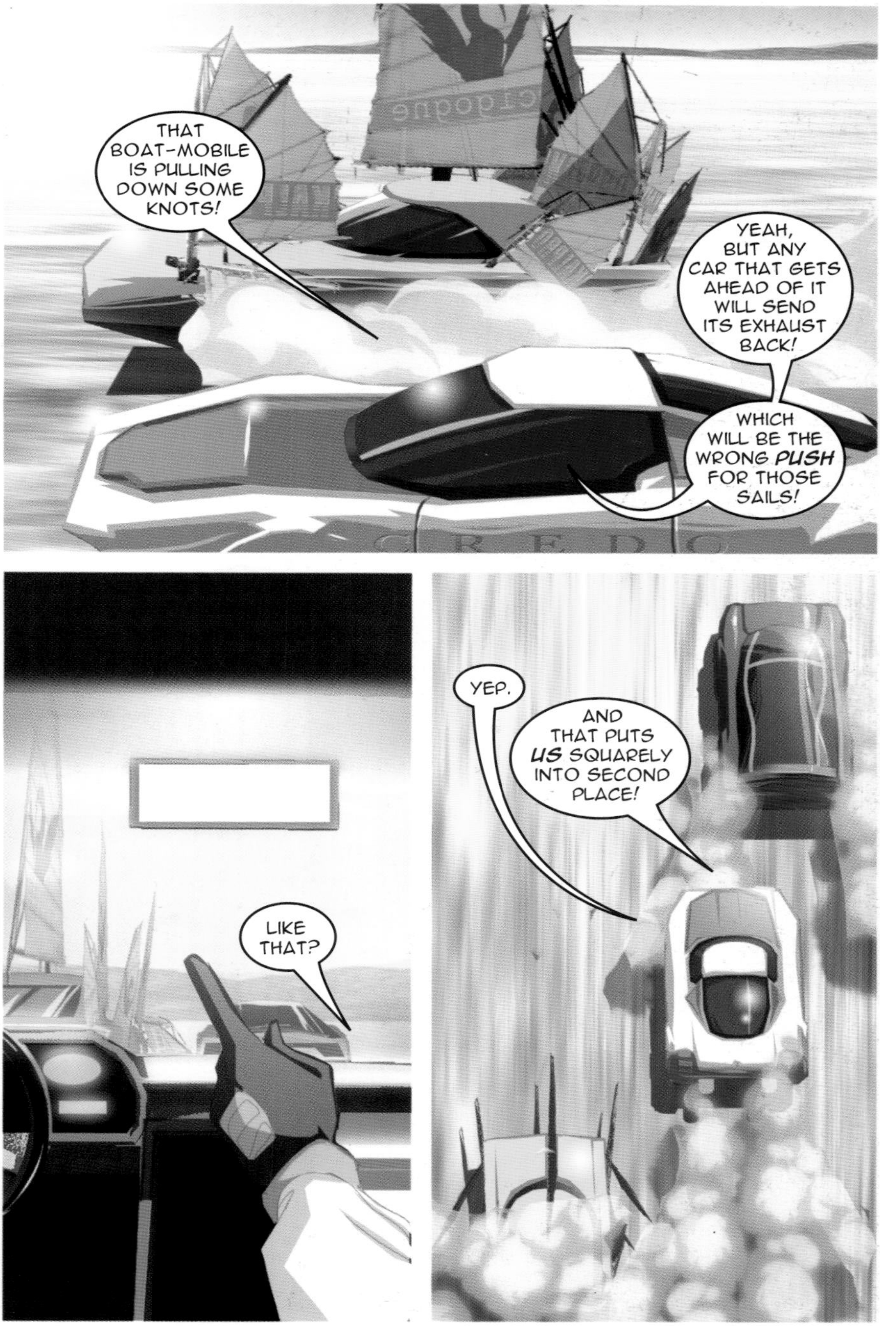
THAT BOAT-MOBILE IS PULLING DOWN SOME KNOTS!
YEAH, BUT ANY CAR THAT GETS AHEAD OF IT WILL SEND ITS EXHAUST BACK!
WHICH WILL BE THE WRONG ***PUSH*** FOR THOSE SAILS!
CREDO
LIKE THAT?
YEP.
AND THAT PUTS ***US*** SQUARELY INTO SECOND PLACE!

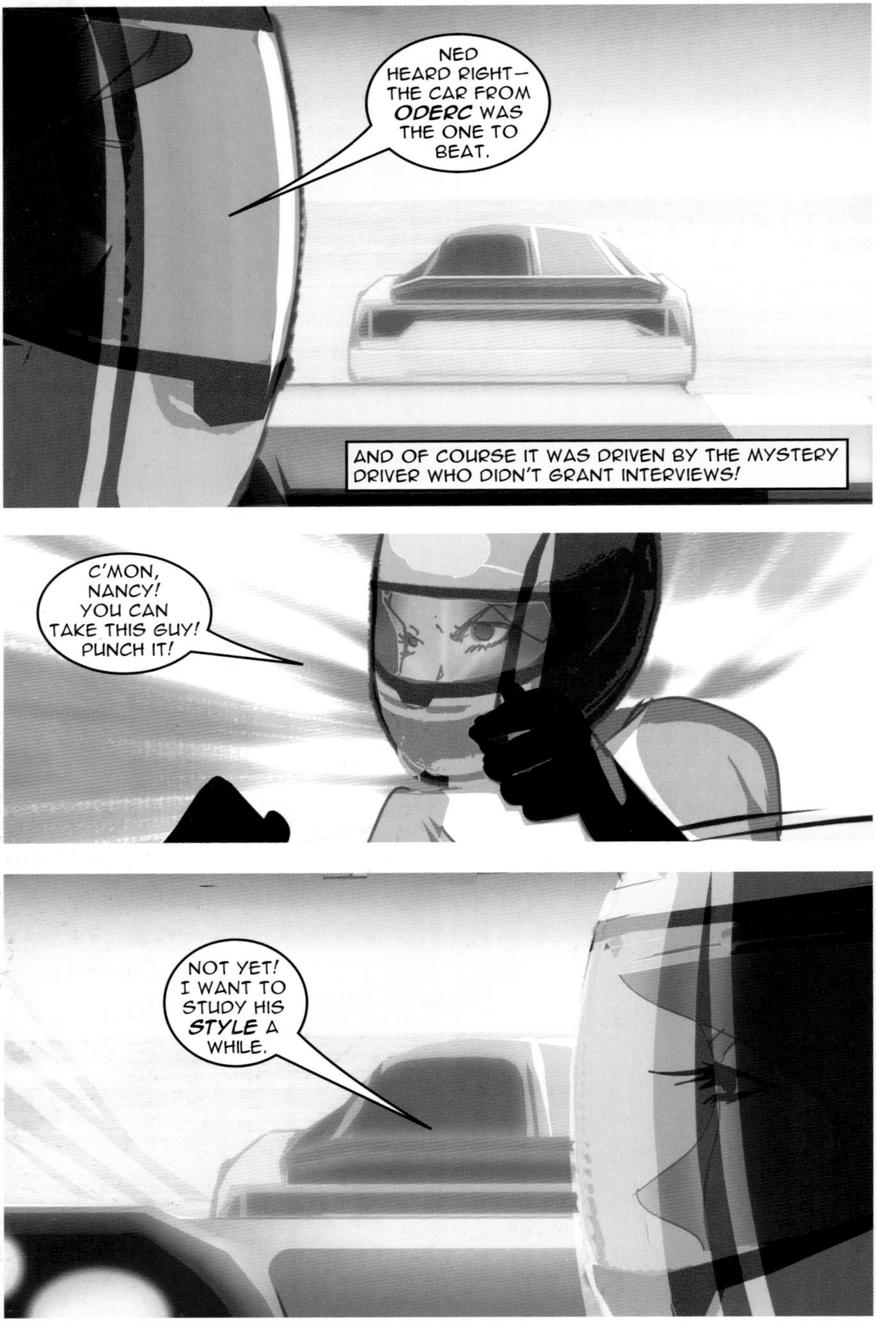
NED HEARD RIGHT— THE CAR FROM ODERC WAS THE ONE TO BEAT.
AND OF COURSE IT WAS DRIVEN BY THE MYSTERY DRIVER WHO DIDN'T GRANT INTERVIEWS!
C'MON, NANCY! YOU CAN TAKE THIS GUY! PUNCH IT!
NOT YET! I WANT TO STUDY HIS STYLE A WHILE.

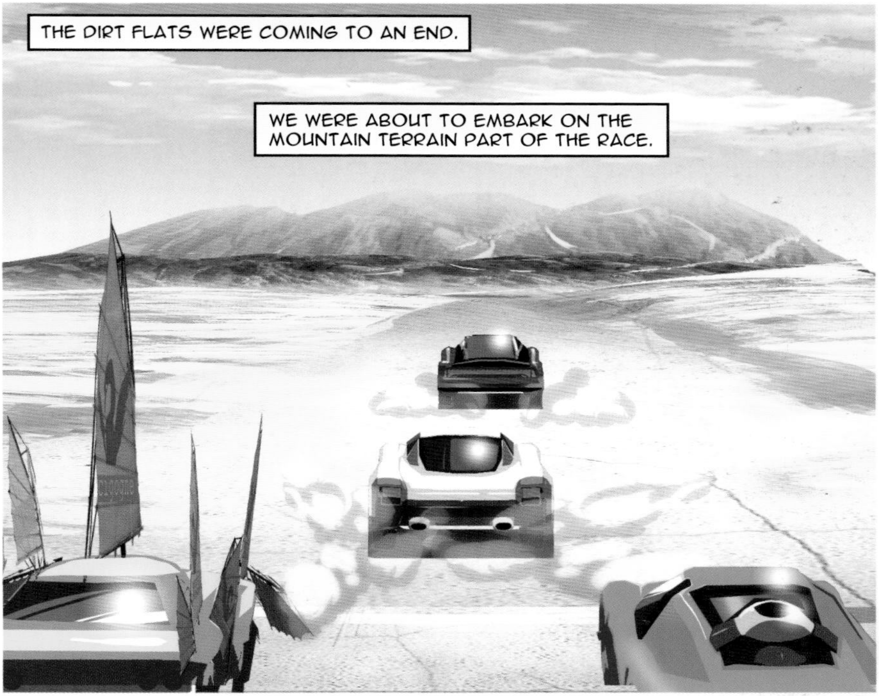
THE DIRT FLATS WERE COMING TO AN END.
WE WERE ABOUT TO EMBARK ON THE MOUNTAIN TERRAIN PART OF THE RACE.

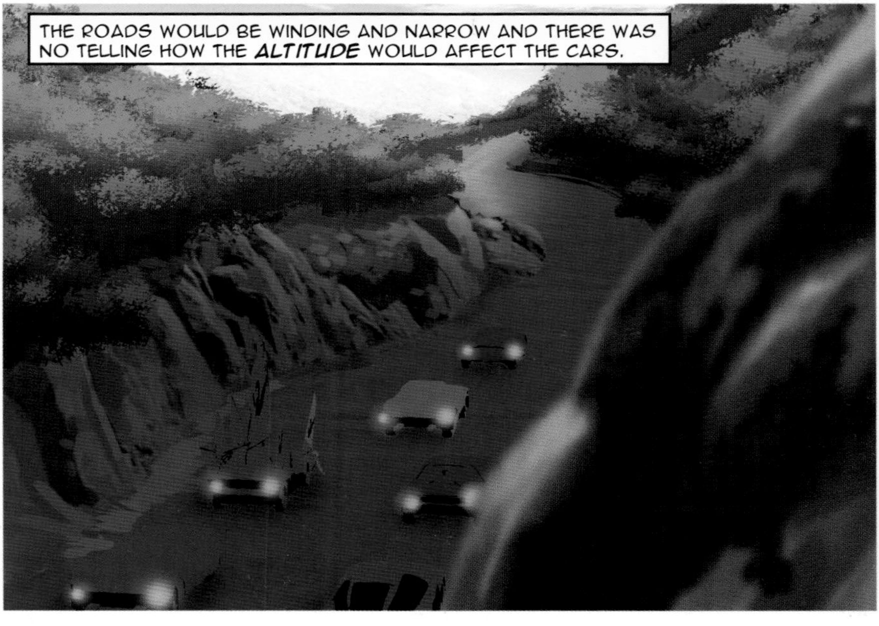
THE ROADS WOULD BE WINDING AND NARROW AND THERE WAS NO TELLING HOW THE *ALTITUDE* WOULD AFFECT THE CARS.

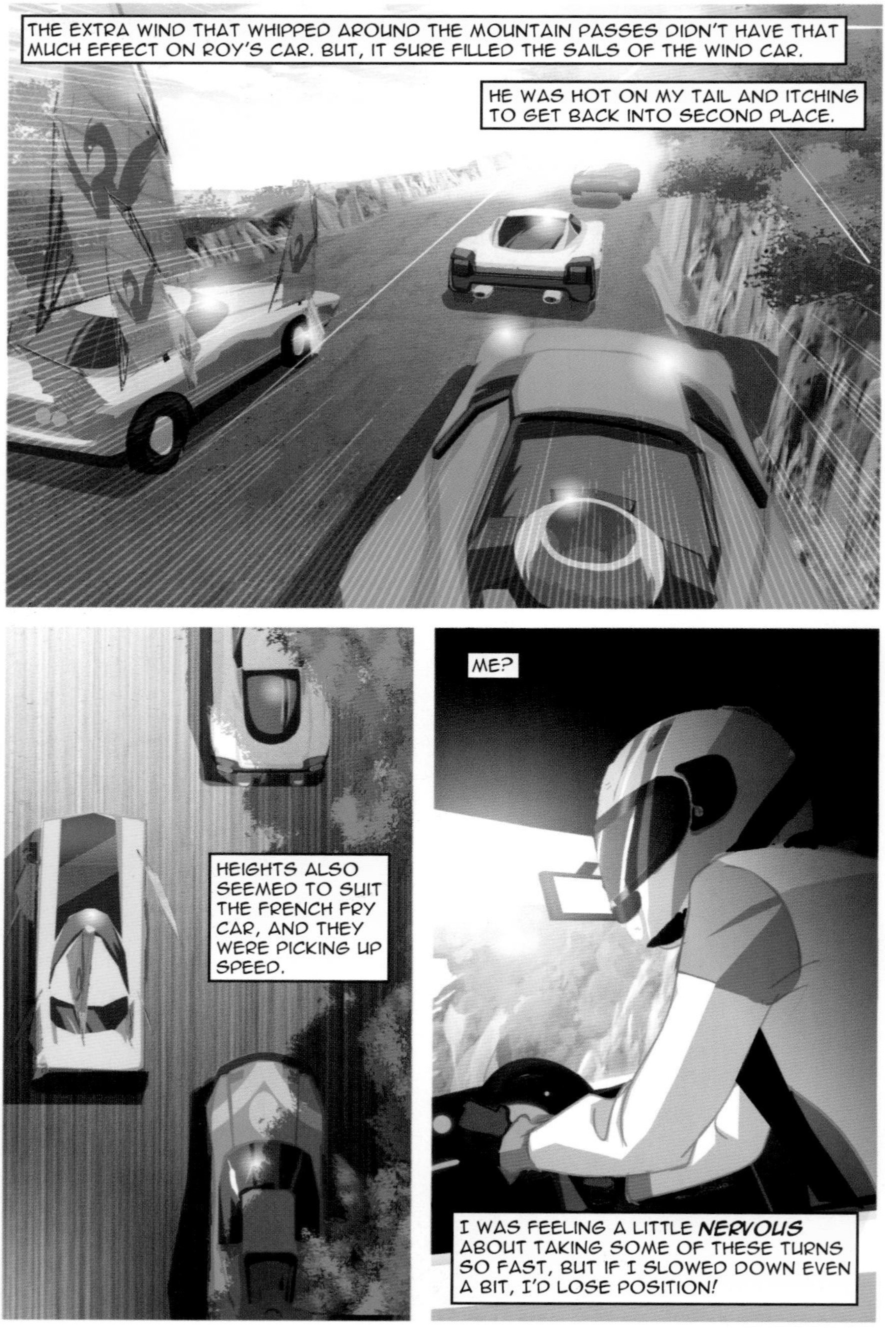
THE EXTRA WIND THAT WHIPPED AROUND THE MOUNTAIN PASSES DIDN'T HAVE THAT MUCH EFFECT ON ROY'S CAR. BUT, IT SURE FILLED THE SAILS OF THE WIND CAR.
HE WAS HOT ON MY TAIL AND ITCHING TO GET BACK INTO SECOND PLACE.
HEIGHTS ALSO SEEMED TO SUIT THE FRENCH FRY CAR, AND THEY WERE PICKING UP SPEED.
ME?
I WAS FEELING A LITTLE ***NERVOUS*** ABOUT TAKING SOME OF THESE TURNS SO FAST, BUT IF I SLOWED DOWN EVEN A BIT, I'D LOSE POSITION!

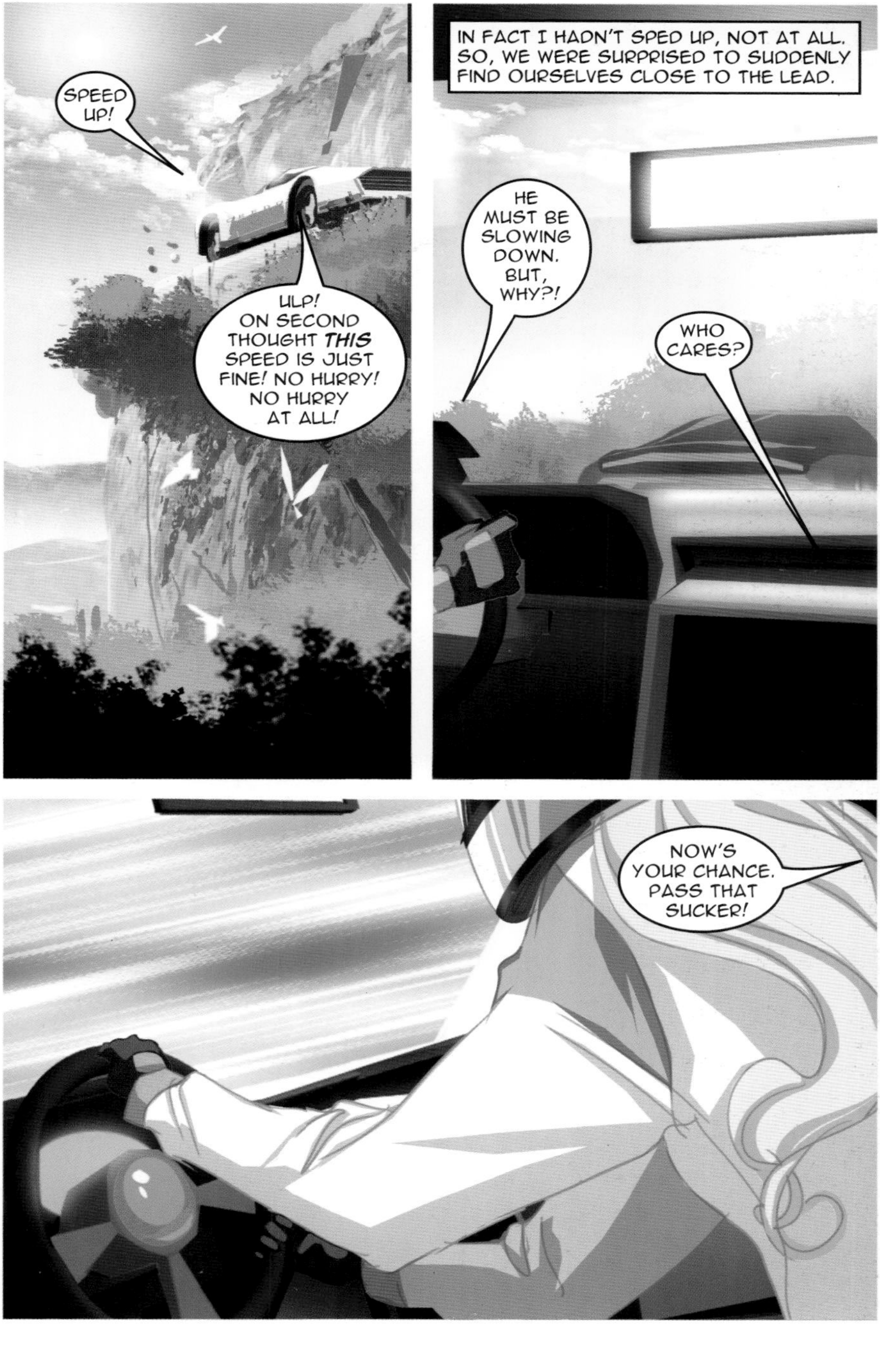
SPEED UP!
ULP! ON SECOND THOUGHT *THIS* SPEED IS JUST FINE! NO HURRY! NO HURRY AT ALL!
IN FACT I HADN'T SPED UP, NOT AT ALL. SO, WE WERE SURPRISED TO SUDDENLY FIND OURSELVES CLOSE TO THE LEAD.
HE MUST BE SLOWING DOWN. BUT, WHY?!
WHO CARES?
NOW'S YOUR CHANCE. PASS THAT SUCKER!

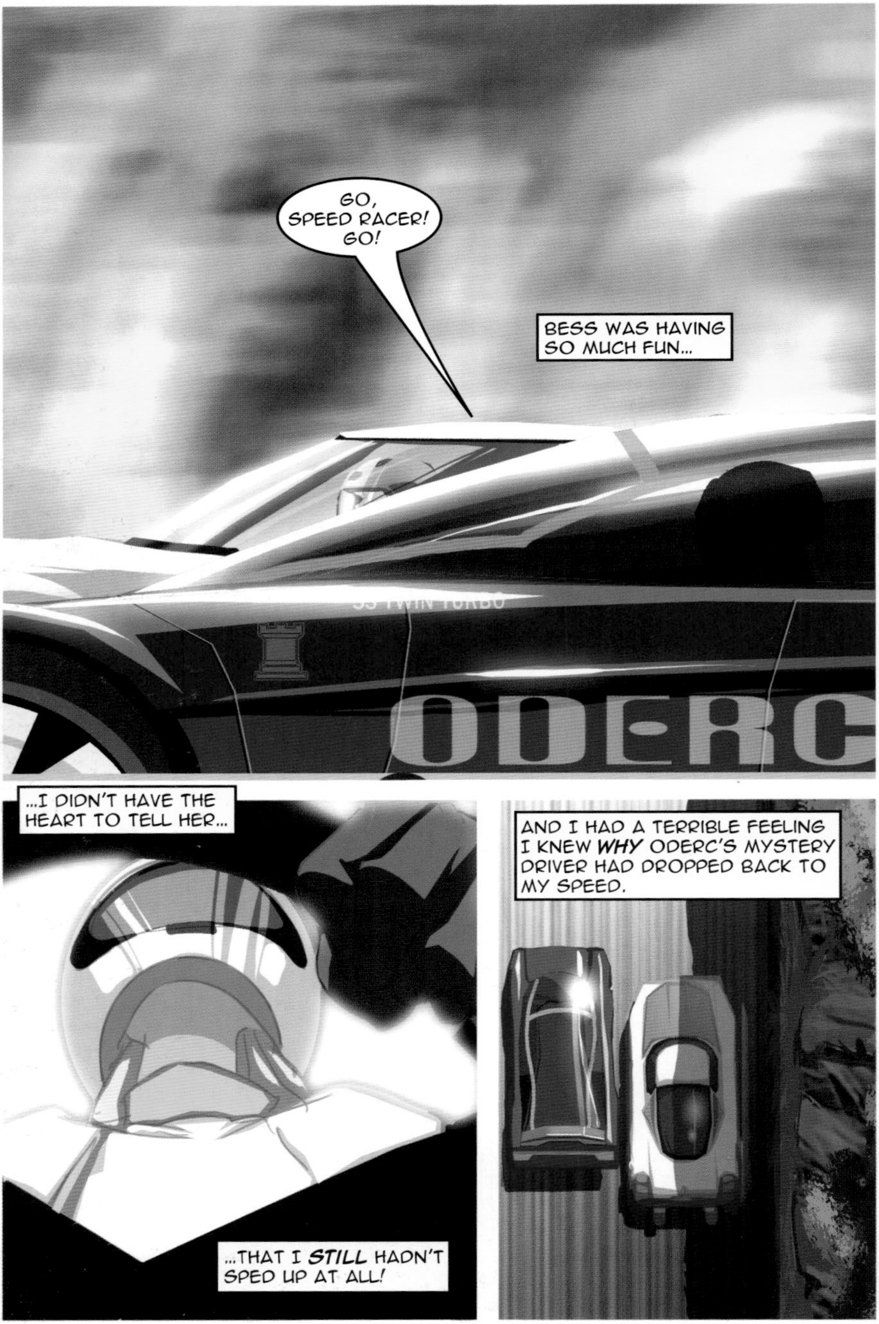
GO, SPEED RACER! GO!
BESS WAS HAVING SO MUCH FUN...
ODERC
...I DIDN'T HAVE THE HEART TO TELL HER...
...THAT I *STILL* HADN'T SPED UP AT ALL!
AND I HAD A TERRIBLE FEELING I KNEW *WHY* ODERC'S MYSTERY DRIVER HAD DROPPED BACK TO MY SPEED.

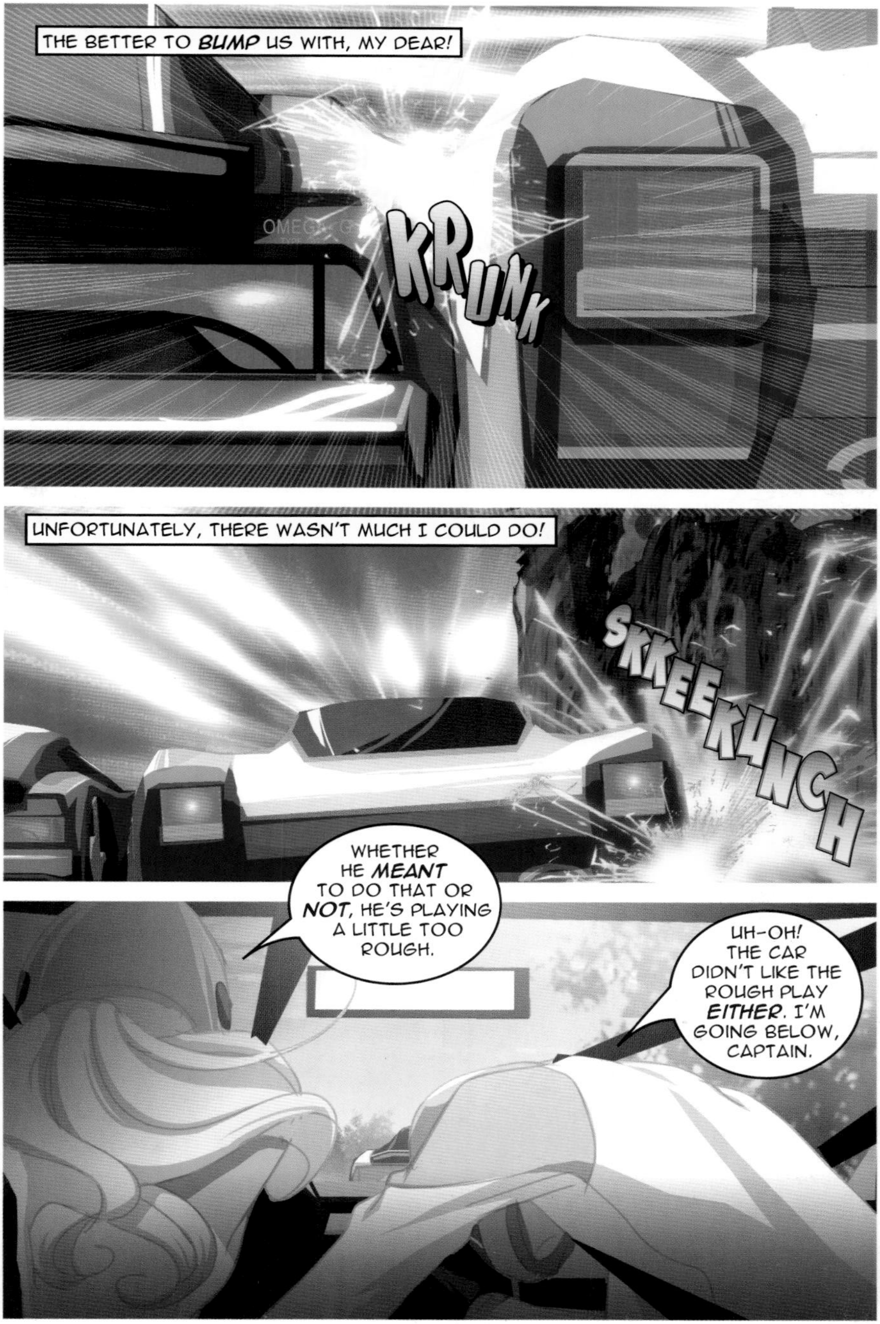
THE BETTER TO ***BUMP*** US WITH, MY DEAR!
KRUNK
UNFORTUNATELY, THERE WASN'T MUCH I COULD DO!
SKKEEKUNCH
WHETHER HE ***MEANT*** TO DO THAT OR ***NOT***, HE'S PLAYING A LITTLE TOO ROUGH.
UH-OH! THE CAR DIDN'T LIKE THE ROUGH PLAY ***EITHER***. I'M GOING BELOW, CAPTAIN.

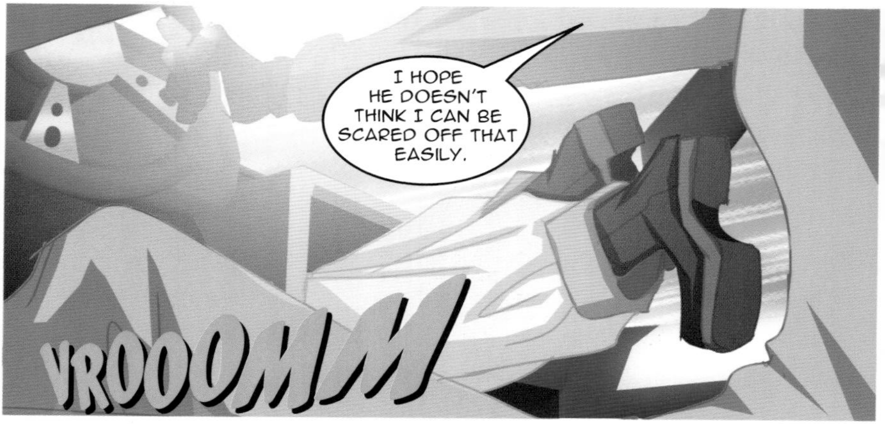
I HOPE HE DOESN'T THINK I CAN BE SCARED OFF THAT EASILY.
VROOOMM

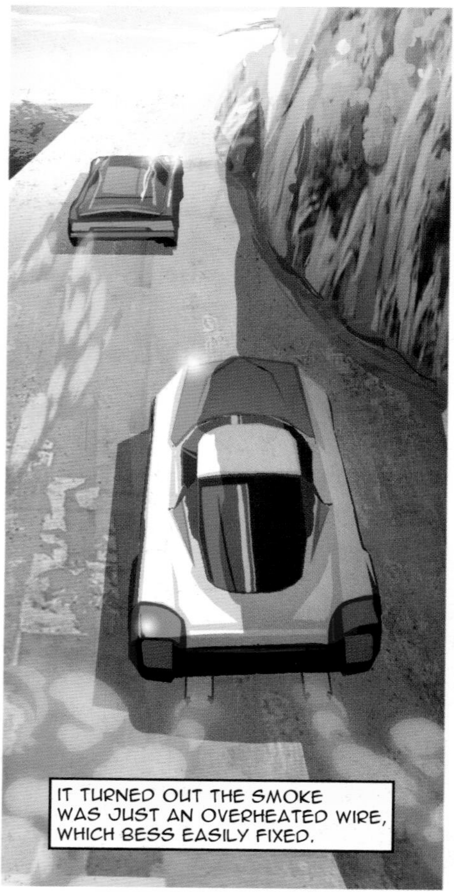
IT TURNED OUT THE SMOKE WAS JUST AN OVERHEATED WIRE, WHICH BESS EASILY FIXED.

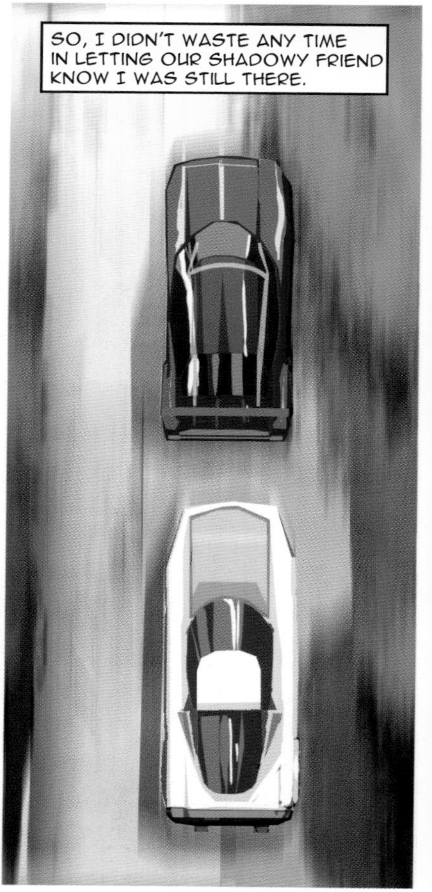
SO, I DIDN'T WASTE ANY TIME IN LETTING OUR SHADOWY FRIEND KNOW I WAS STILL THERE.

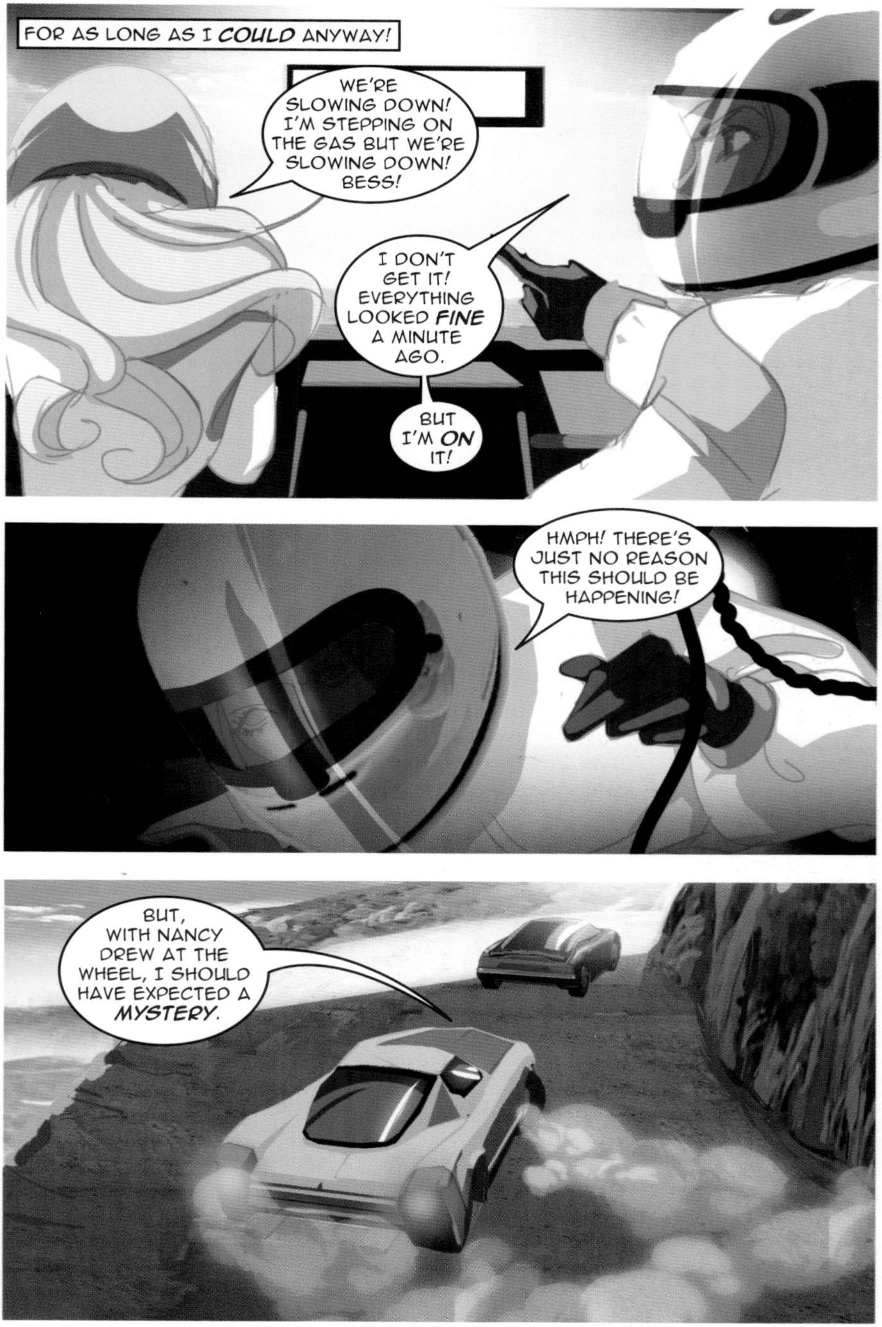
FOR AS LONG AS I COULD ANYWAY!
WE'RE SLOWING DOWN! I'M STEPPING ON THE GAS BUT WE'RE SLOWING DOWN! BESS!
I DON'T GET IT! EVERYTHING LOOKED FINE A MINUTE AGO.
BUT I'M ON IT!
HMPH! THERE'S JUST NO REASON THIS SHOULD BE HAPPENING!
BUT, WITH NANCY DREW AT THE WHEEL, I SHOULD HAVE EXPECTED A MYSTERY.

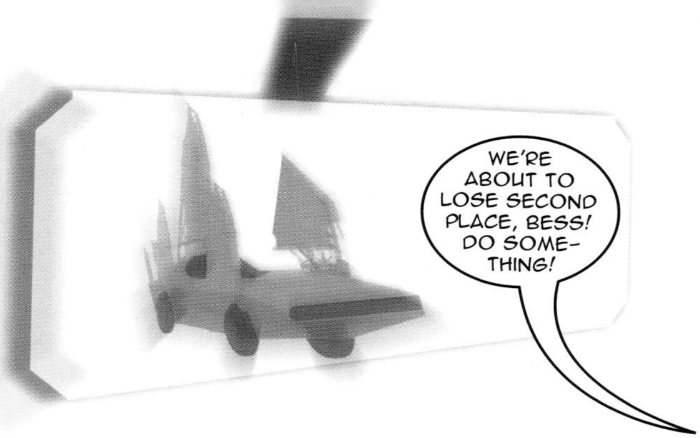
WE'RE ABOUT TO LOSE SECOND PLACE, BESS! DO SOME-THING!

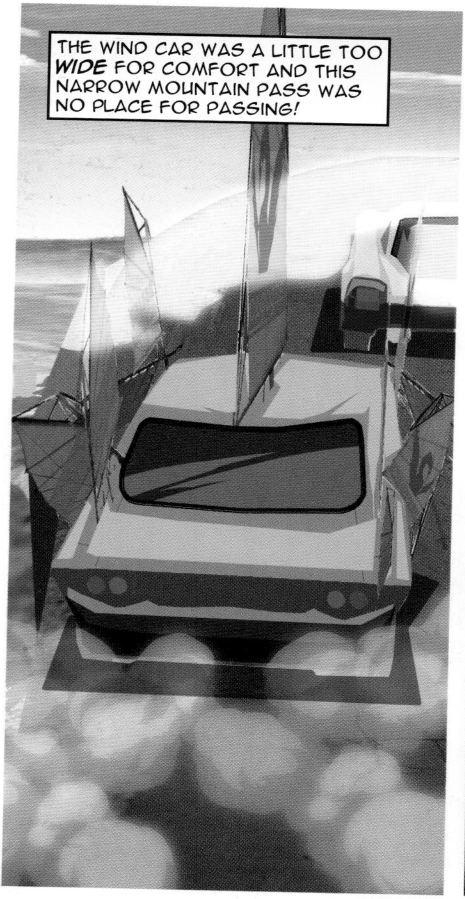
THE WIND CAR WAS A LITTLE TOO WIDE FOR COMFORT AND THIS NARROW MOUNTAIN PASS WAS NO PLACE FOR PASSING!

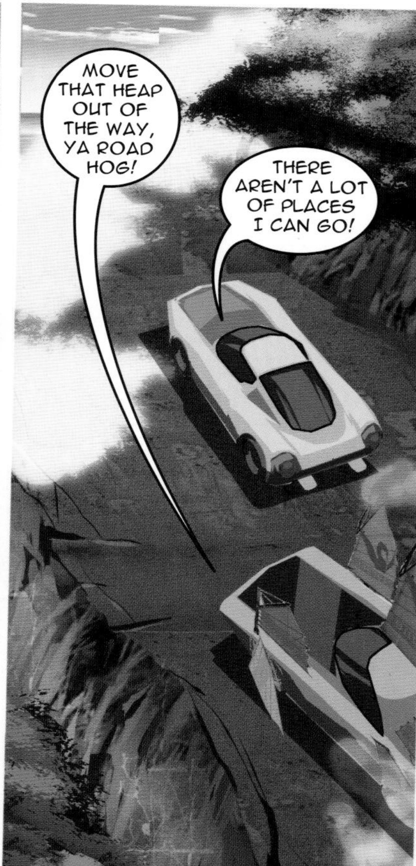
MOVE THAT HEAP OUT OF THE WAY, YA ROAD HOG!
THERE AREN'T A LOT OF PLACES I CAN GO!

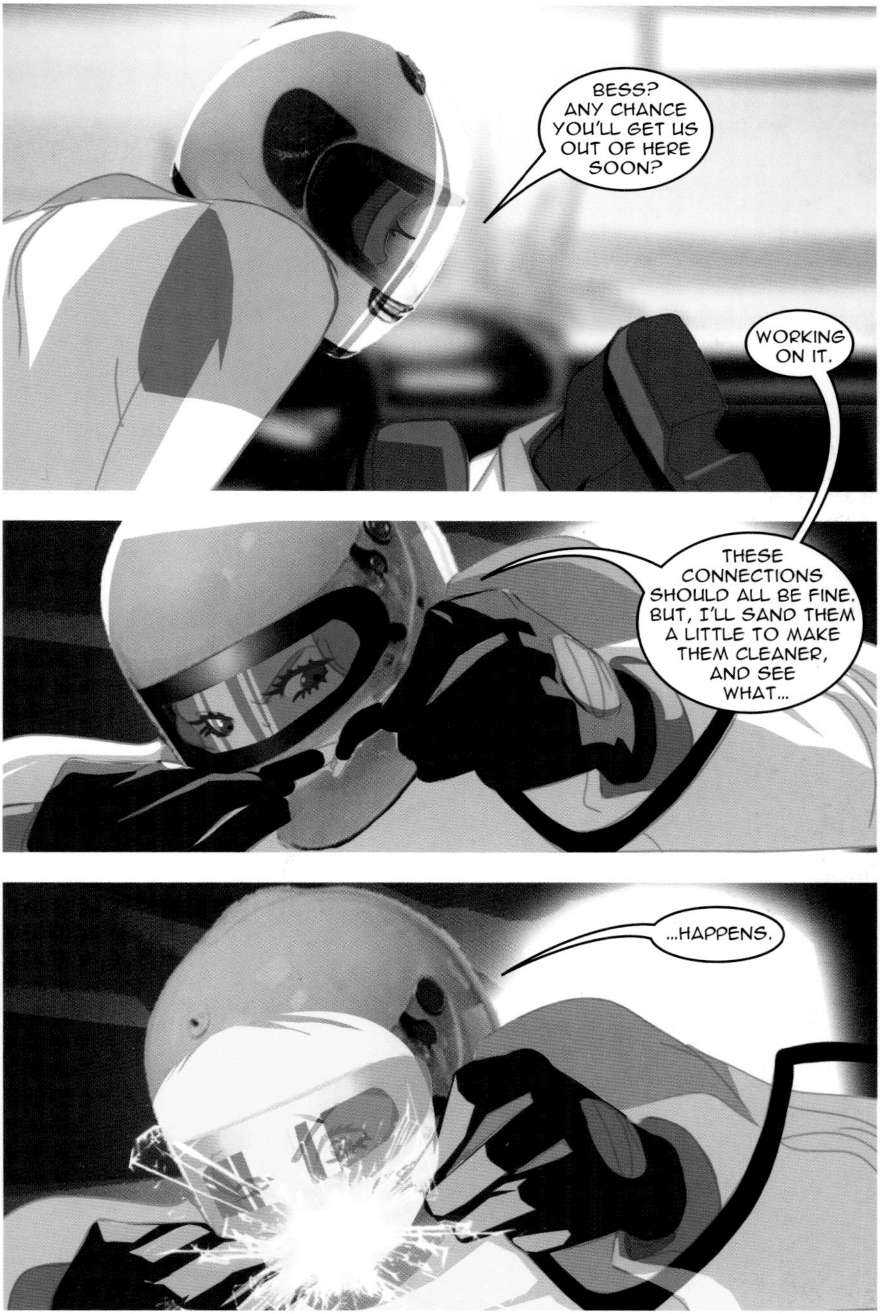
BESS? ANY CHANCE YOU'LL GET US OUT OF HERE SOON?
WORKING ON IT.
THESE CONNECTIONS SHOULD ALL BE FINE. BUT, I'LL SAND THEM A LITTLE TO MAKE THEM CLEANER, AND SEE WHAT...
...HAPPENS.

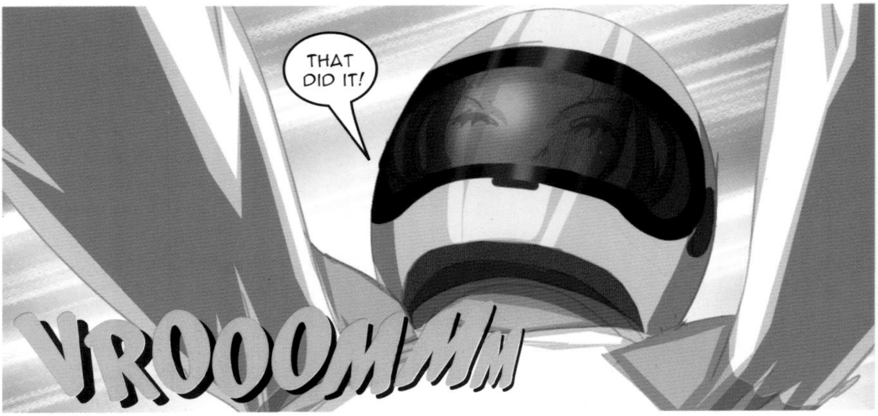
THAT DID IT!
VROOOMMM

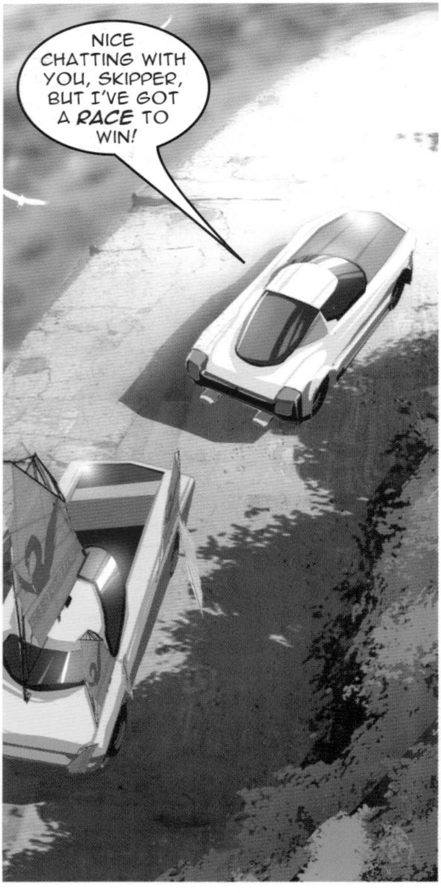
NICE CHATTING WITH YOU, SKIPPER, BUT I'VE GOT A RACE TO WIN!

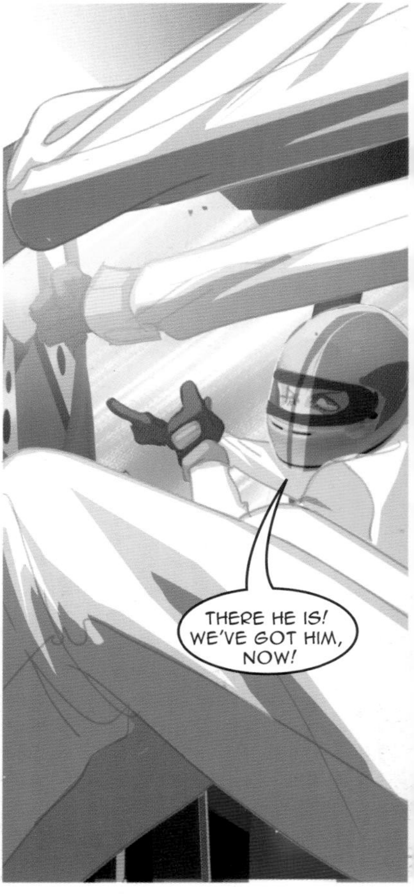
THERE HE IS! WE'VE GOT HIM, NOW!

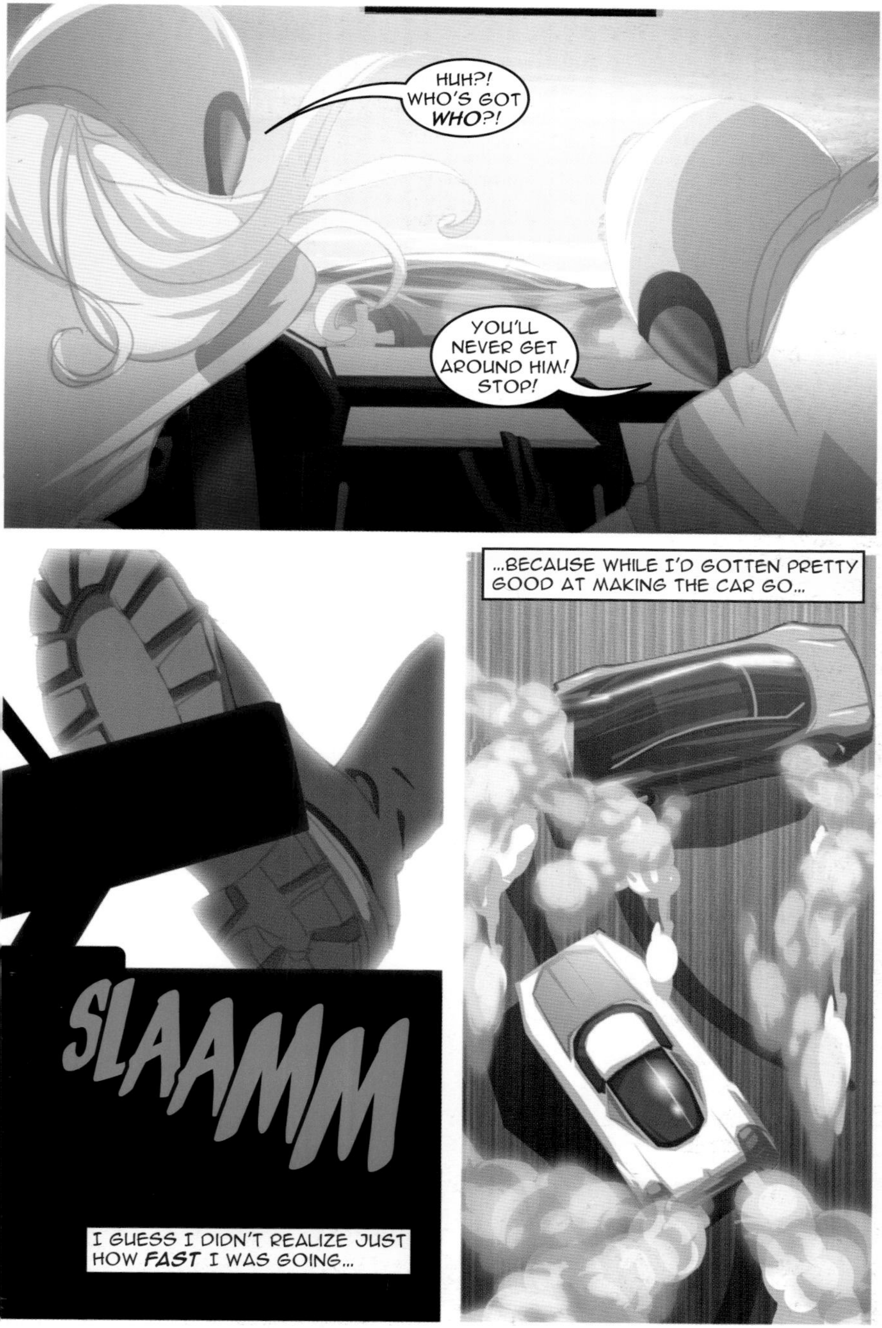
HUH?! WHO'S GOT WHO?!
YOU'LL NEVER GET AROUND HIM! STOP!
SLAAMM
I GUESS I DIDN'T REALIZE JUST HOW FAST I WAS GOING...
...BECAUSE WHILE I'D GOTTEN PRETTY GOOD AT MAKING THE CAR GO...

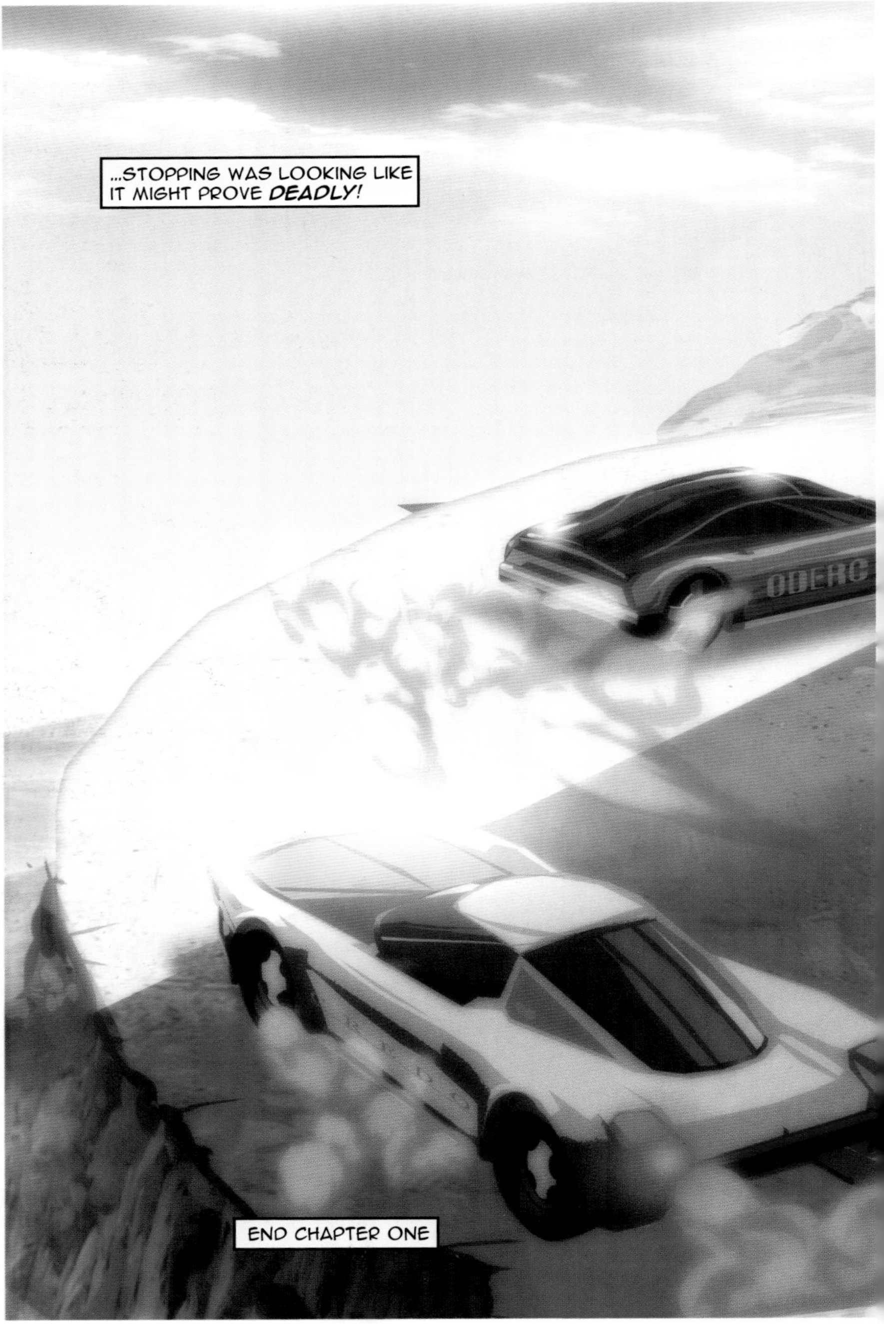
...STOPPING WAS LOOKING LIKE IT MIGHT PROVE DEADLY!
ODERC
END CHAPTER ONE

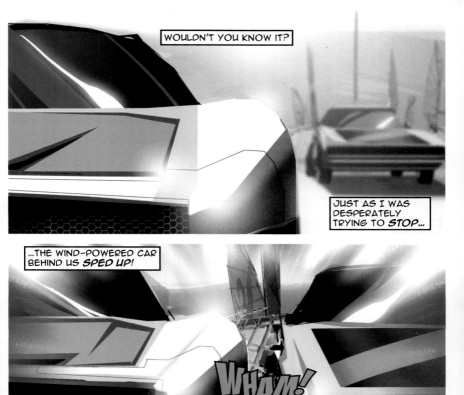

WOULDN'T YOU KNOW IT?

JUST AS I WAS DESPERATELY TRYING TO **STOP**...

...THE WIND-POWERED CAR BEHIND US **SPED UP!**

WHAM!

AND WE WERE SLAMMED BACK **ONTO** THE ROAD! WHICH WAS MUCH BETTER DIRECTION THAN THE ONE WE WERE GOING IN!

CHAPTER 2: RACING GRIPES

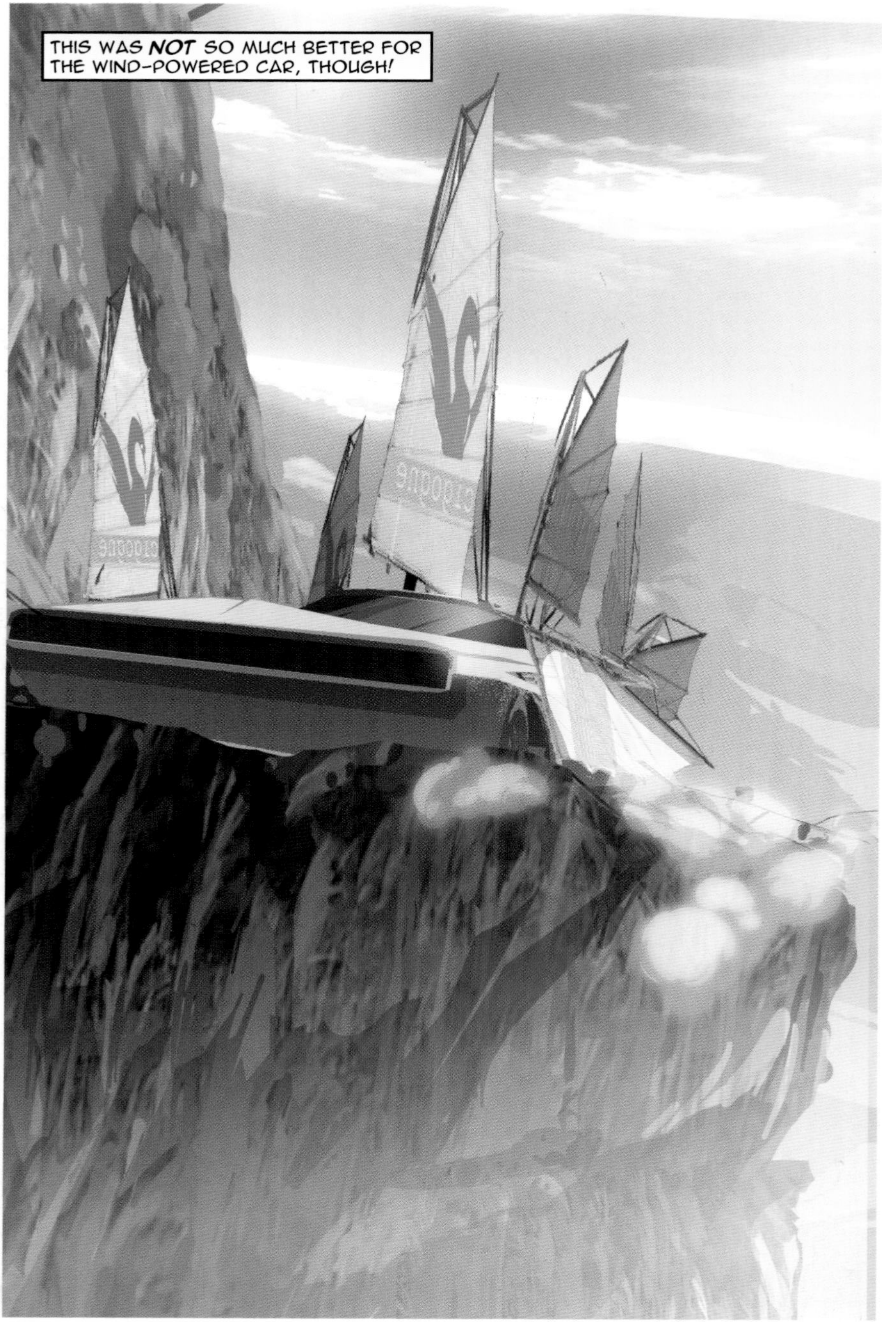
THIS WAS NOT SO MUCH BETTER FOR THE WIND-POWERED CAR, THOUGH!

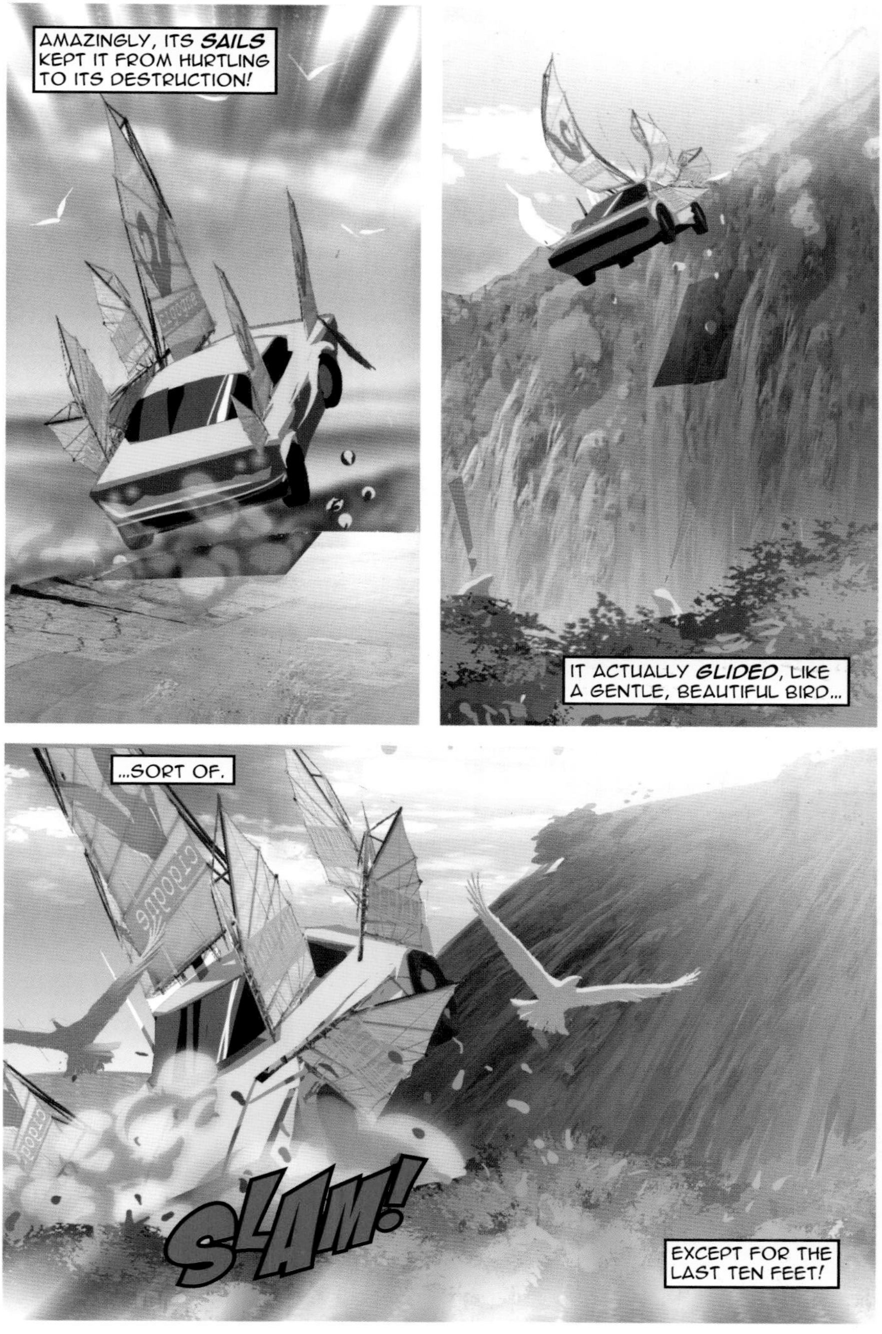
AMAZINGLY, ITS SAILS KEPT IT FROM HURTLING TO ITS DESTRUCTION!
IT ACTUALLY GLIDED, LIKE A GENTLE, BEAUTIFUL BIRD...
...SORT OF.
SLAM!
EXCEPT FOR THE LAST TEN FEET!

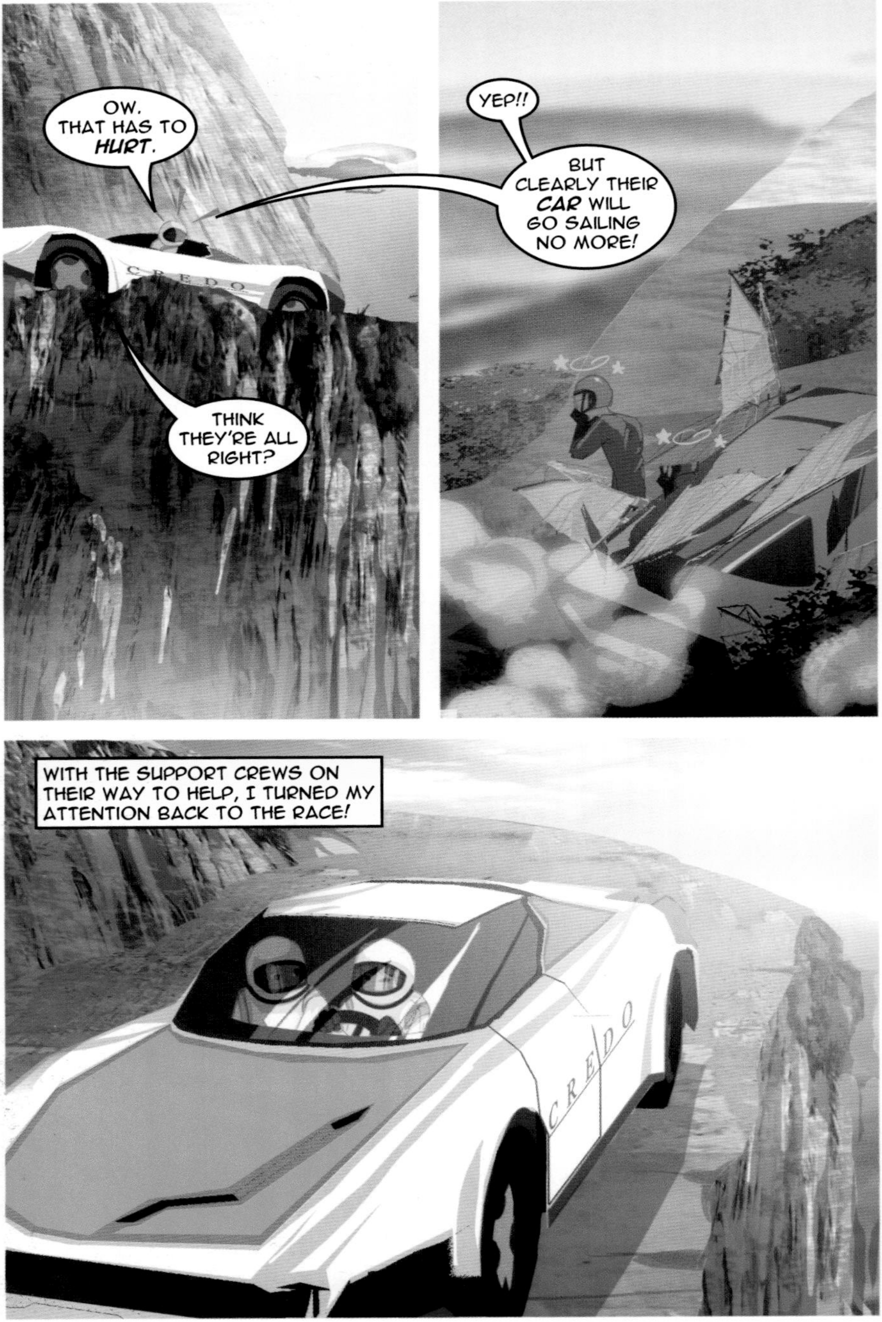
OW. THAT HAS TO HURT.
THINK THEY'RE ALL RIGHT?
YEP!!
BUT CLEARLY THEIR CAR WILL GO SAILING NO MORE!
CREDO
WITH THE SUPPORT CREWS ON THEIR WAY TO HELP, I TURNED MY ATTENTION BACK TO THE RACE!
CREDO

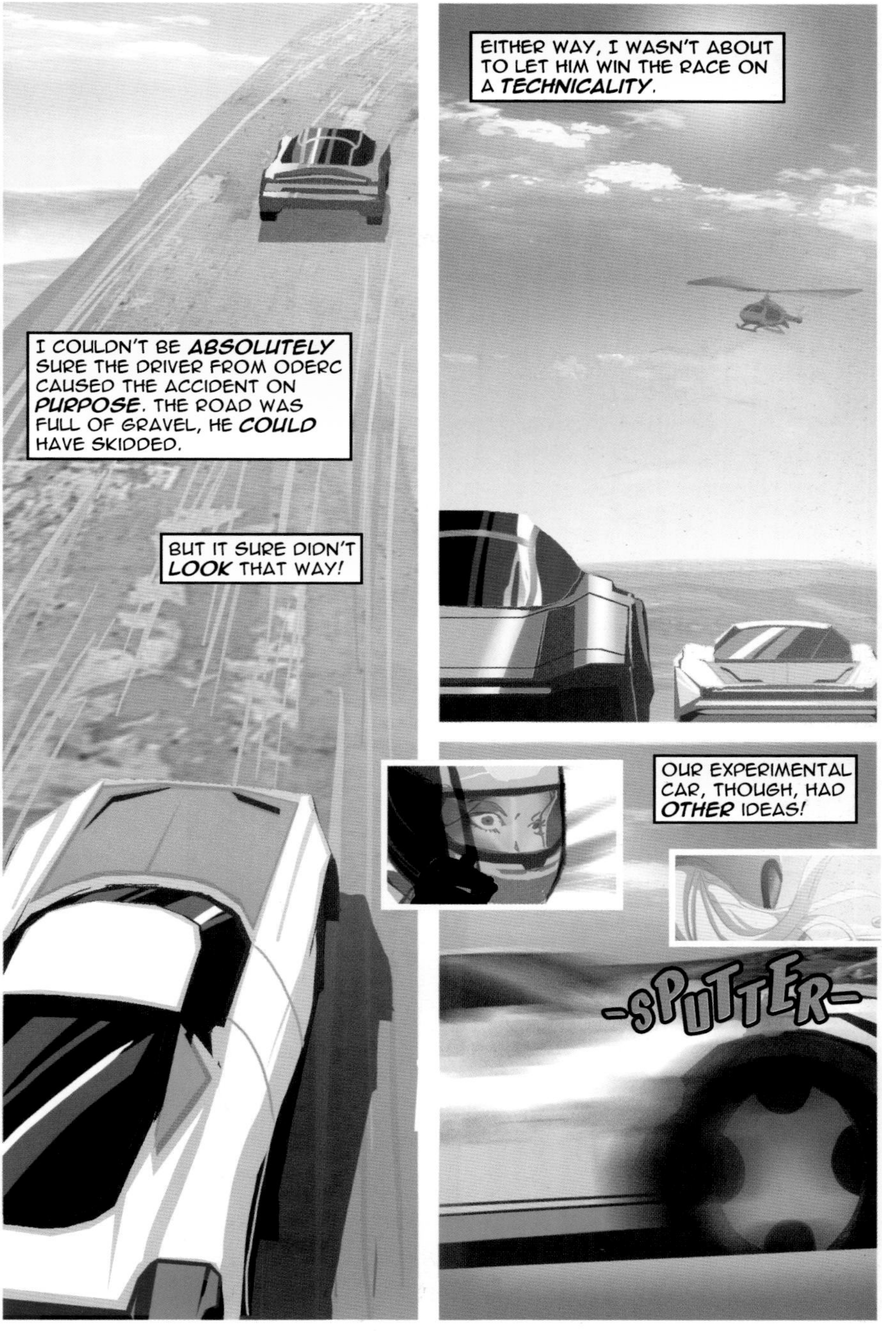
I COULDN'T BE ABSOLUTELY SURE THE DRIVER FROM ODERC CAUSED THE ACCIDENT ON PURPOSE. THE ROAD WAS FULL OF GRAVEL, HE COULD HAVE SKIDDED.
BUT IT SURE DIDN'T LOOK THAT WAY!
EITHER WAY, I WASN'T ABOUT TO LET HIM WIN THE RACE ON A TECHNICALITY.
OUR EXPERIMENTAL CAR, THOUGH, HAD OTHER IDEAS!
-SPUTTER-

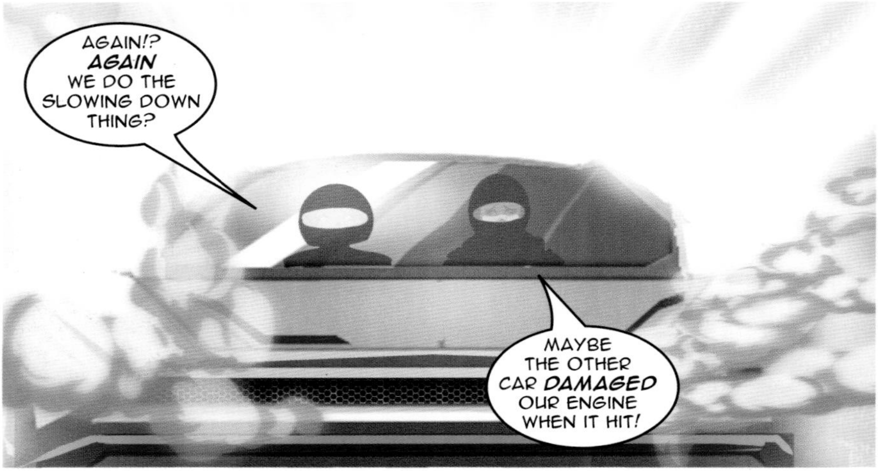
AGAIN!? **AGAIN** WE DO THE SLOWING DOWN THING?
MAYBE THE OTHER CAR **DAMAGED** OUR ENGINE WHEN IT HIT!

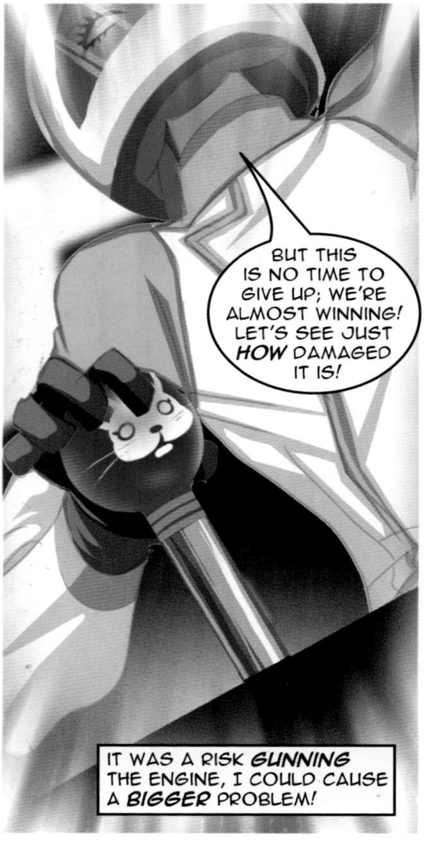
BUT THIS IS NO TIME TO GIVE UP; WE'RE ALMOST WINNING! LET'S SEE JUST **HOW** DAMAGED IT IS!
IT WAS A RISK **GUNNING** THE ENGINE, I COULD CAUSE A **BIGGER** PROBLEM!

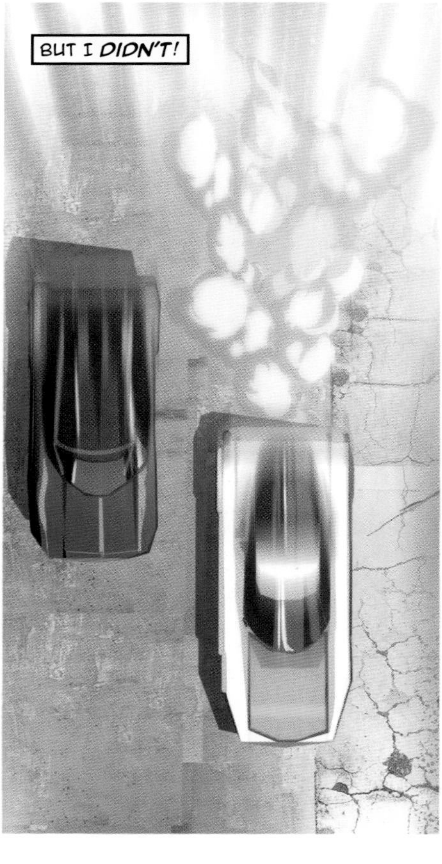
BUT I **DIDN'T**!

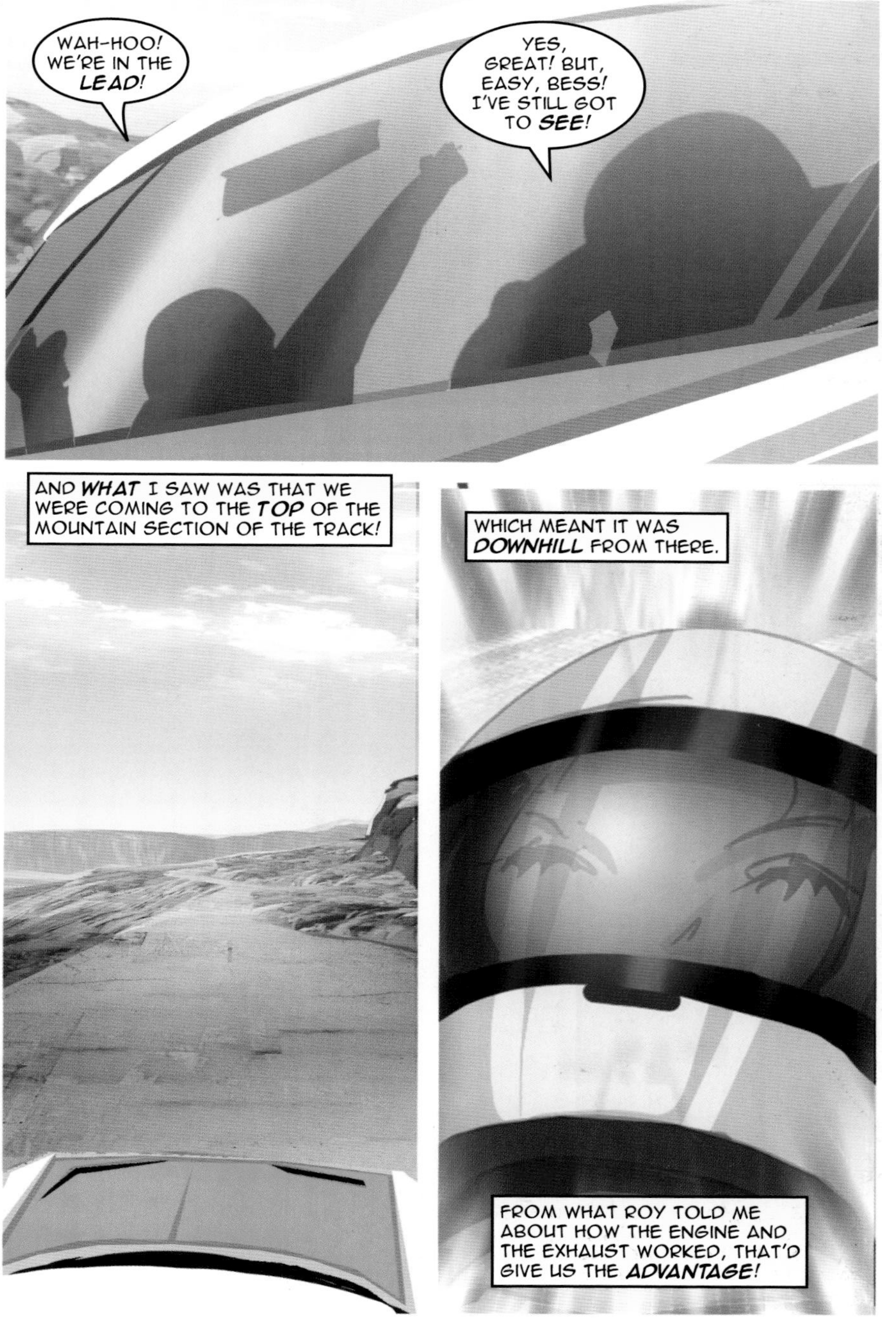
WAH-HOO! WE'RE IN THE LEAD!
YES, GREAT! BUT, EASY, BESS! I'VE STILL GOT TO SEE!
AND WHAT I SAW WAS THAT WE WERE COMING TO THE TOP OF THE MOUNTAIN SECTION OF THE TRACK!
WHICH MEANT IT WAS DOWNHILL FROM THERE.
FROM WHAT ROY TOLD ME ABOUT HOW THE ENGINE AND THE EXHAUST WORKED, THAT'D GIVE US THE ADVANTAGE!

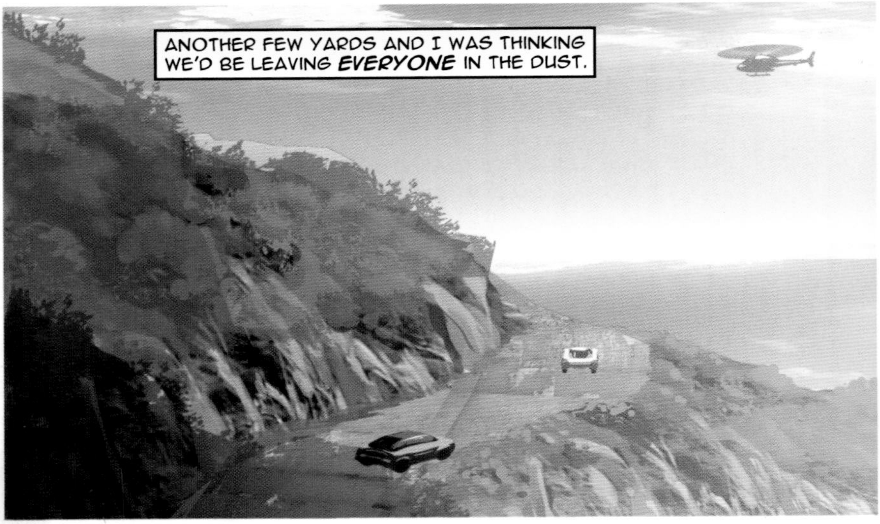
ANOTHER FEW YARDS AND I WAS THINKING WE'D BE LEAVING *EVERYONE* IN THE DUST.

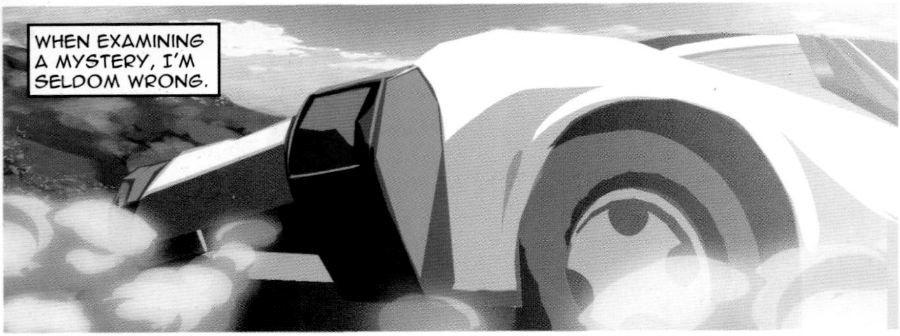
WHEN EXAMINING A MYSTERY, I'M SELDOM WRONG.

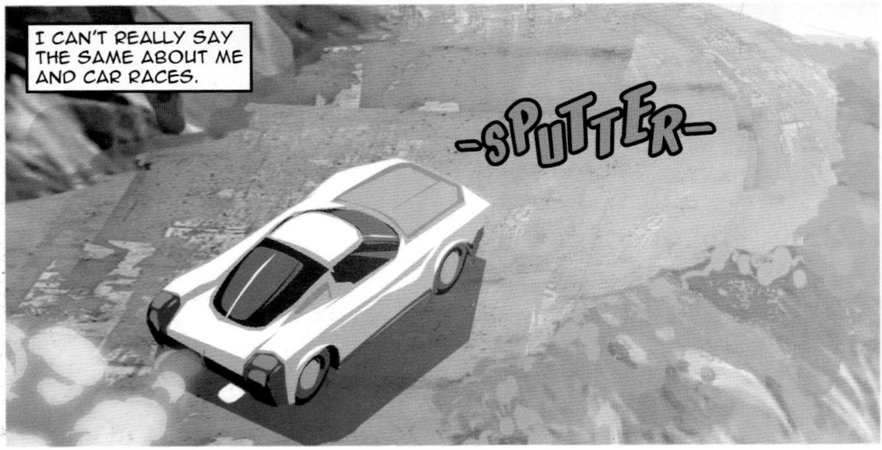
I CAN'T REALLY SAY THE SAME ABOUT ME AND CAR RACES.
-SPUTTER-

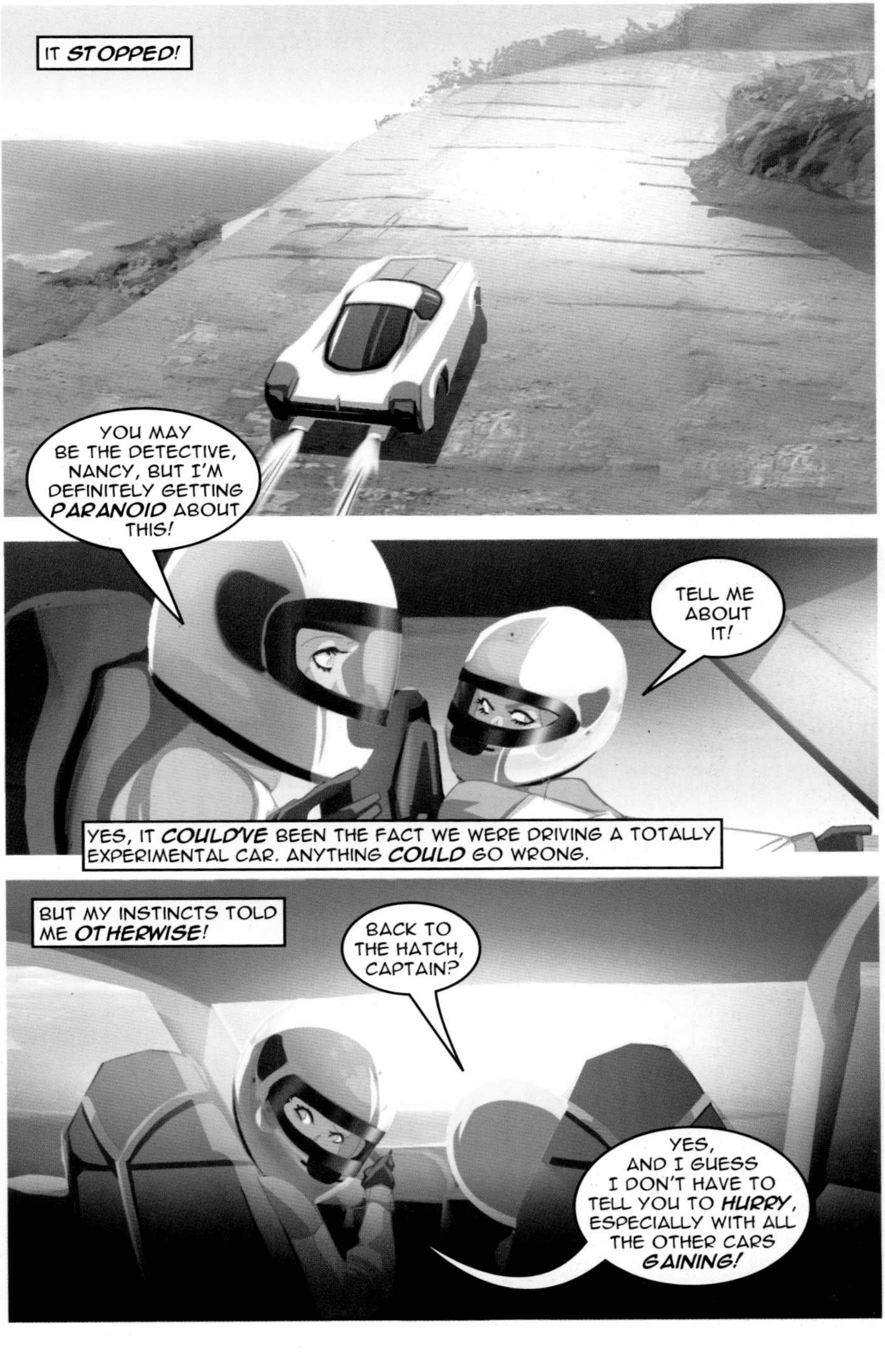
IT STOPPED!
YOU MAY BE THE DETECTIVE, NANCY, BUT I'M DEFINITELY GETTING PARANOID ABOUT THIS!
TELL ME ABOUT IT!
YES, IT COULD'VE BEEN THE FACT WE WERE DRIVING A TOTALLY EXPERIMENTAL CAR. ANYTHING COULD GO WRONG.
BUT MY INSTINCTS TOLD ME OTHERWISE!
BACK TO THE HATCH, CAPTAIN?
YES, AND I GUESS I DON'T HAVE TO TELL YOU TO HURRY, ESPECIALLY WITH ALL THE OTHER CARS GAINING!

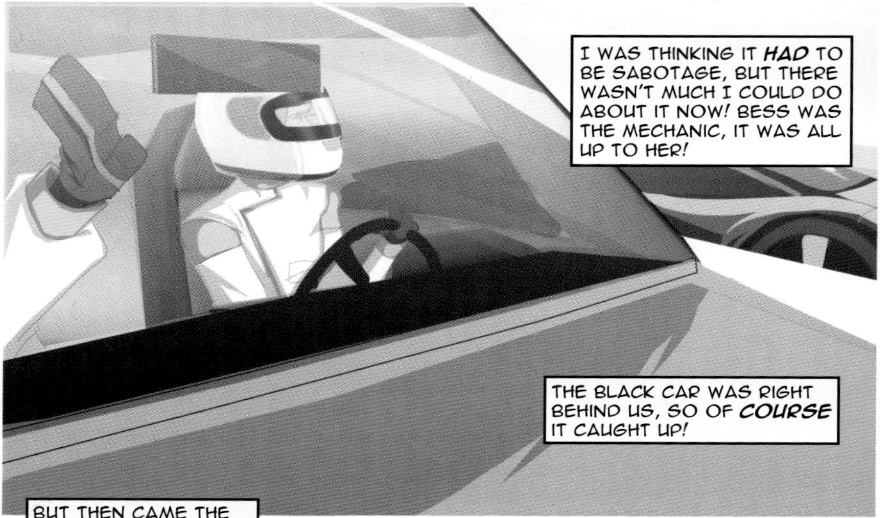
I WAS THINKING IT ***HAD*** TO BE SABOTAGE, BUT THERE WASN'T MUCH I COULD DO ABOUT IT NOW! BESS WAS THE MECHANIC, IT WAS ALL UP TO HER!
THE BLACK CAR WAS RIGHT BEHIND US, SO OF ***COURSE*** IT CAUGHT UP!

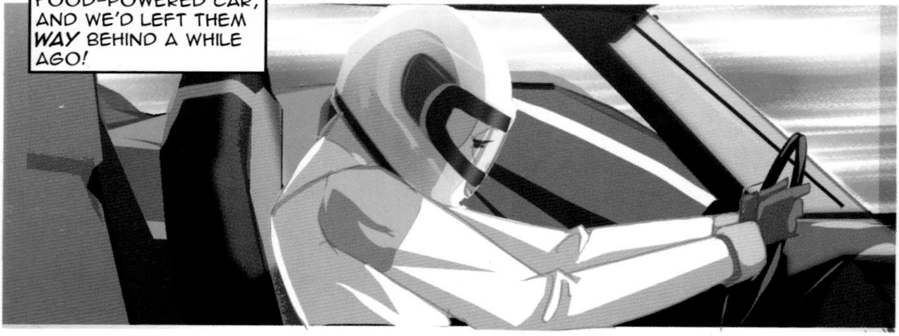
BUT THEN CAME THE FOOD-POWERED CAR, AND WE'D LEFT THEM ***WAY*** BEHIND A WHILE AGO!

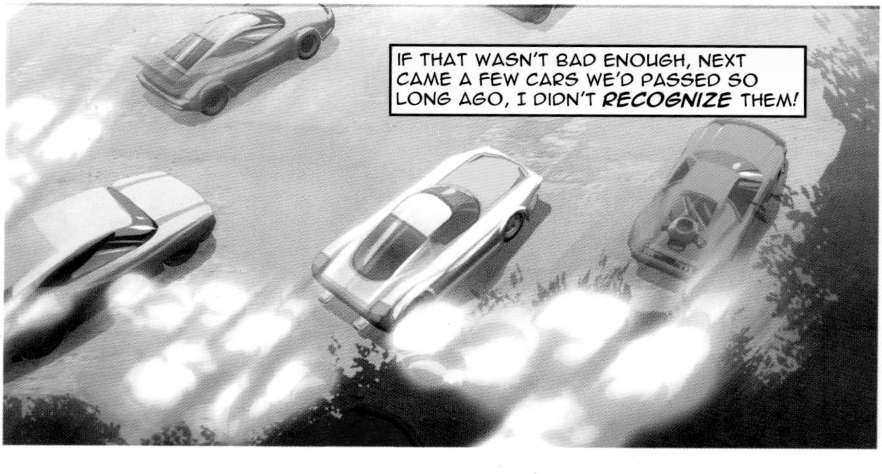
IF THAT WASN'T BAD ENOUGH, NEXT CAME A FEW CARS WE'D PASSED SO LONG AGO, I DIDN'T ***RECOGNIZE*** THEM!

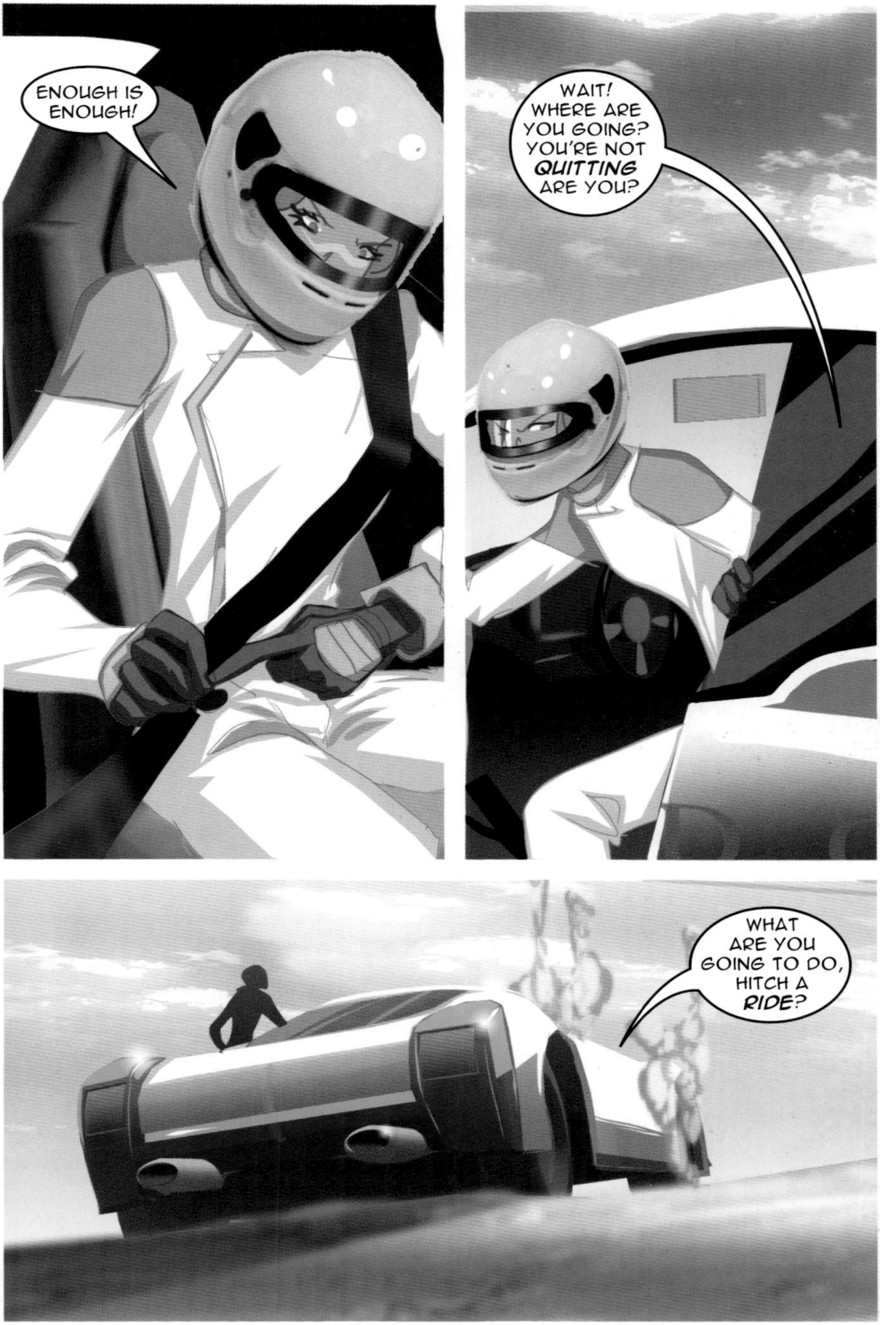
ENOUGH IS ENOUGH!
WAIT! WHERE ARE YOU GOING? YOU'RE NOT *QUITTING* ARE YOU?
WHAT ARE YOU GOING TO DO, HITCH A *RIDE*?

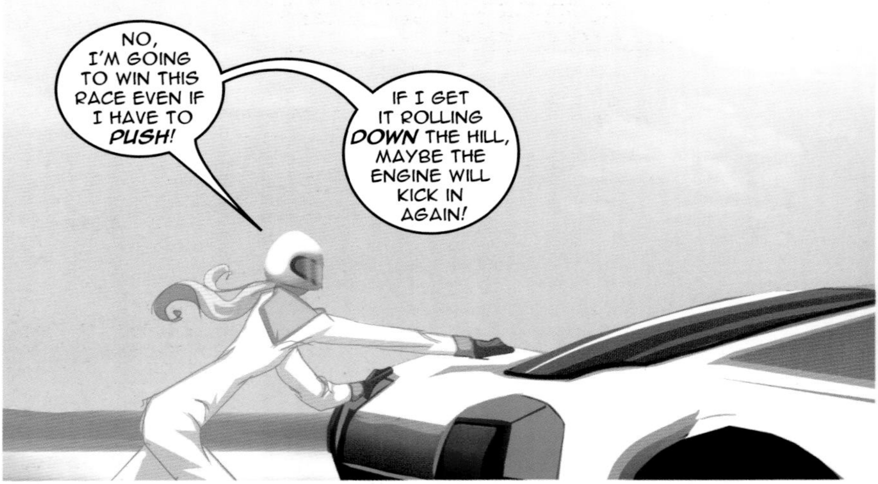
NO, I'M GOING TO WIN THIS RACE EVEN IF I HAVE TO PUSH!
IF I GET IT ROLLING DOWN THE HILL, MAYBE THE ENGINE WILL KICK IN AGAIN!

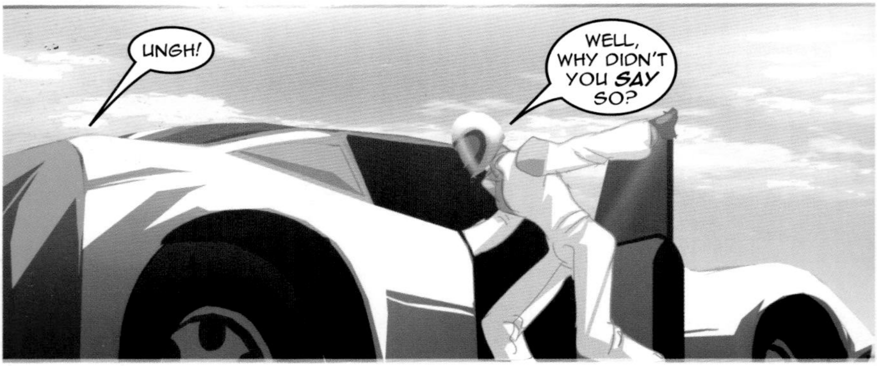
UNGH!
WELL, WHY DIDN'T YOU SAY SO?

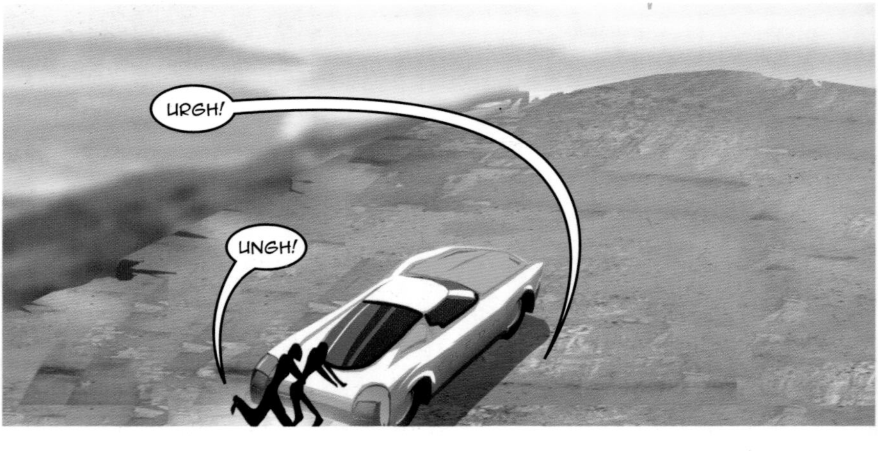
URGH!
UNGH!

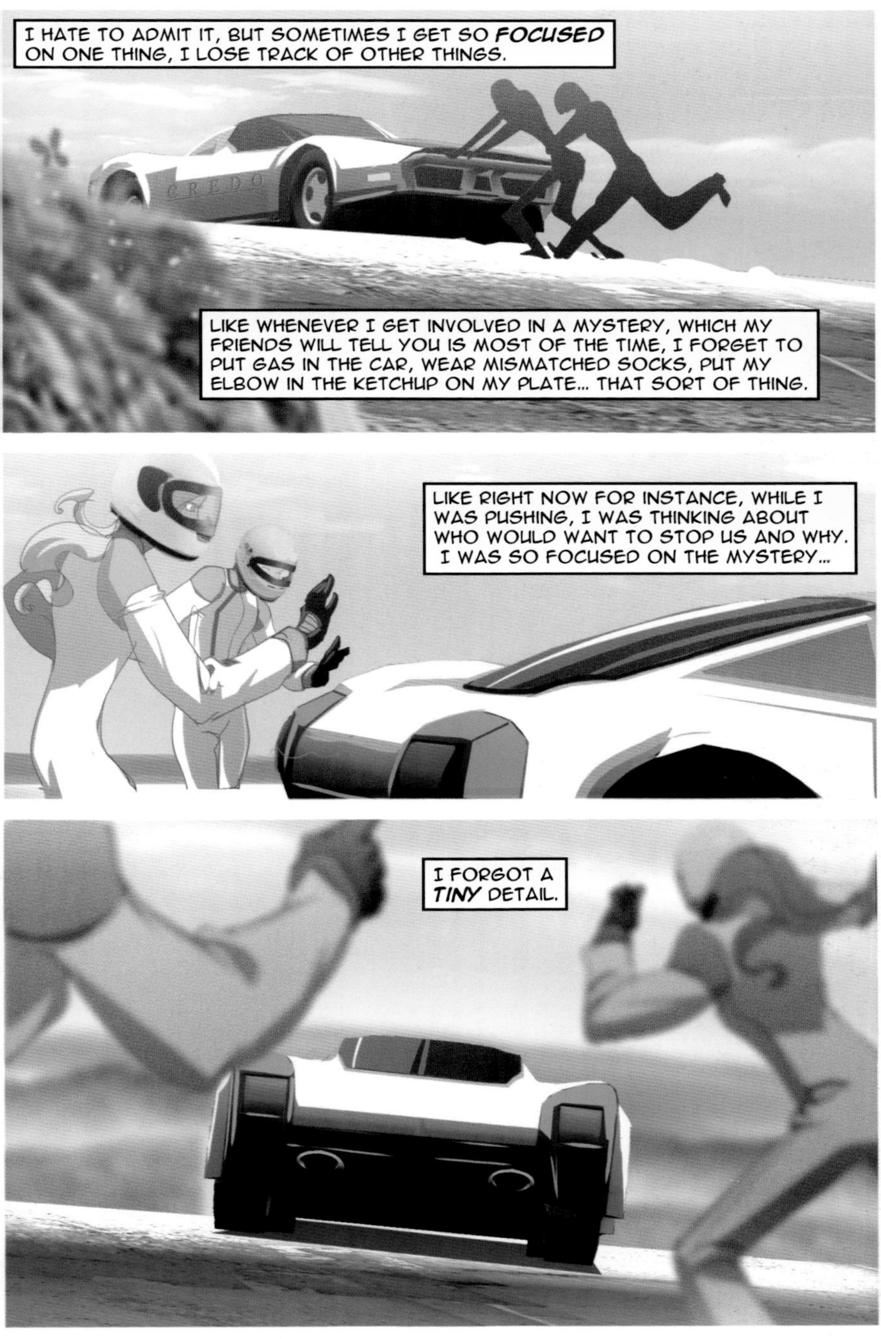
I HATE TO ADMIT IT, BUT SOMETIMES I GET SO *FOCUSED* ON ONE THING, I LOSE TRACK OF OTHER THINGS.
CREDO
LIKE WHENEVER I GET INVOLVED IN A MYSTERY, WHICH MY FRIENDS WILL TELL YOU IS MOST OF THE TIME, I FORGET TO PUT GAS IN THE CAR, WEAR MISMATCHED SOCKS, PUT MY ELBOW IN THE KETCHUP ON MY PLATE... THAT SORT OF THING.
LIKE RIGHT NOW FOR INSTANCE, WHILE I WAS PUSHING, I WAS THINKING ABOUT WHO WOULD WANT TO STOP US AND WHY. I WAS SO FOCUSED ON THE MYSTERY...
I FORGOT A *TINY* DETAIL.

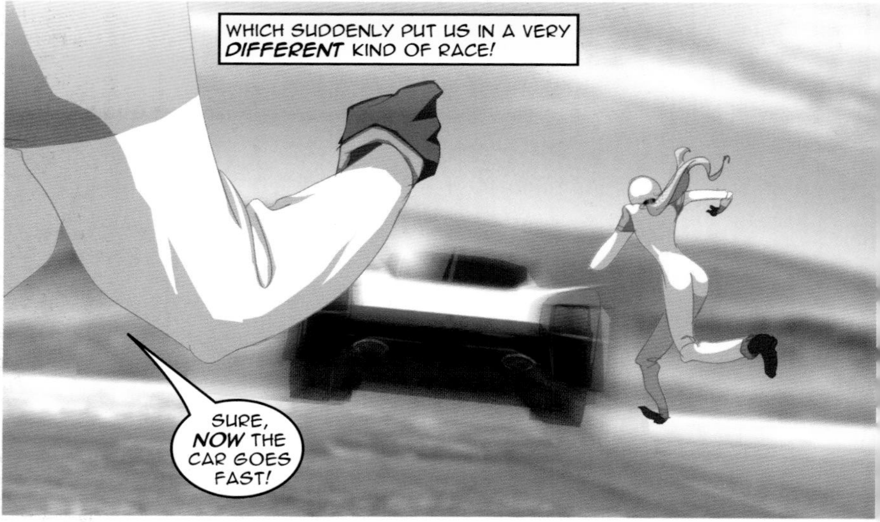
WHICH SUDDENLY PUT US IN A VERY *DIFFERENT* KIND OF RACE!
SURE, **NOW** THE CAR GOES FAST!

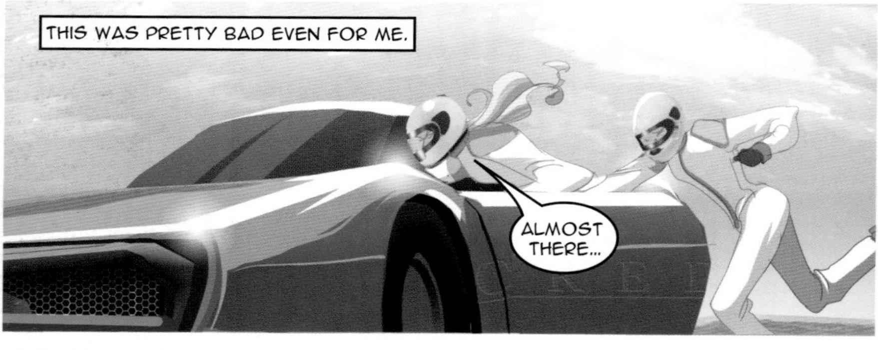
THIS WAS PRETTY BAD EVEN FOR ME.
ALMOST THERE...

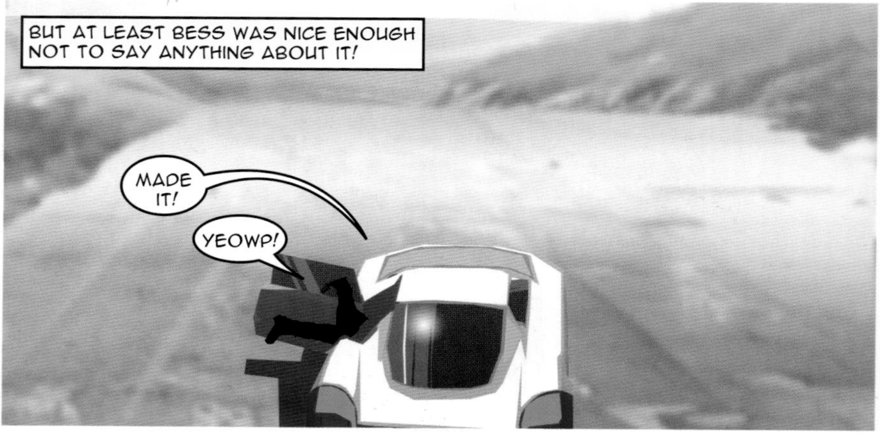
BUT AT LEAST BESS WAS NICE ENOUGH NOT TO SAY ANYTHING ABOUT IT!
MADE IT!
YEOWP!

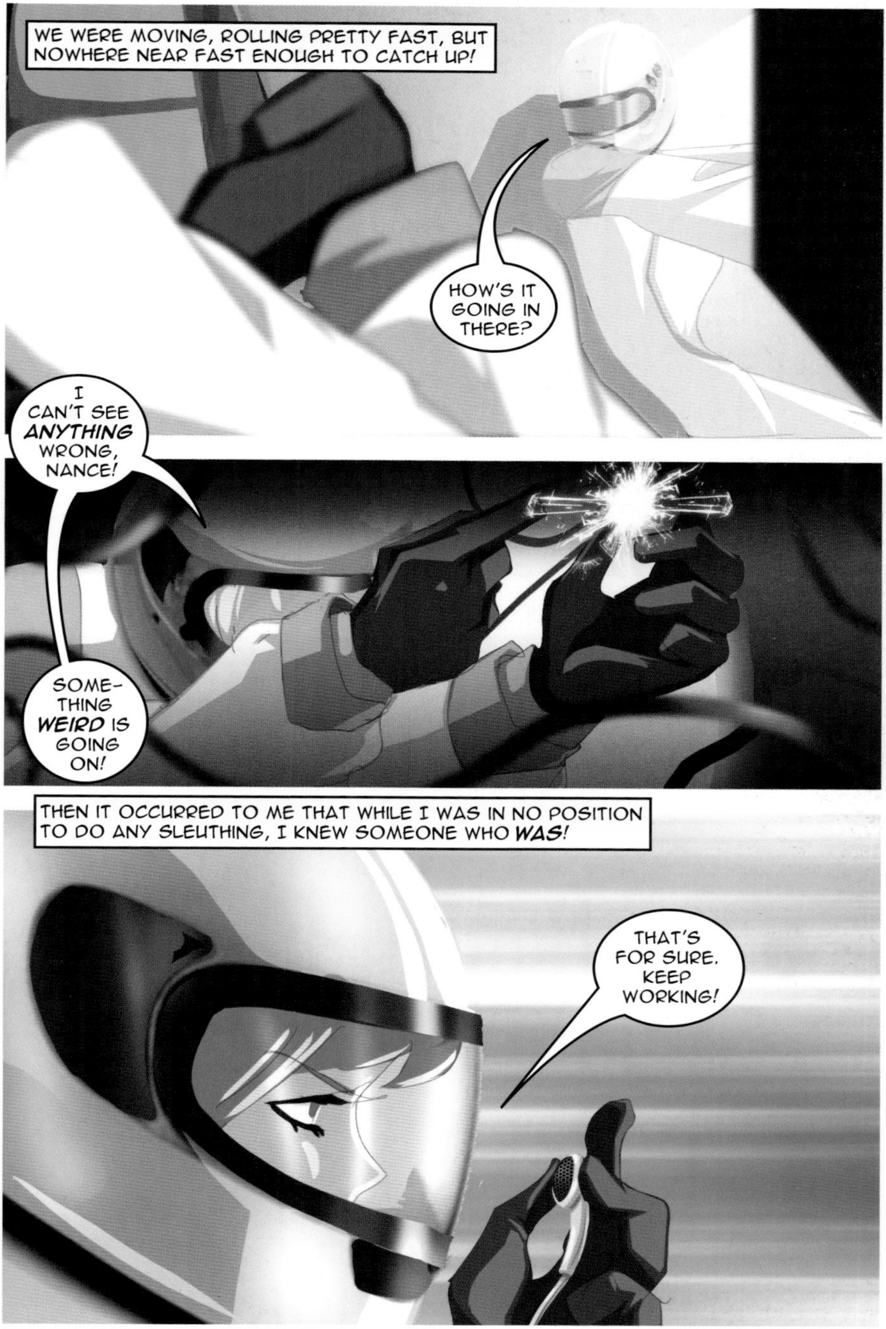
WE WERE MOVING, ROLLING PRETTY FAST, BUT NOWHERE NEAR FAST ENOUGH TO CATCH UP!
HOW'S IT GOING IN THERE?
I CAN'T SEE *ANYTHING* WRONG, NANCE!
SOMETHING *WEIRD* IS GOING ON!
THEN IT OCCURRED TO ME THAT WHILE I WAS IN NO POSITION TO DO ANY SLEUTHING, I KNEW SOMEONE WHO *WAS*!
THAT'S FOR SURE. KEEP WORKING!

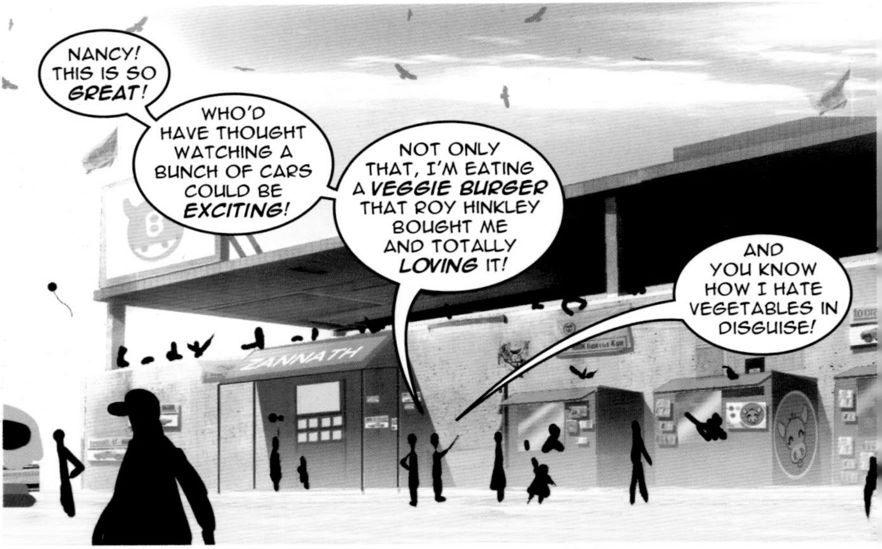
NANCY! THIS IS SO **GREAT**!
WHO'D HAVE THOUGHT WATCHING A BUNCH OF CARS COULD BE **EXCITING**!
NOT ONLY THAT, I'M EATING A **VEGGIE BURGER** THAT ROY HINKLEY BOUGHT ME AND TOTALLY **LOVING** IT!
AND YOU KNOW HOW I HATE VEGETABLES IN DISGUISE!
ZANNATH

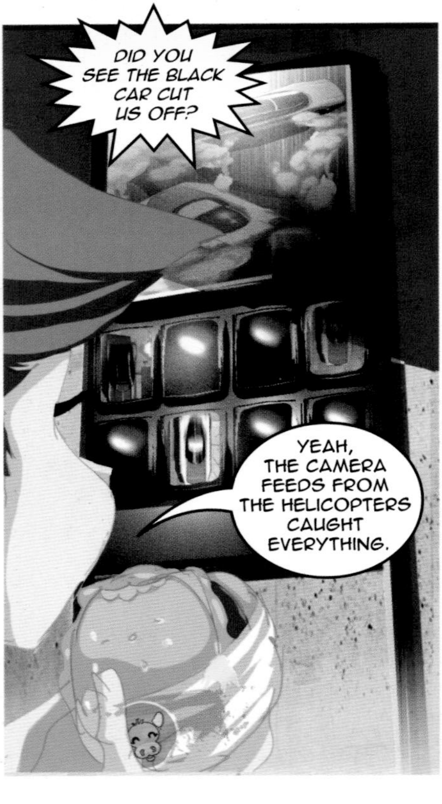
DID YOU SEE THE BLACK CAR CUT US OFF?
YEAH, THE CAMERA FEEDS FROM THE HELICOPTERS CAUGHT EVERYTHING.

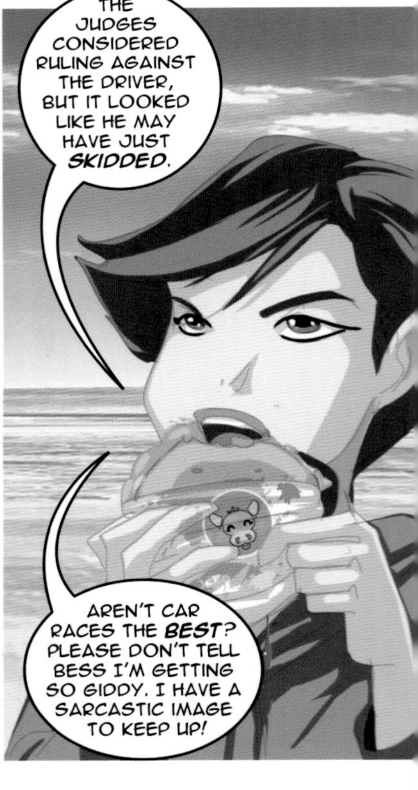
THE JUDGES CONSIDERED RULING AGAINST THE DRIVER, BUT IT LOOKED LIKE HE MAY HAVE JUST **SKIDDED**.
AREN'T CAR RACES THE **BEST**? PLEASE DON'T TELL BESS I'M GETTING SO GIDDY. I HAVE A SARCASTIC IMAGE TO KEEP UP!

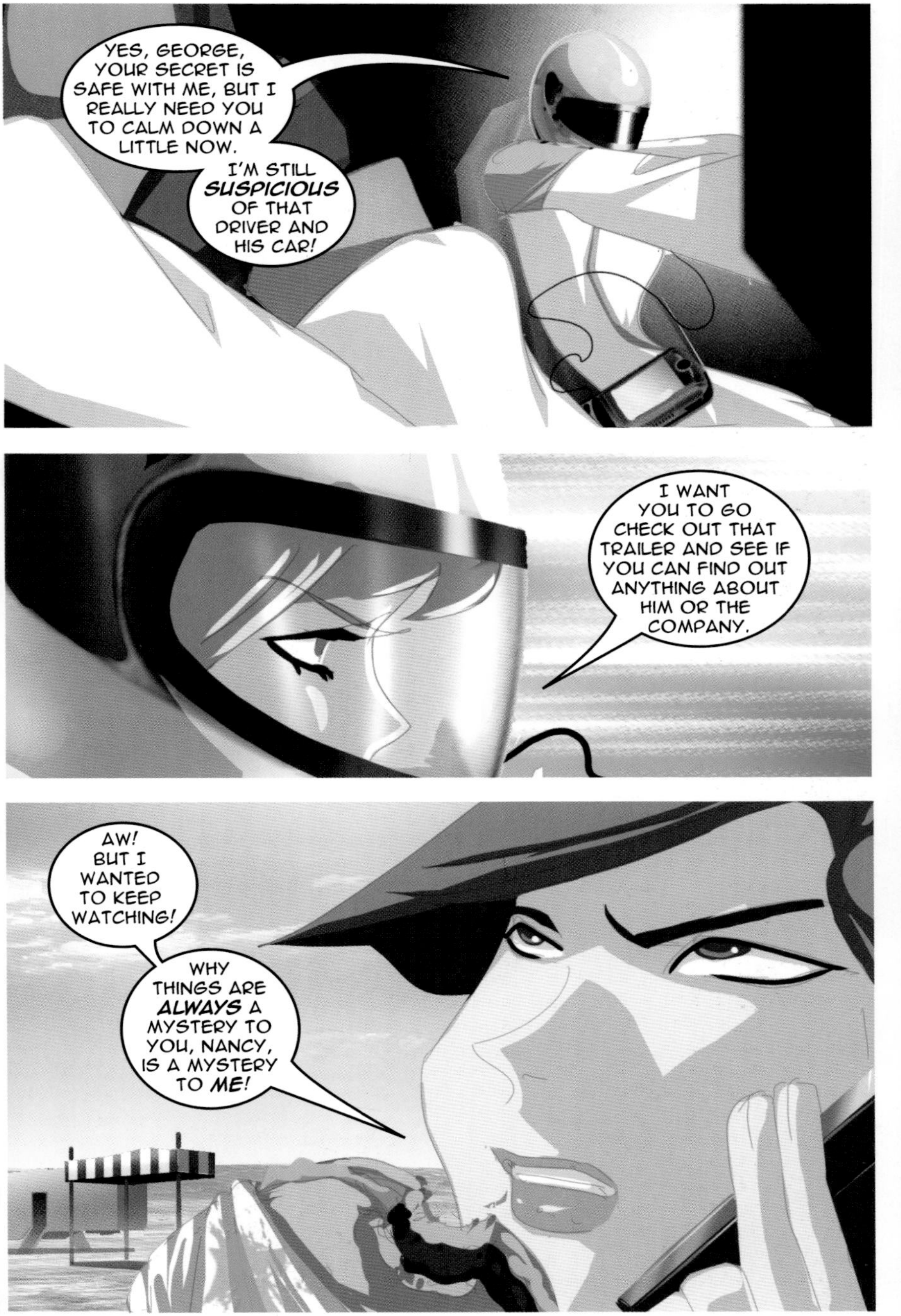
YES, GEORGE, YOUR SECRET IS SAFE WITH ME, BUT I REALLY NEED YOU TO CALM DOWN A LITTLE NOW.
I'M STILL *SUSPICIOUS* OF THAT DRIVER AND HIS CAR!
I WANT YOU TO GO CHECK OUT THAT TRAILER AND SEE IF YOU CAN FIND OUT ANYTHING ABOUT HIM OR THE COMPANY.
AW! BUT I WANTED TO KEEP WATCHING!
WHY THINGS ARE *ALWAYS* A MYSTERY TO YOU, NANCY, IS A MYSTERY TO *ME*!

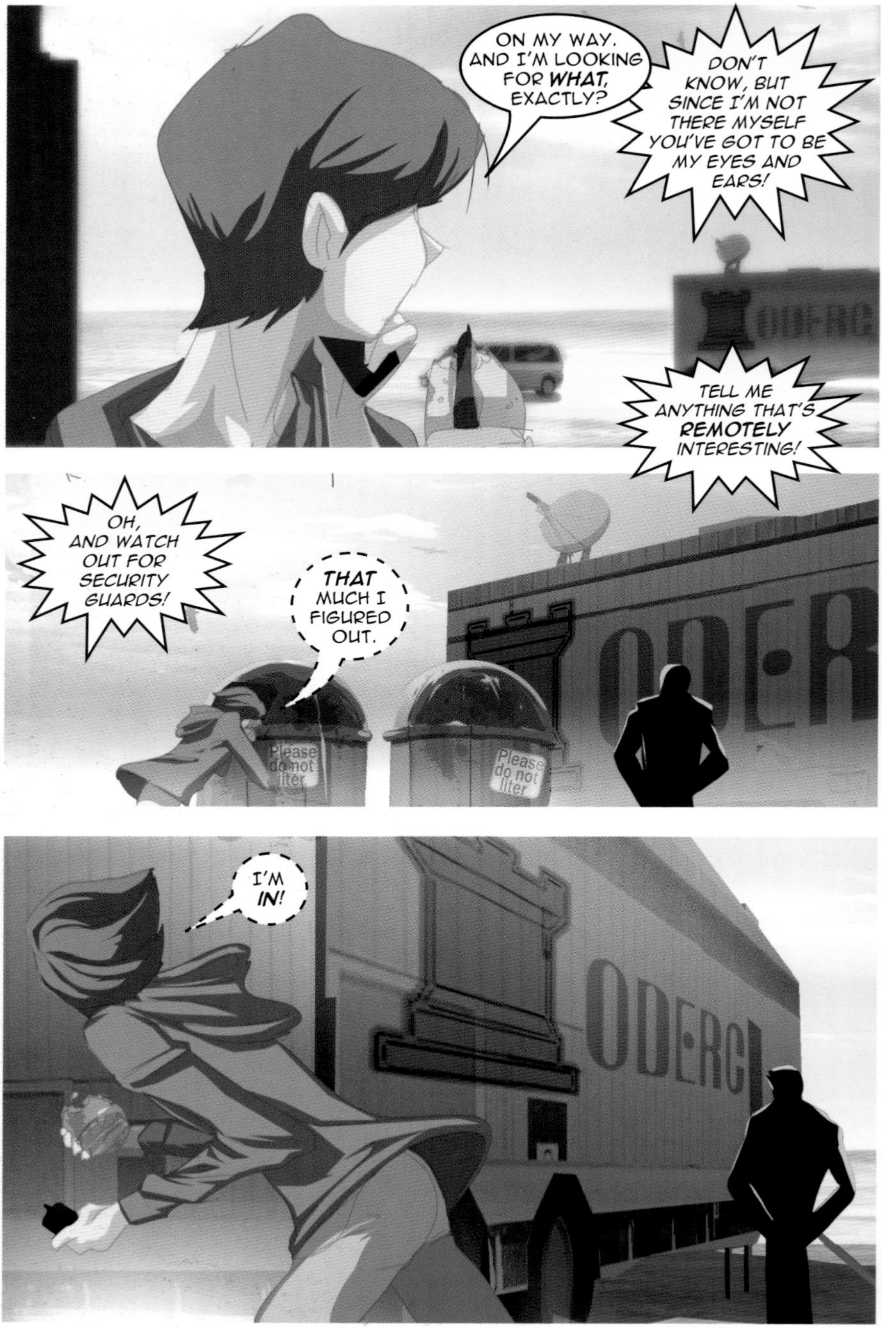
ON MY WAY. AND I'M LOOKING FOR **WHAT,** EXACTLY?
DON'T KNOW, BUT SINCE I'M NOT THERE MYSELF YOU'VE GOT TO BE MY EYES AND EARS!
TELL ME ANYTHING THAT'S **REMOTELY** INTERESTING!
OH, AND WATCH OUT FOR SECURITY GUARDS!
THAT MUCH I FIGURED OUT.
Please do not liter
Please do not liter
I'M **IN!**

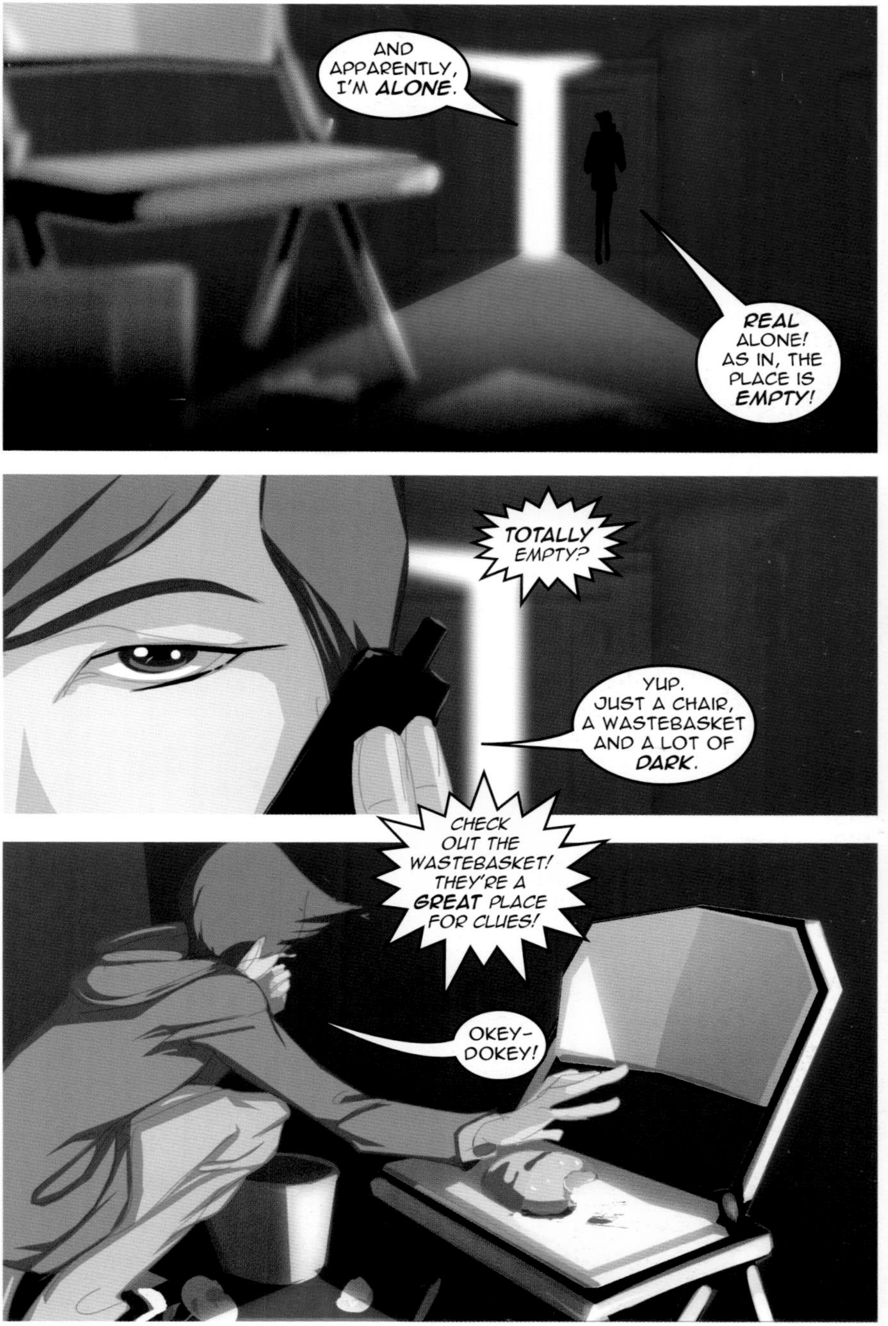
AND APPARENTLY, I'M ALONE.
REAL ALONE! AS IN, THE PLACE IS EMPTY!
TOTALLY EMPTY?
YUP. JUST A CHAIR, A WASTEBASKET AND A LOT OF DARK.
CHECK OUT THE WASTEBASKET! THEY'RE A GREAT PLACE FOR CLUES!
OKEY-DOKEY!

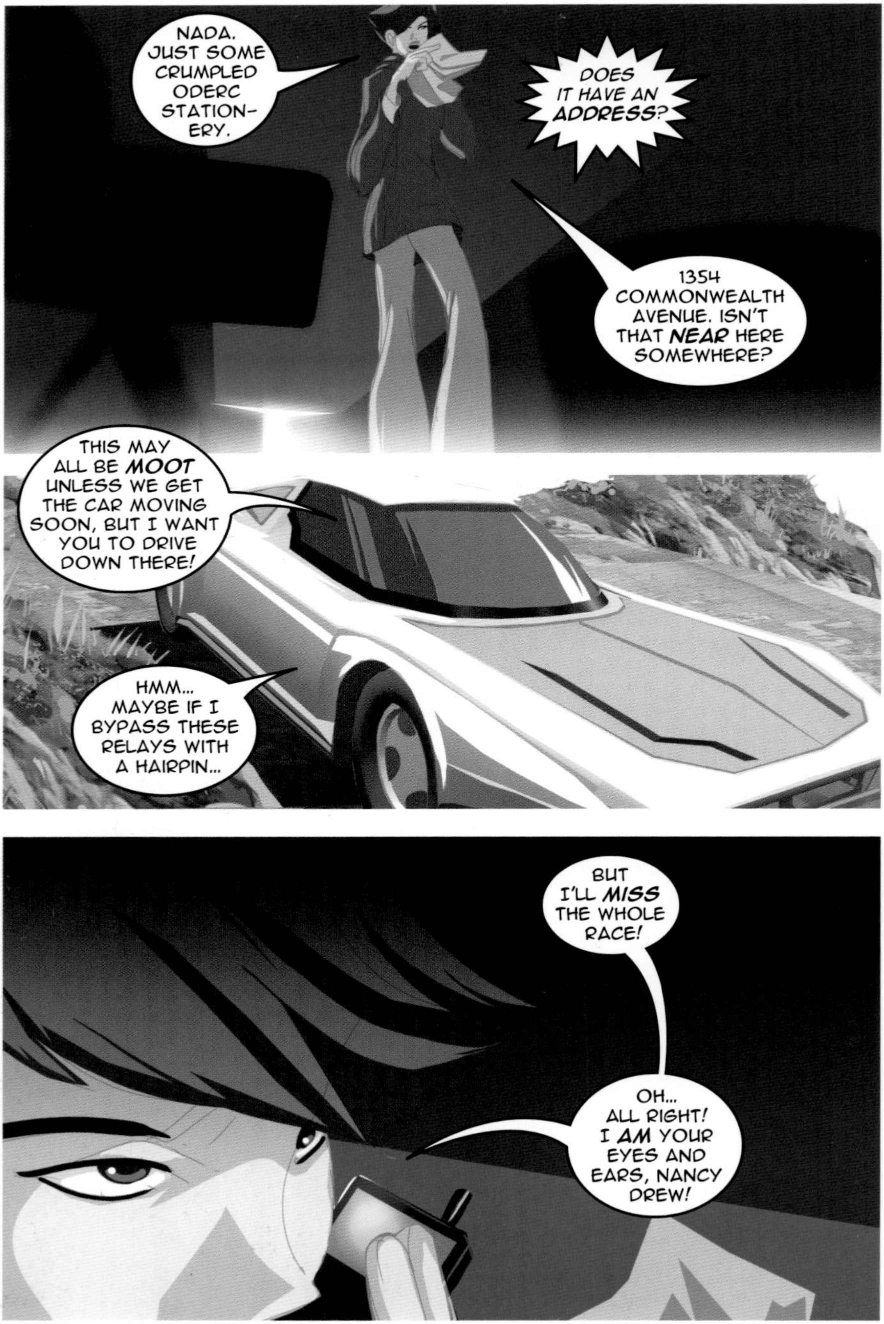
NADA. JUST SOME CRUMPLED ODERC STATION-ERY.
DOES IT HAVE AN ADDRESS?
1354 COMMONWEALTH AVENUE. ISN'T THAT NEAR HERE SOMEWHERE?
THIS MAY ALL BE MOOT UNLESS WE GET THE CAR MOVING SOON, BUT I WANT YOU TO DRIVE DOWN THERE!
HMM... MAYBE IF I BYPASS THESE RELAYS WITH A HAIRPIN...
BUT I'LL MISS THE WHOLE RACE!
OH... ALL RIGHT! I AM YOUR EYES AND EARS, NANCY DREW!

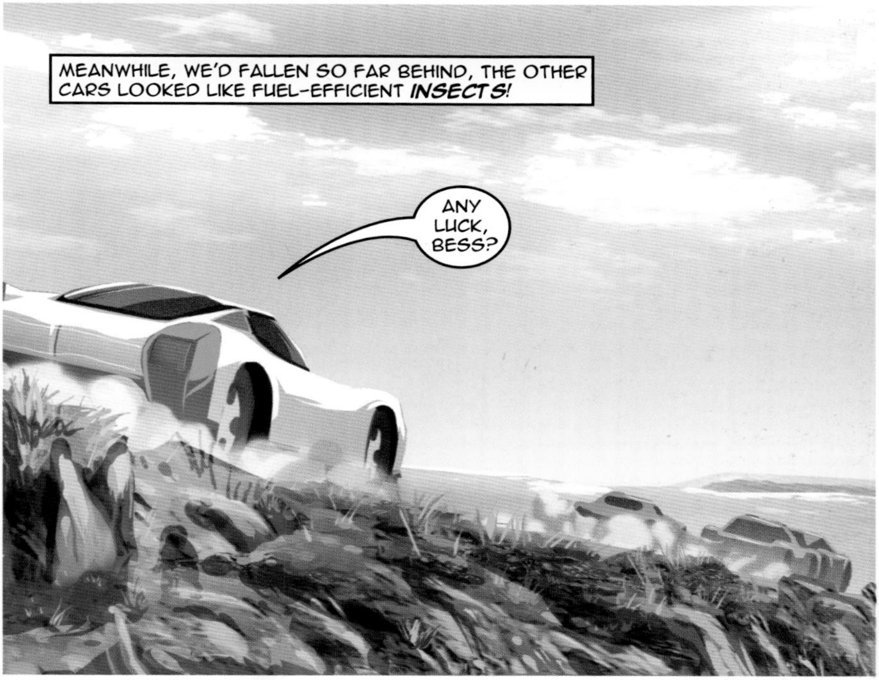
MEANWHILE, WE'D FALLEN SO FAR BEHIND, THE OTHER CARS LOOKED LIKE FUEL-EFFICIENT INSECTS!
ANY LUCK, BESS?

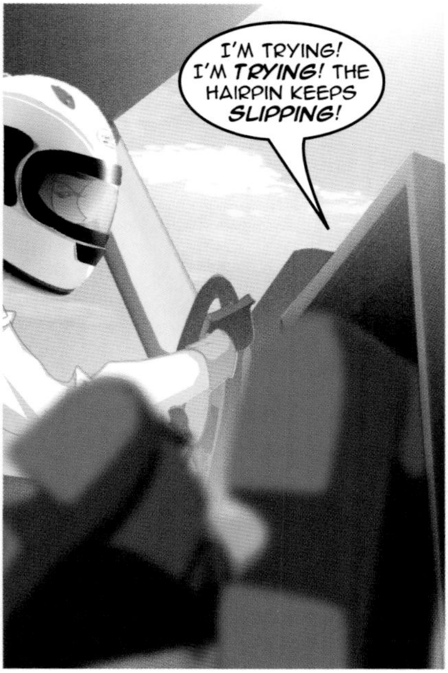
I'M TRYING! I'M TRYING! THE HAIRPIN KEEPS SLIPPING!

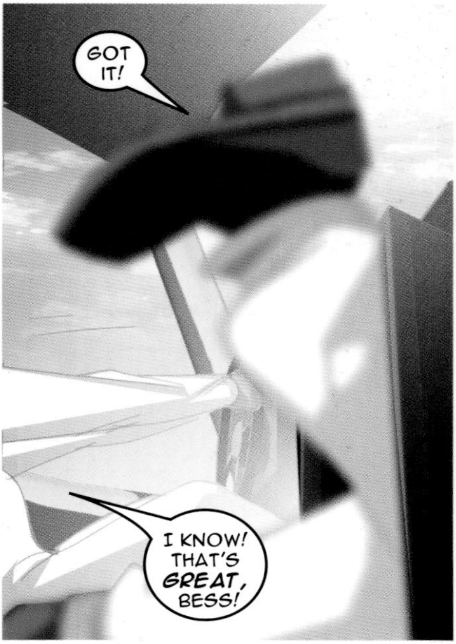
GOT IT!
I KNOW! THAT'S GREAT, BESS!

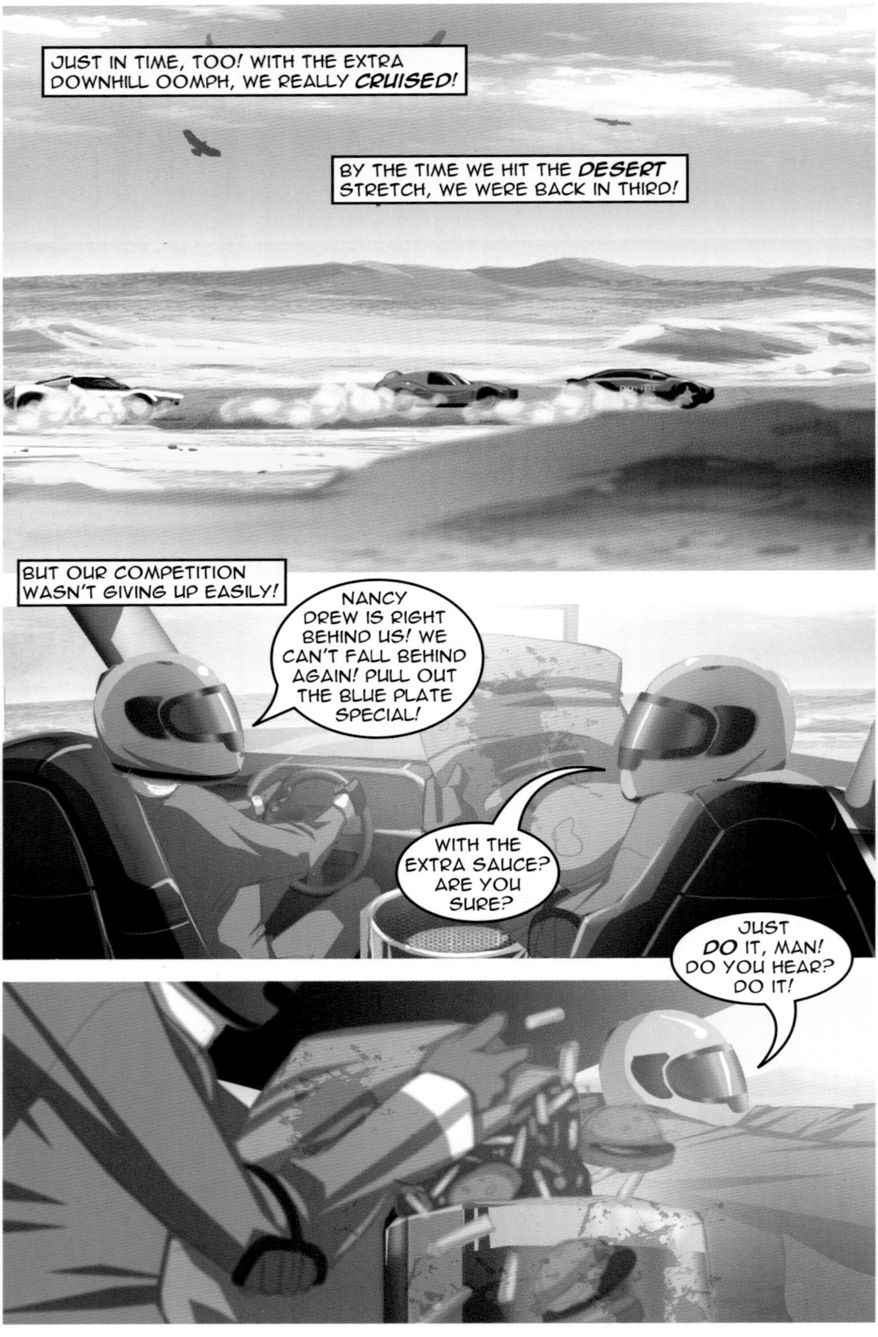
JUST IN TIME, TOO! WITH THE EXTRA DOWNHILL OOMPH, WE REALLY CRUISED!
BY THE TIME WE HIT THE DESERT STRETCH, WE WERE BACK IN THIRD!
BUT OUR COMPETITION WASN'T GIVING UP EASILY!
NANCY DREW IS RIGHT BEHIND US! WE CAN'T FALL BEHIND AGAIN! PULL OUT THE BLUE PLATE SPECIAL!
WITH THE EXTRA SAUCE? ARE YOU SURE?
JUST DO IT, MAN! DO YOU HEAR? DO IT!

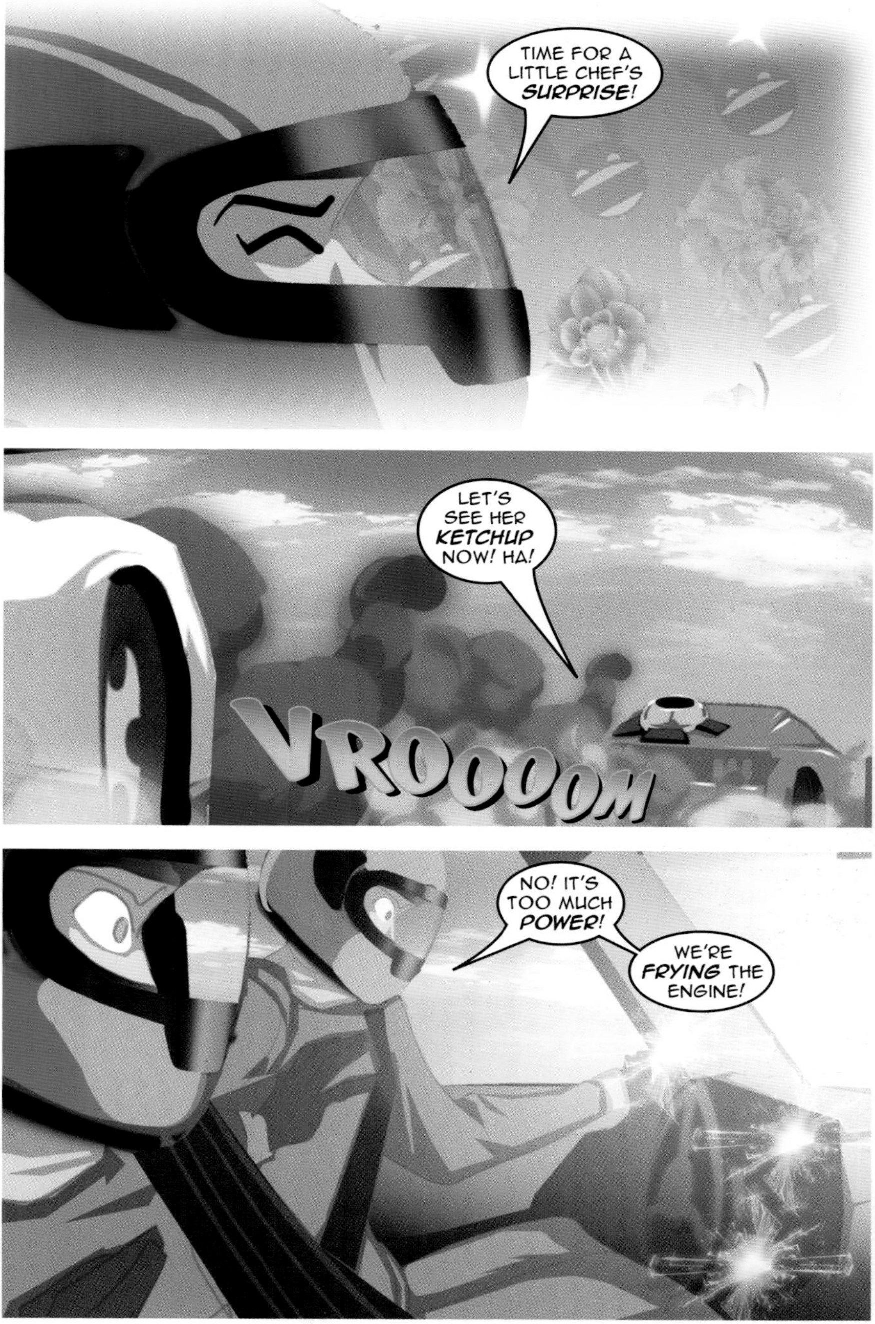
TIME FOR A LITTLE CHEF'S *SURPRISE!*
LET'S SEE HER *KETCHUP* NOW! HA!
VROOOOM
NO! IT'S TOO MUCH *POWER!*
WE'RE *FRYING* THE ENGINE!

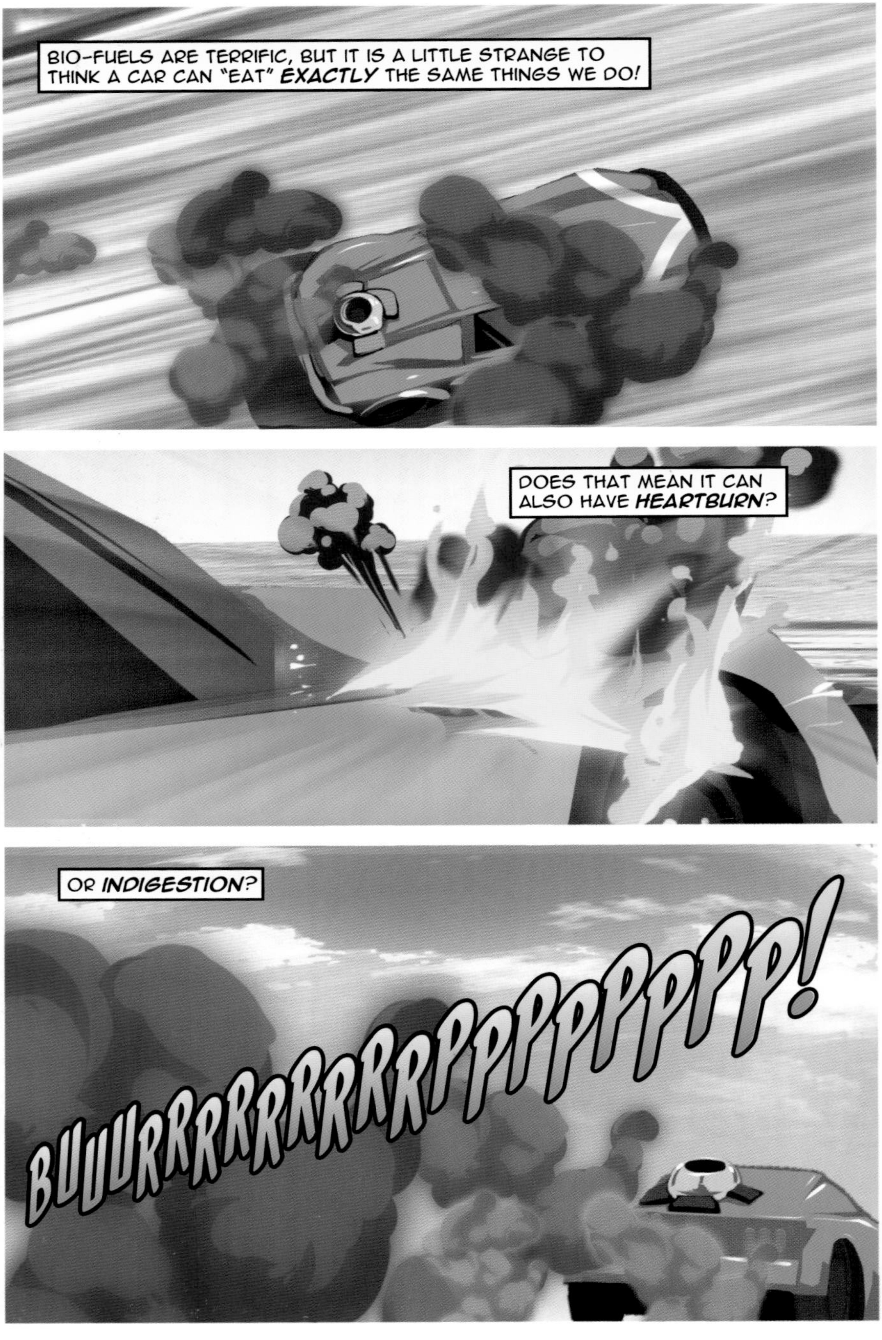
BIO-FUELS ARE TERRIFIC, BUT IT IS A LITTLE STRANGE TO THINK A CAR CAN "EAT" EXACTLY THE SAME THINGS WE DO!
DOES THAT MEAN IT CAN ALSO HAVE HEARTBURN?
OR INDIGESTION?
BUUURRRRRRRRRRPPPPPPPPP!

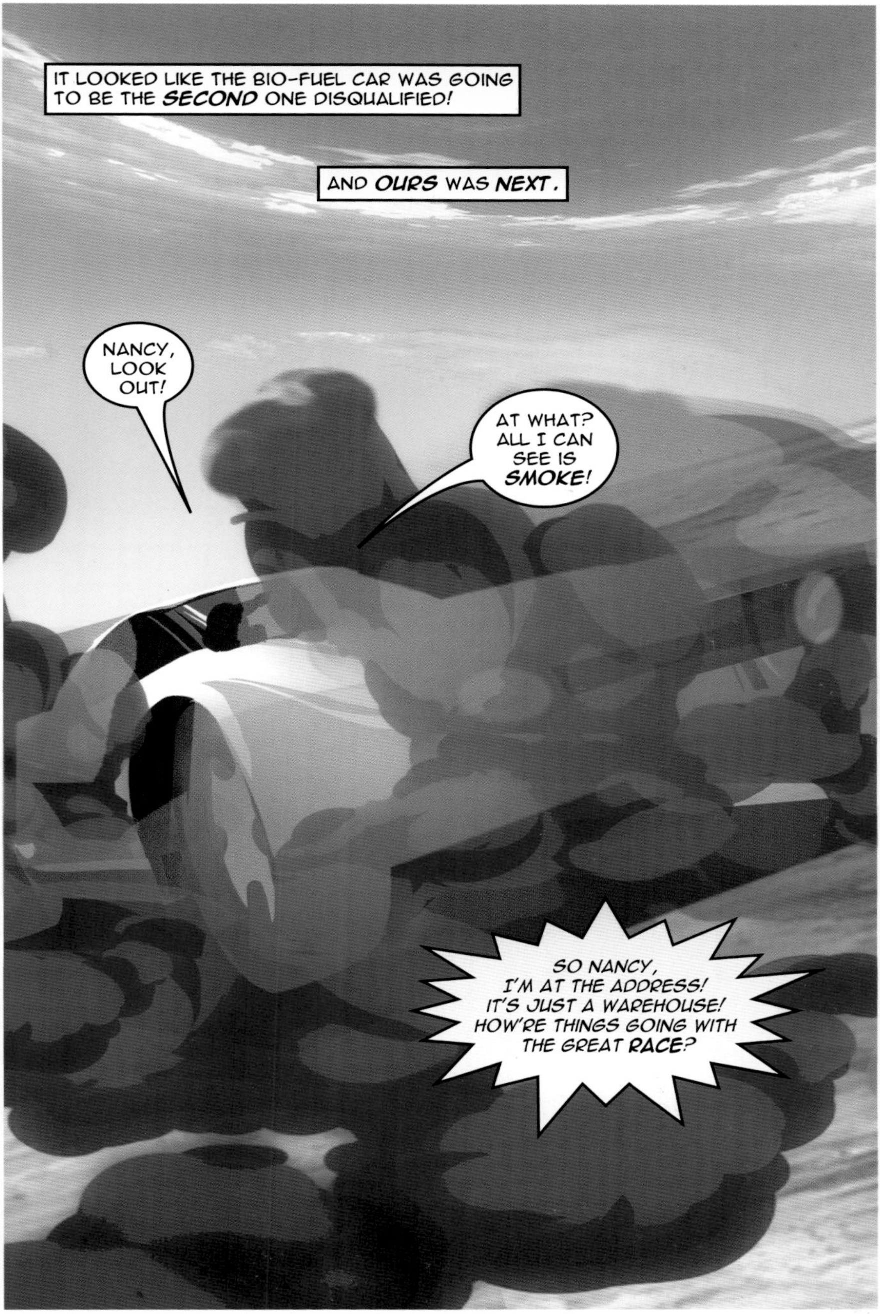
IT LOOKED LIKE THE BIO-FUEL CAR WAS GOING TO BE THE *SECOND* ONE DISQUALIFIED!
AND *OURS* WAS *NEXT*.
NANCY, LOOK OUT!
AT WHAT? ALL I CAN SEE IS *SMOKE*!
SO NANCY, I'M AT THE ADDRESS! IT'S JUST A WAREHOUSE! HOW'RE THINGS GOING WITH THE GREAT *RACE*?

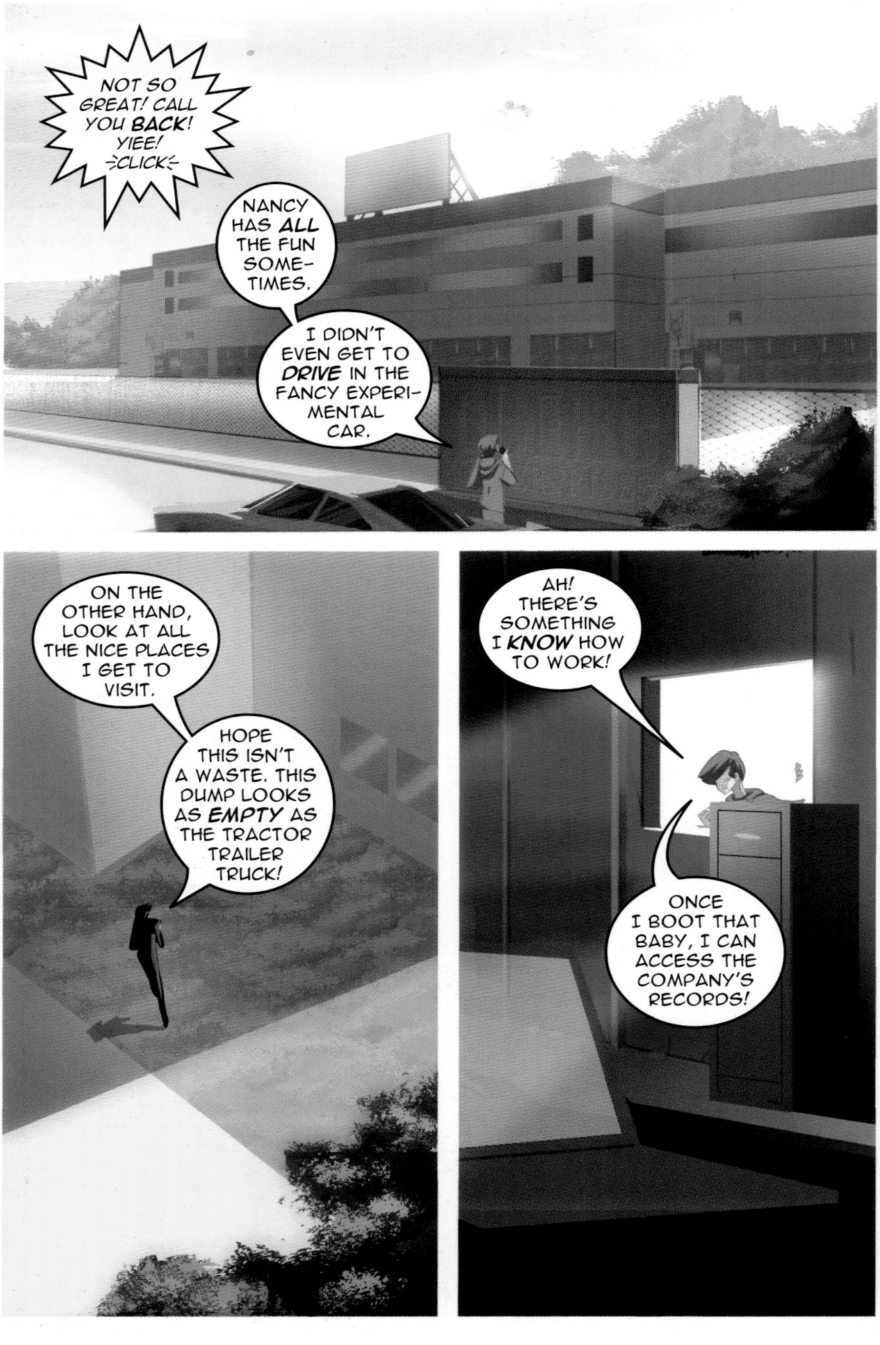
NOT SO GREAT! CALL YOU BACK! YIEE! ⪢CLICK⪡
NANCY HAS ALL THE FUN SOME-TIMES.
I DIDN'T EVEN GET TO DRIVE IN THE FANCY EXPERI-MENTAL CAR.
ON THE OTHER HAND, LOOK AT ALL THE NICE PLACES I GET TO VISIT.
HOPE THIS ISN'T A WASTE. THIS DUMP LOOKS AS EMPTY AS THE TRACTOR TRAILER TRUCK!
AH! THERE'S SOMETHING I KNOW HOW TO WORK!
ONCE I BOOT THAT BABY, I CAN ACCESS THE COMPANY'S RECORDS!

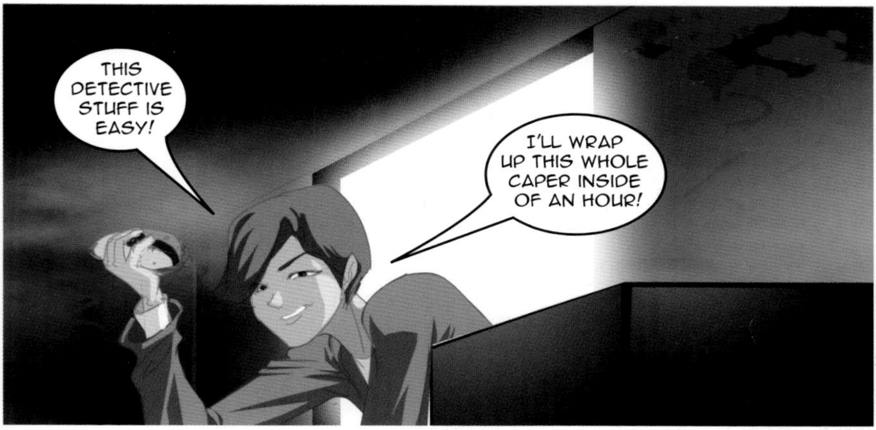
THIS DETECTIVE STUFF IS EASY!
I'LL WRAP UP THIS WHOLE CAPER INSIDE OF AN HOUR!

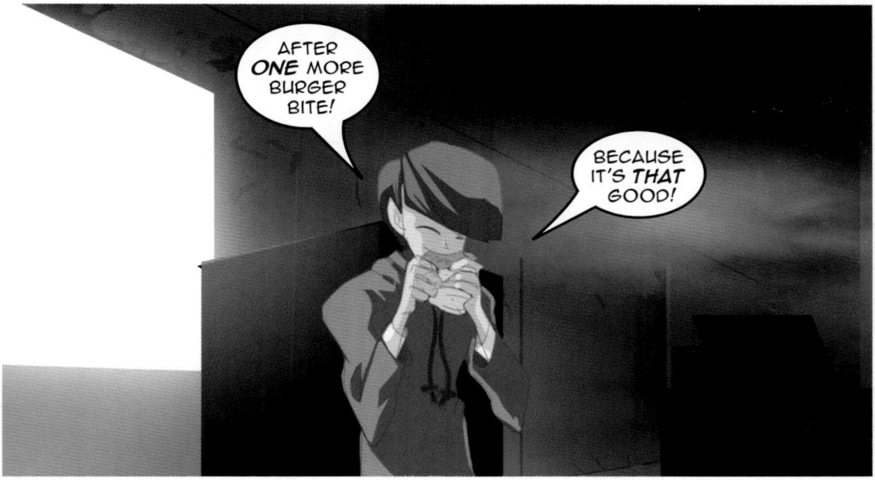
AFTER *ONE* MORE BURGER BITE!
BECAUSE IT'S *THAT* GOOD!

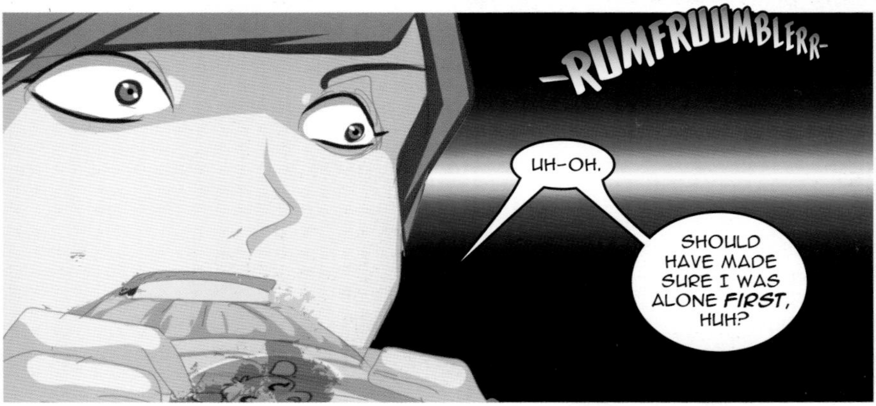
-RUMFRUUMBLERR-
UH-OH.
SHOULD HAVE MADE SURE I WAS ALONE *FIRST*, HUH?

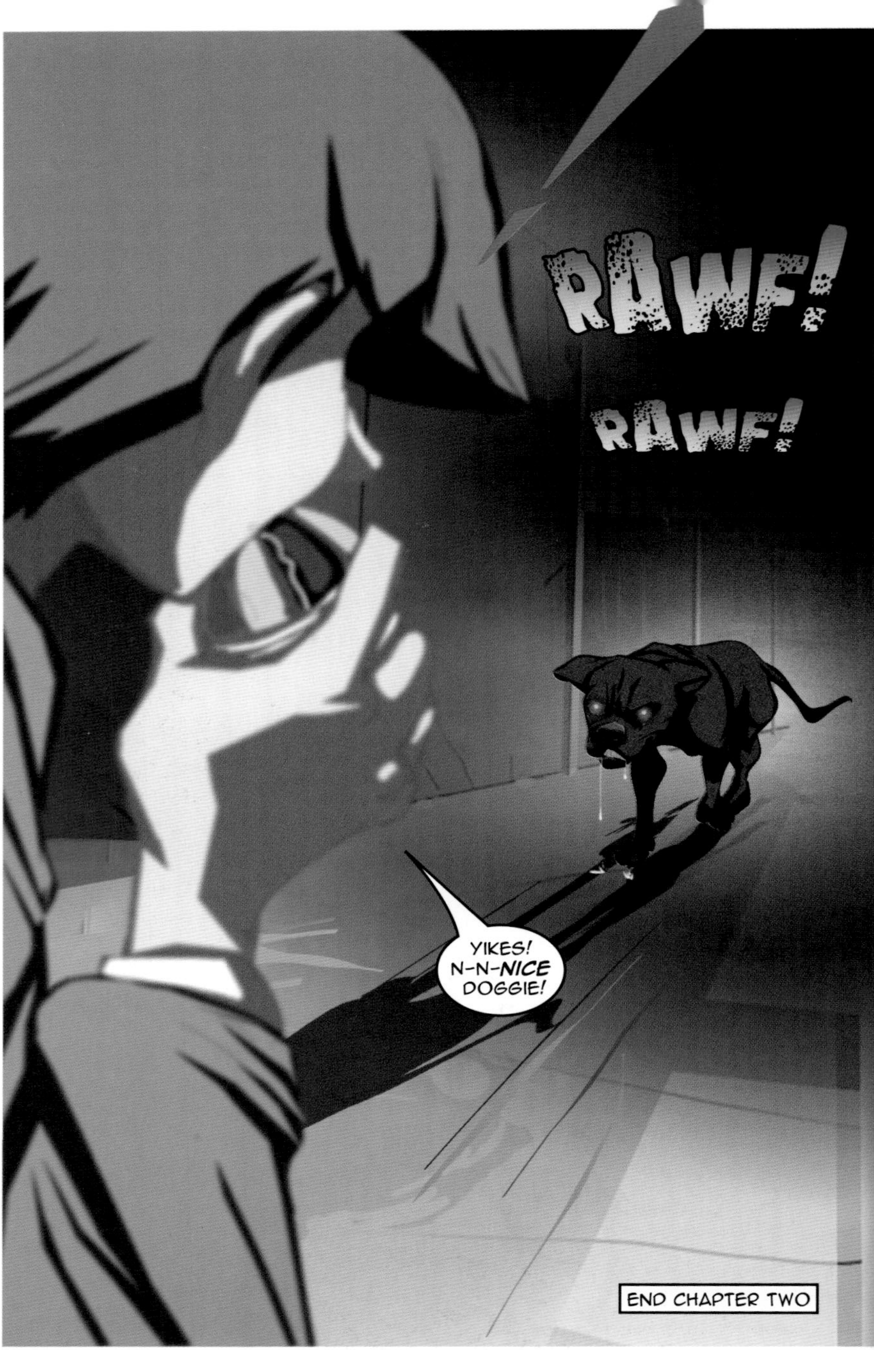
RAWF!
RAWF!
YIKES! N-N-NICE DOGGIE!
END CHAPTER TWO

I CAN'T SEE!
I ALWAYS SAY, WHEN YOU CAN'T SEE WHERE YOU'RE GOING... STOP!
THAT SEEMED SMART TO ME!
I JUST HOPED I COULD STOP BEFORE THE INVISIBLE CAR STOPPED US!
ROY HAD SAID IN AN EMERGENCY I MIGHT HAVE TO SPIN THE CAR, AND THIS SEEMED LIKE IT!
CHAPTER THREE: STALL'S WELL

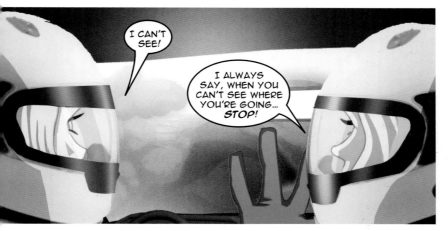

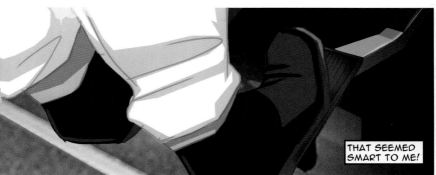

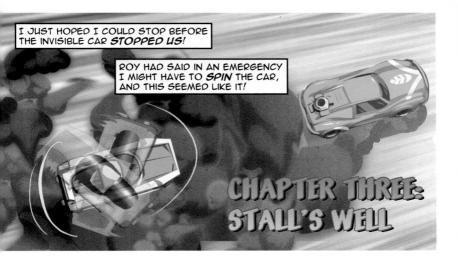

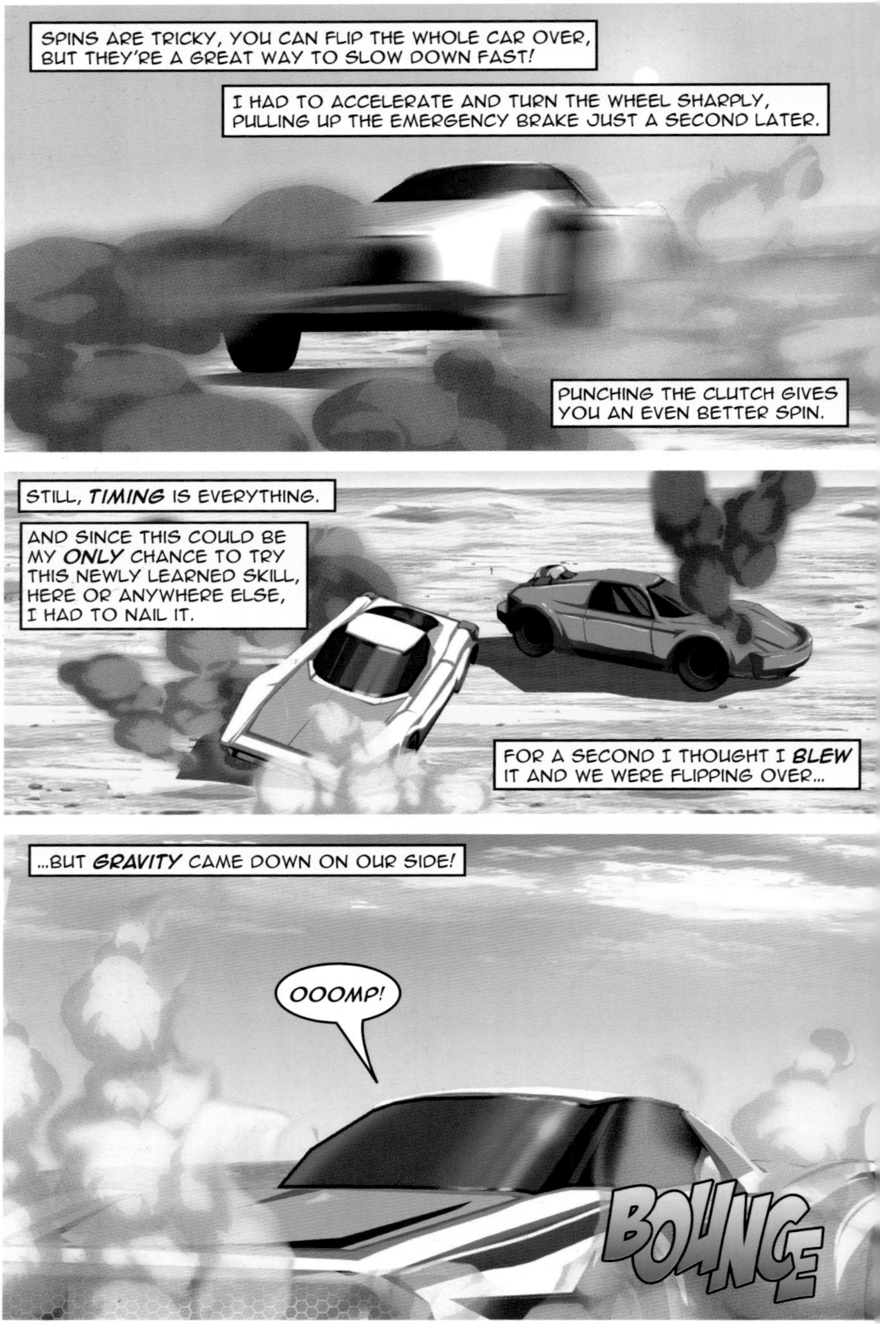
SPINS ARE TRICKY, YOU CAN FLIP THE WHOLE CAR OVER, BUT THEY'RE A GREAT WAY TO SLOW DOWN FAST!
I HAD TO ACCELERATE AND TURN THE WHEEL SHARPLY, PULLING UP THE EMERGENCY BRAKE JUST A SECOND LATER.
PUNCHING THE CLUTCH GIVES YOU AN EVEN BETTER SPIN.
STILL, *TIMING* IS EVERYTHING.
AND SINCE THIS COULD BE MY *ONLY* CHANCE TO TRY THIS NEWLY LEARNED SKILL, HERE OR ANYWHERE ELSE, I HAD TO NAIL IT.
FOR A SECOND I THOUGHT I *BLEW* IT AND WE WERE FLIPPING OVER...
...BUT *GRAVITY* CAME DOWN ON OUR SIDE!
OOOMP!
BOUNCE

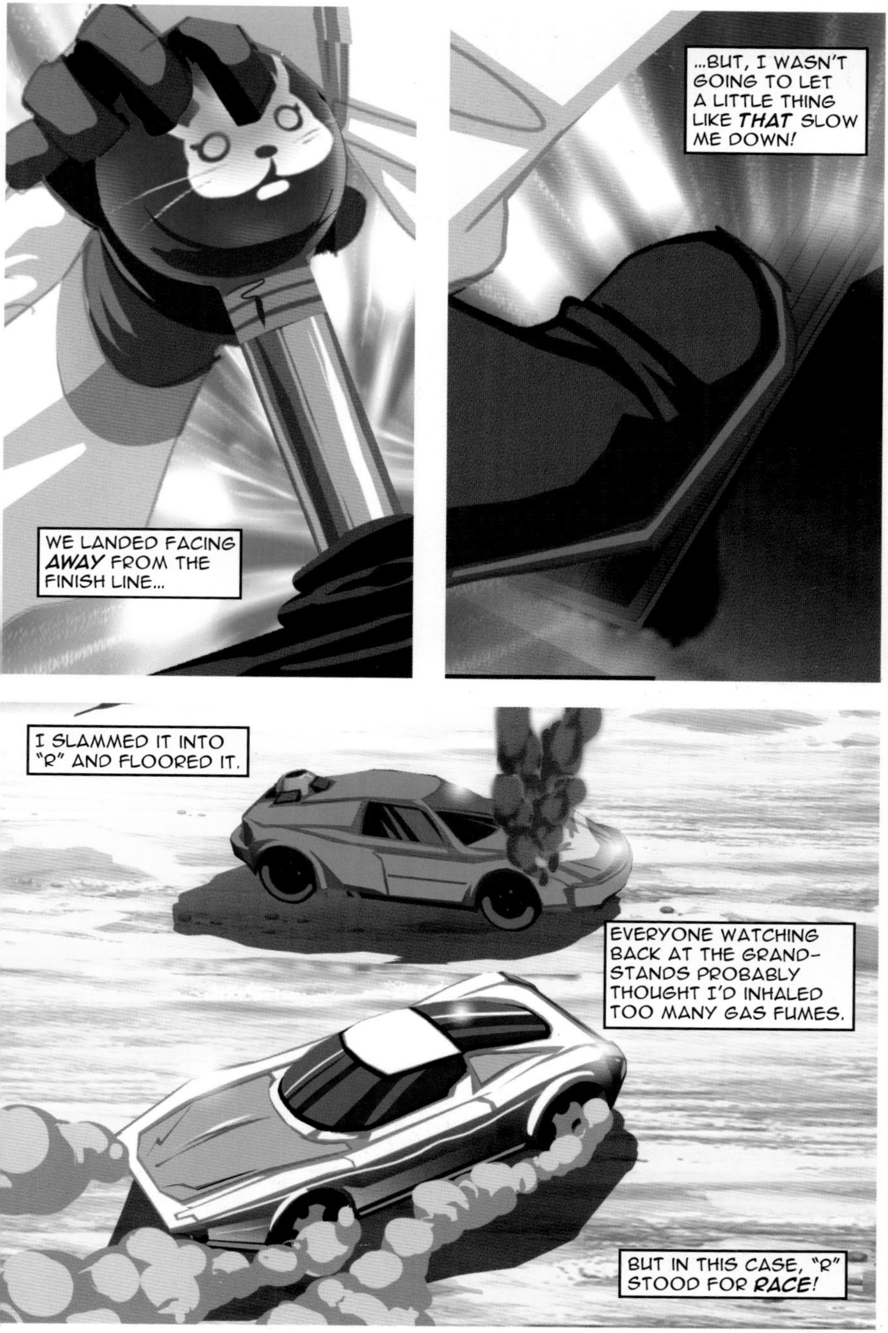
WE LANDED FACING **AWAY** FROM THE FINISH LINE...
...BUT, I WASN'T GOING TO LET A LITTLE THING LIKE **THAT** SLOW ME DOWN!
I SLAMMED IT INTO "R" AND FLOORED IT.
EVERYONE WATCHING BACK AT THE GRAND-STANDS PROBABLY THOUGHT I'D INHALED TOO MANY GAS FUMES.
BUT IN THIS CASE, "R" STOOD FOR **RACE**!

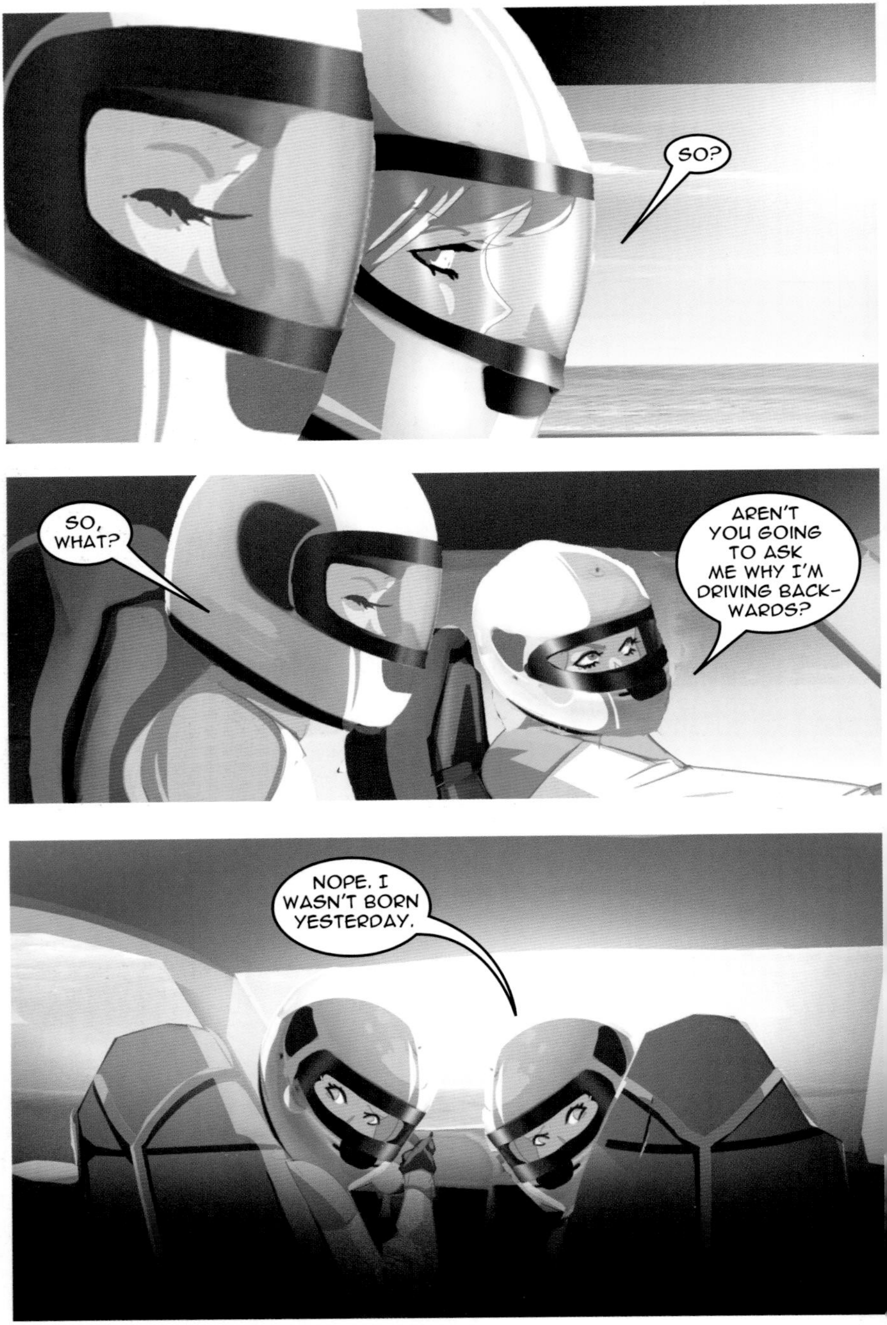
SO?
SO, WHAT?
AREN'T YOU GOING TO ASK ME WHY I'M DRIVING BACK-WARDS?
NOPE. I WASN'T BORN YESTERDAY.

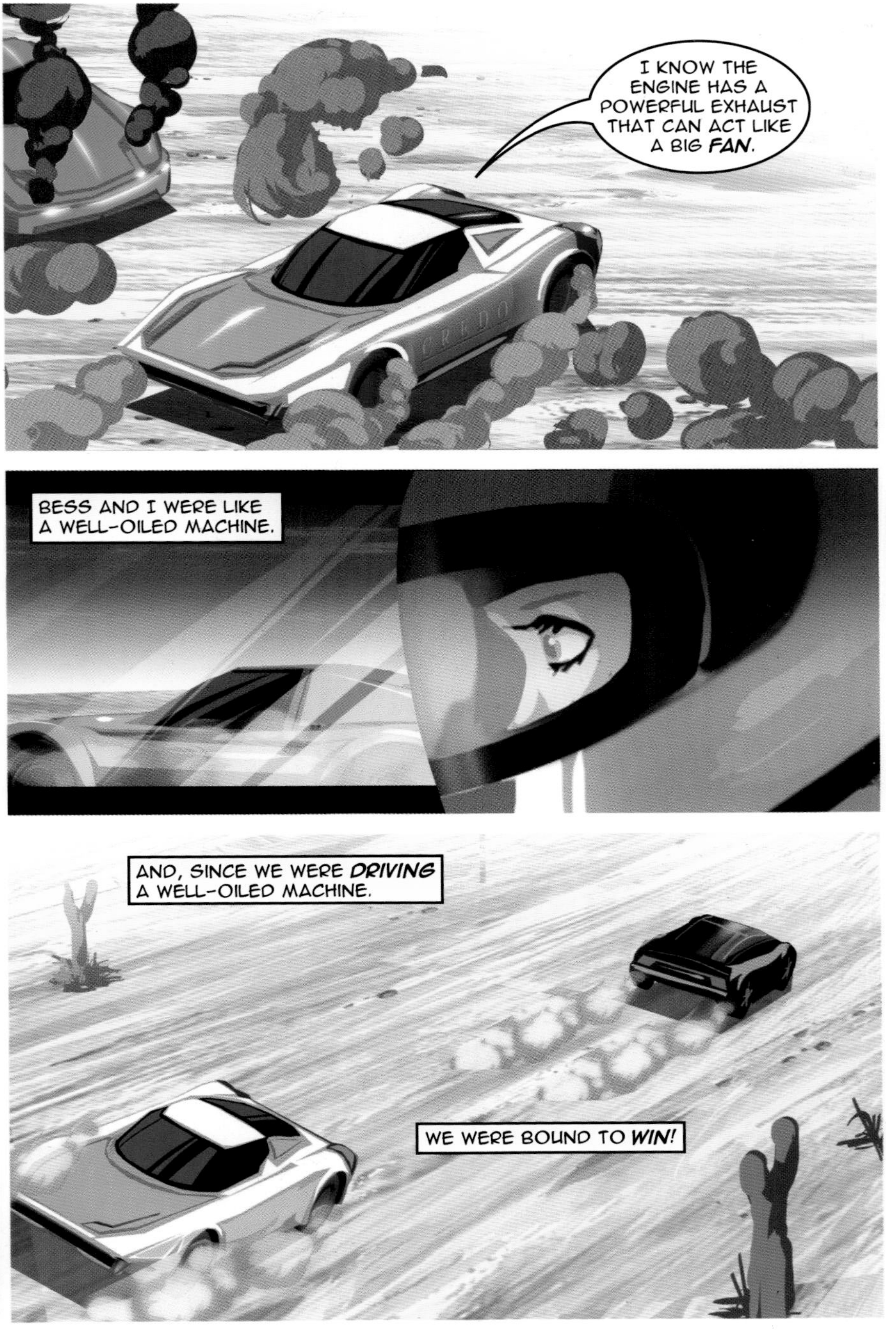
I KNOW THE ENGINE HAS A POWERFUL EXHAUST THAT CAN ACT LIKE A BIG FAN.
BESS AND I WERE LIKE A WELL-OILED MACHINE.
AND, SINCE WE WERE DRIVING A WELL-OILED MACHINE.
WE WERE BOUND TO WIN!

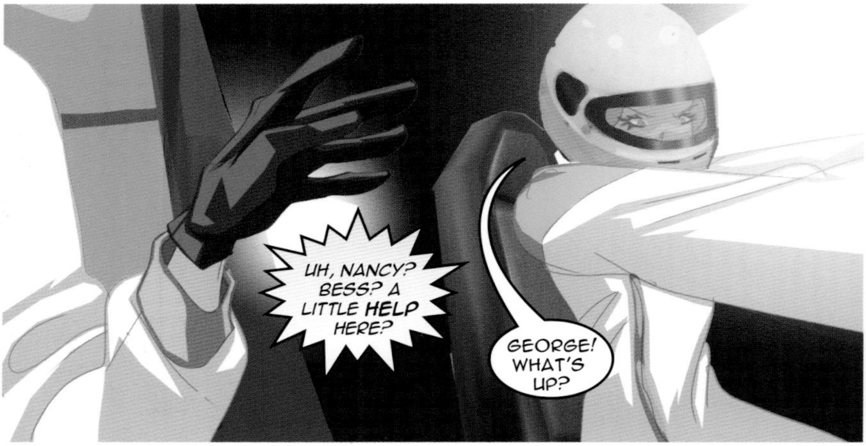
UH, NANCY? BESS? A LITTLE HELP HERE?
GEORGE! WHAT'S UP?

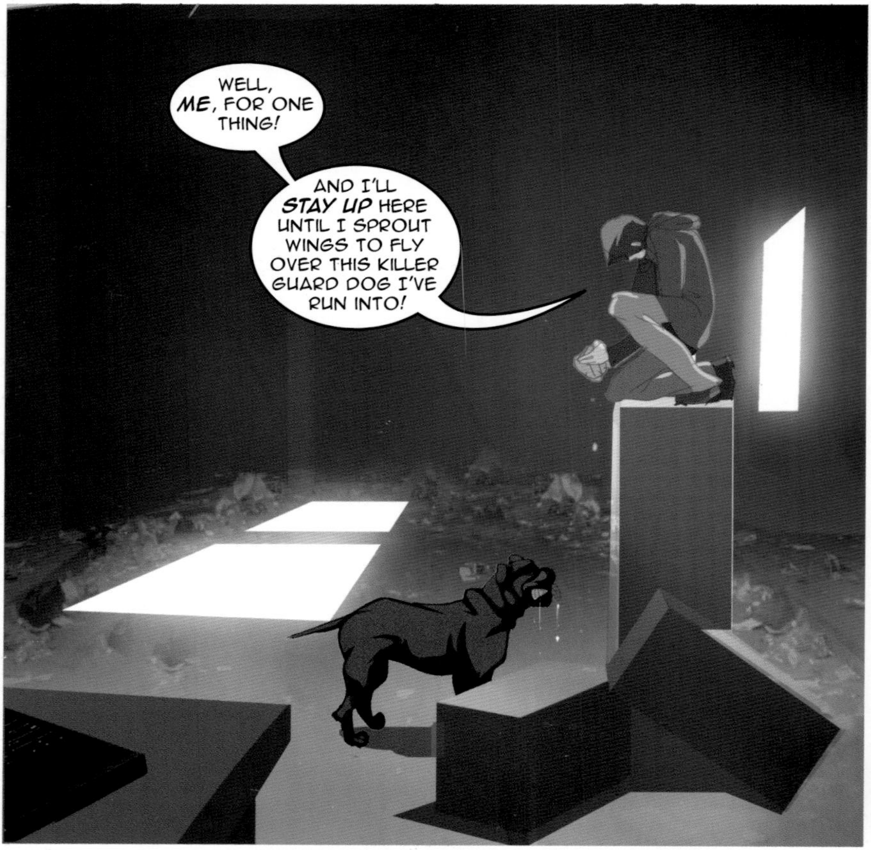
WELL, ME, FOR ONE THING!
AND I'LL STAY UP HERE UNTIL I SPROUT WINGS TO FLY OVER THIS KILLER GUARD DOG I'VE RUN INTO!

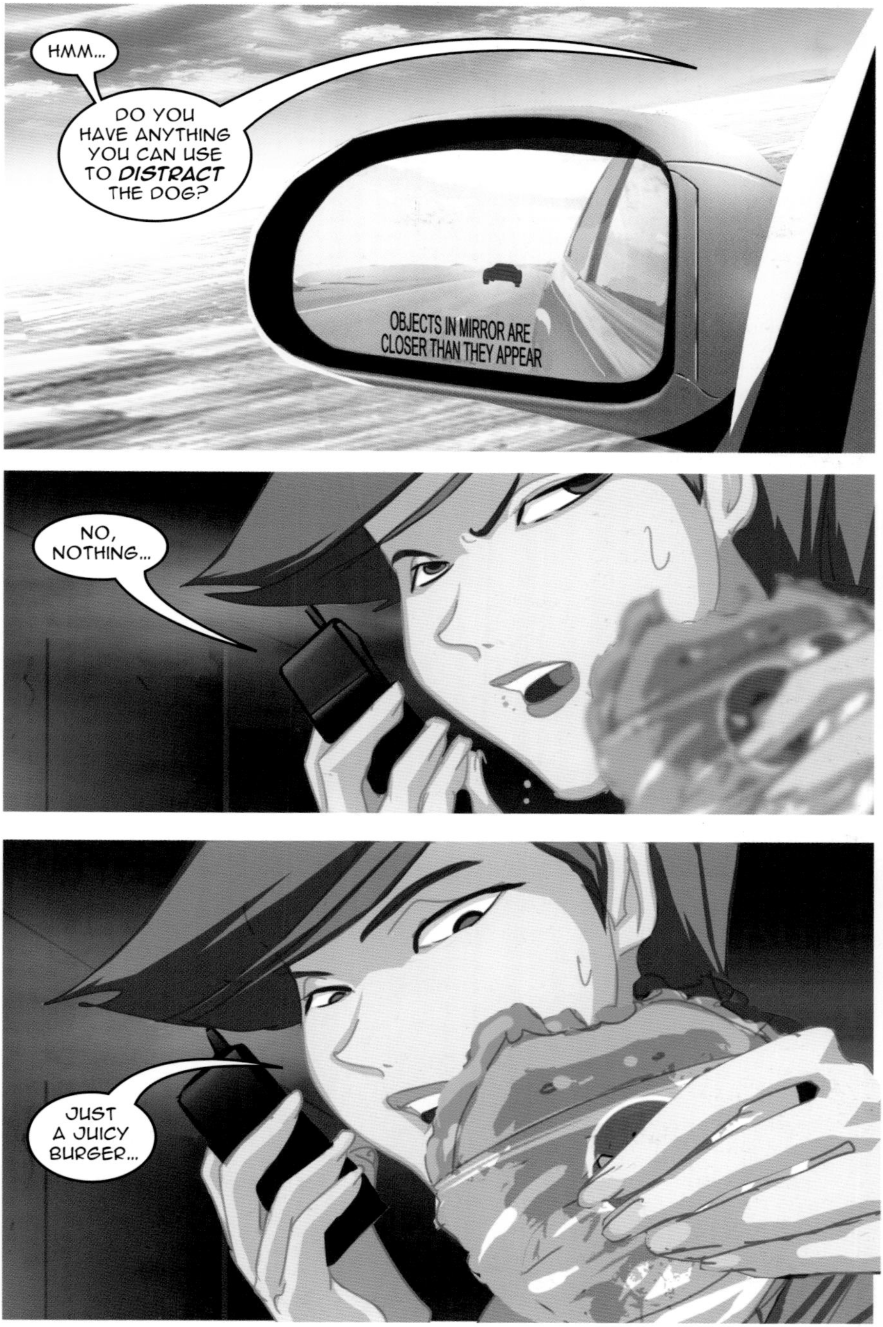
HMM...
DO YOU HAVE ANYTHING YOU CAN USE TO DISTRACT THE DOG?
OBJECTS IN MIRROR ARE CLOSER THAN THEY APPEAR
NO, NOTHING...
JUST A JUICY BURGER...

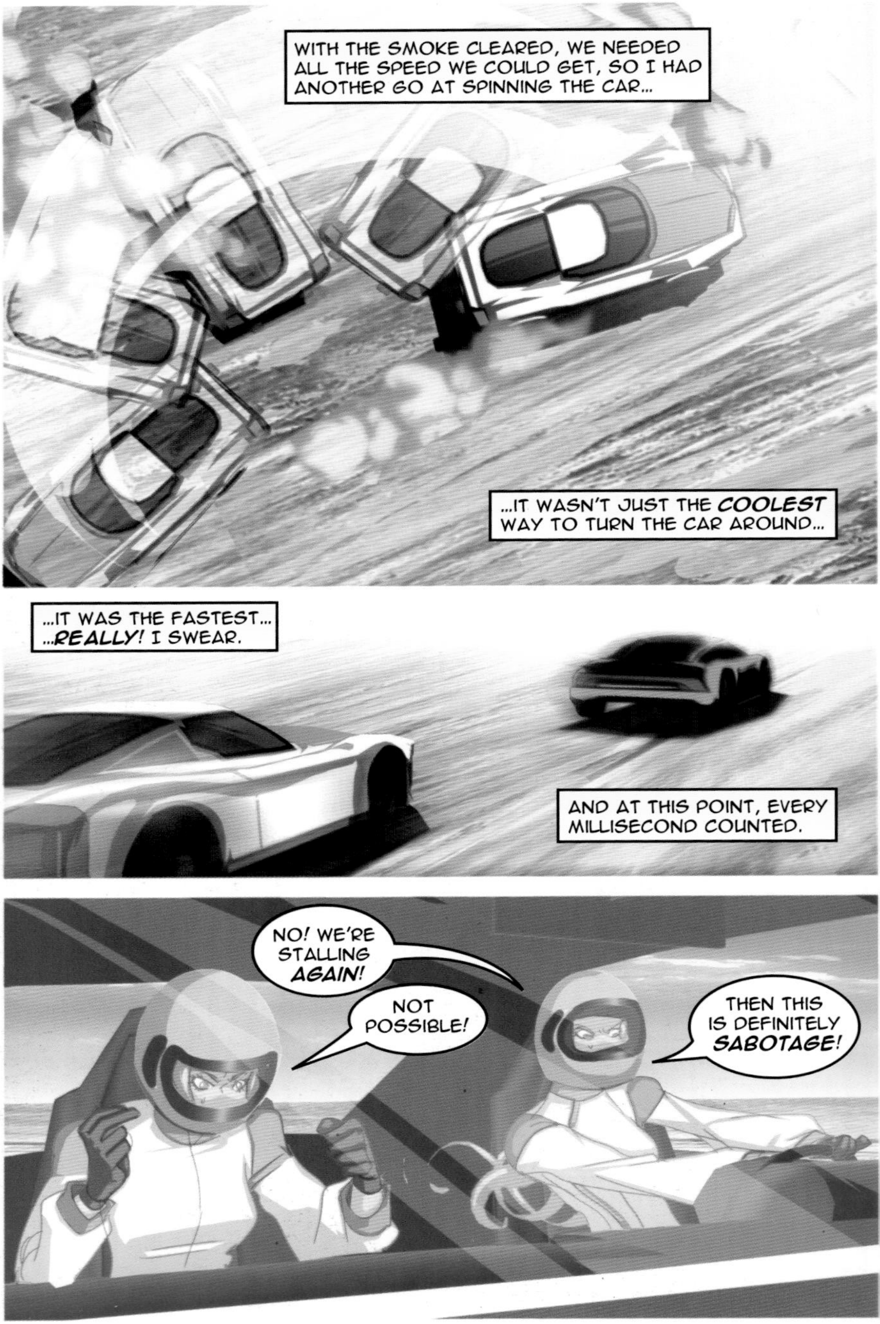
WITH THE SMOKE CLEARED, WE NEEDED ALL THE SPEED WE COULD GET, SO I HAD ANOTHER GO AT SPINNING THE CAR...
...IT WASN'T JUST THE COOLEST WAY TO TURN THE CAR AROUND...
...IT WAS THE FASTEST... ...REALLY! I SWEAR.
AND AT THIS POINT, EVERY MILLISECOND COUNTED.
NO! WE'RE STALLING AGAIN!
NOT POSSIBLE!
THEN THIS IS DEFINITELY SABOTAGE!

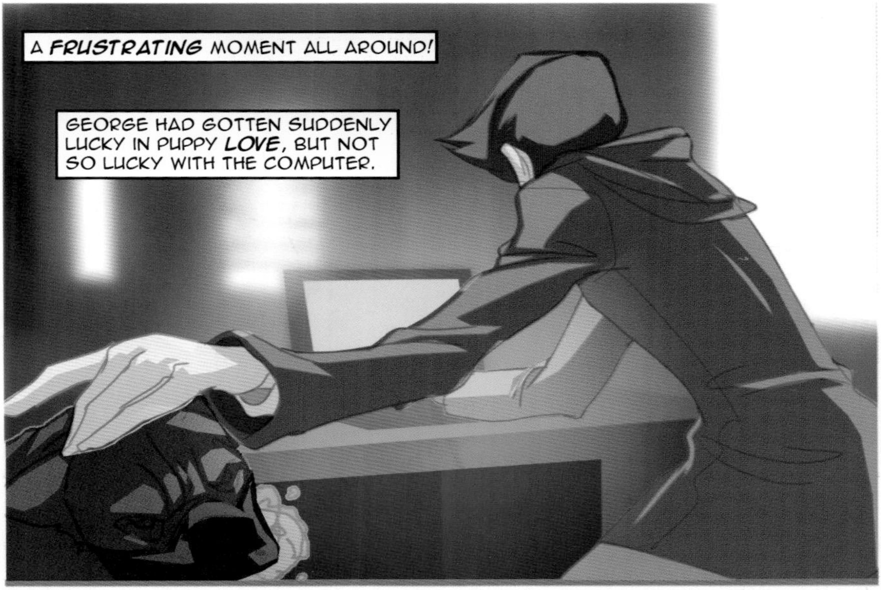
A FRUSTRATING MOMENT ALL AROUND!
GEORGE HAD GOTTEN SUDDENLY LUCKY IN PUPPY LOVE, BUT NOT SO LUCKY WITH THE COMPUTER.

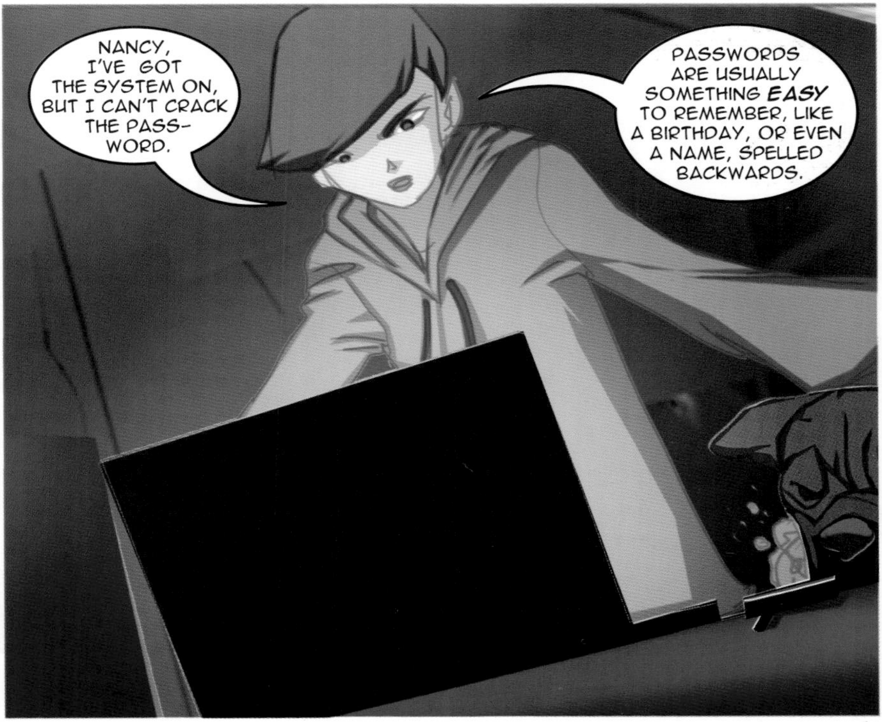
NANCY, I'VE GOT THE SYSTEM ON, BUT I CAN'T CRACK THE PASS-WORD.
PASSWORDS ARE USUALLY SOMETHING EASY TO REMEMBER, LIKE A BIRTHDAY, OR EVEN A NAME, SPELLED BACKWARDS.

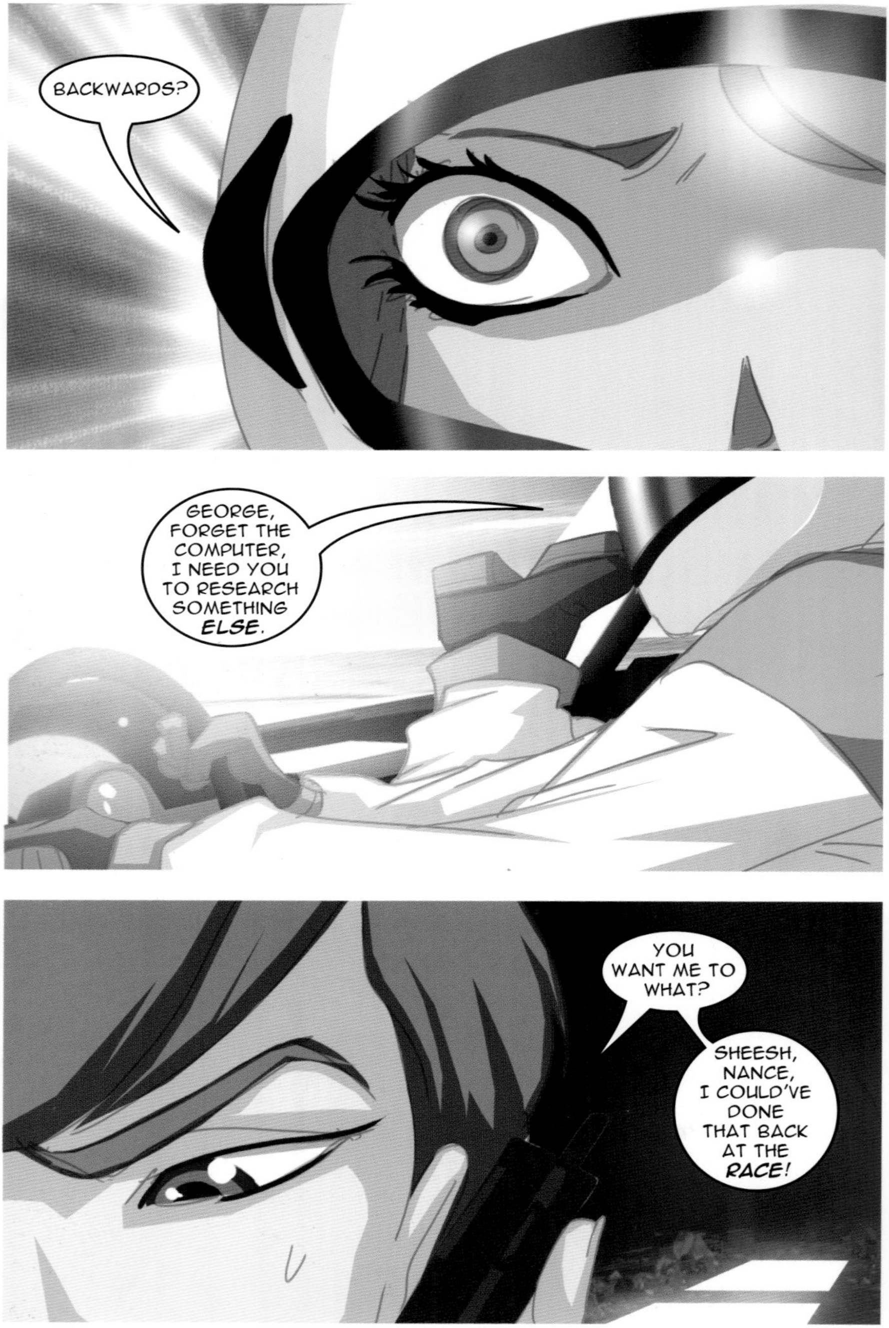
BACKWARDS?
GEORGE, FORGET THE COMPUTER, I NEED YOU TO RESEARCH SOMETHING *ELSE*.
YOU WANT ME TO WHAT?
SHEESH, NANCE, I COULD'VE DONE THAT BACK AT THE *RACE*!

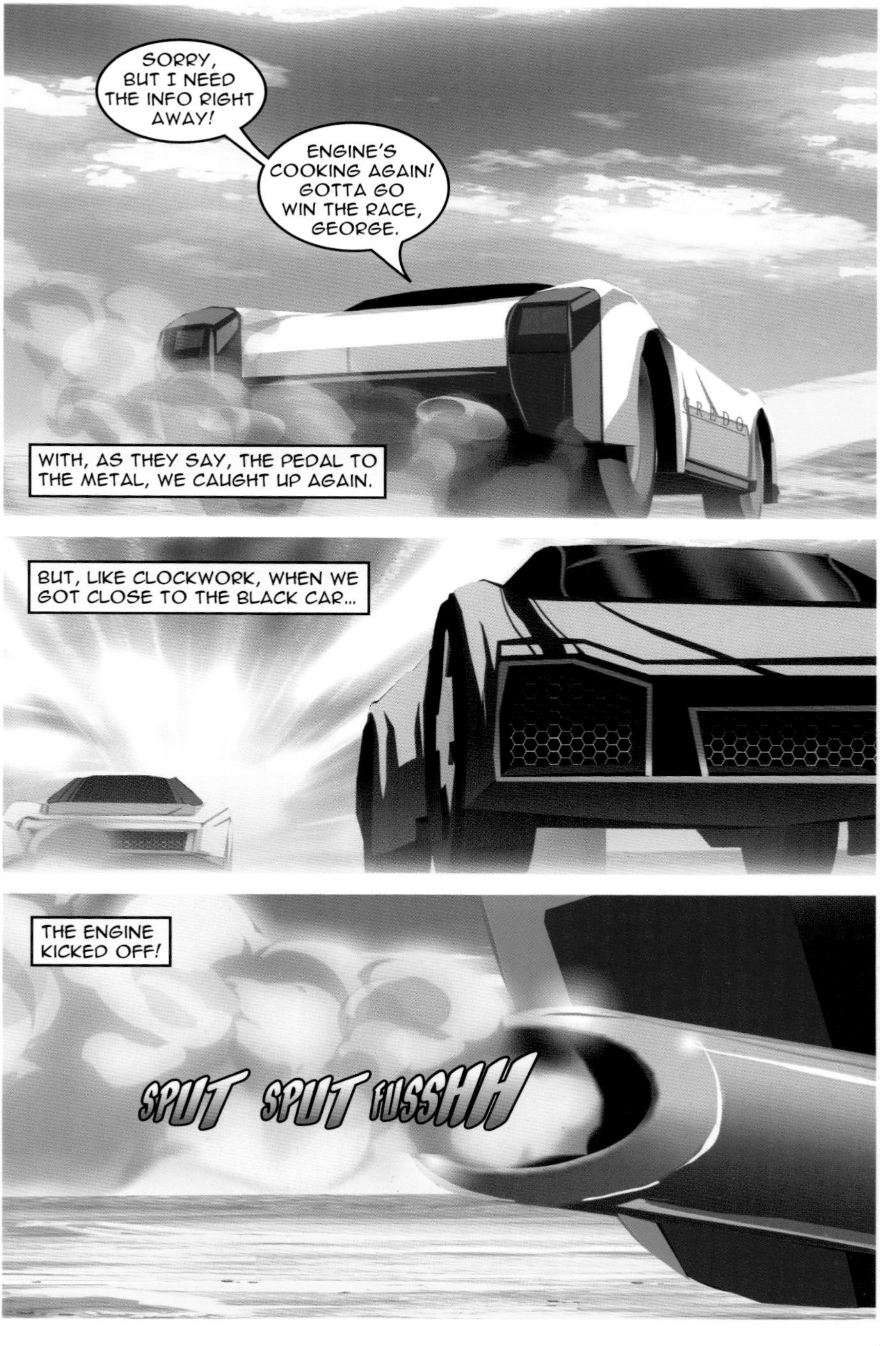
SORRY, BUT I NEED THE INFO RIGHT AWAY!
ENGINE'S COOKING AGAIN! GOTTA GO WIN THE RACE, GEORGE.
CREDO
WITH, AS THEY SAY, THE PEDAL TO THE METAL, WE CAUGHT UP AGAIN.
BUT, LIKE CLOCKWORK, WHEN WE GOT CLOSE TO THE BLACK CAR...
THE ENGINE KICKED OFF!
SPUT SPUT FUSSHH

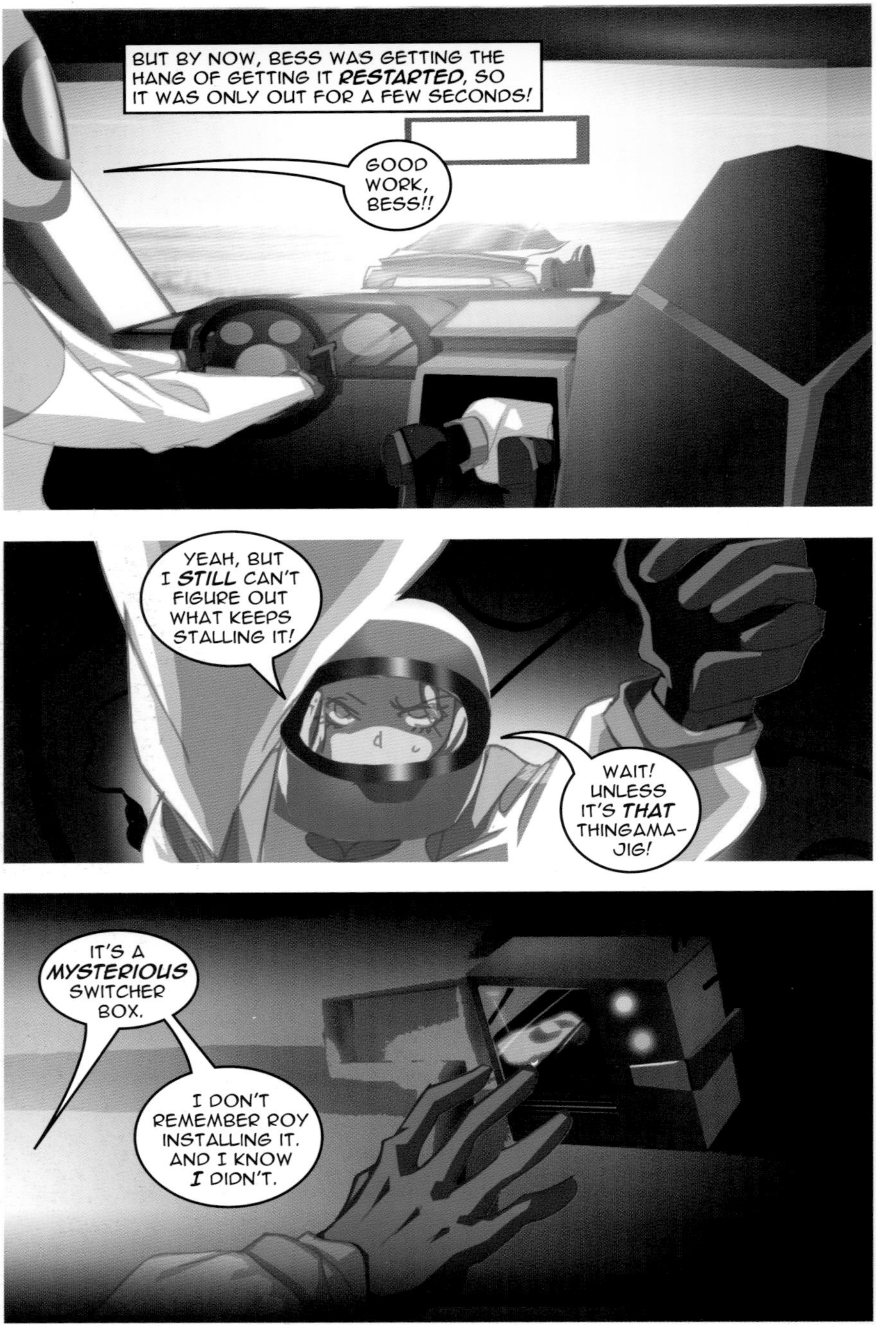
BUT BY NOW, BESS WAS GETTING THE HANG OF GETTING IT RESTARTED, SO IT WAS ONLY OUT FOR A FEW SECONDS!
GOOD WORK, BESS!!
YEAH, BUT I STILL CAN'T FIGURE OUT WHAT KEEPS STALLING IT!
WAIT! UNLESS IT'S THAT THINGAMA-JIG!
IT'S A MYSTERIOUS SWITCHER BOX.
I DON'T REMEMBER ROY INSTALLING IT. AND I KNOW I DIDN'T.

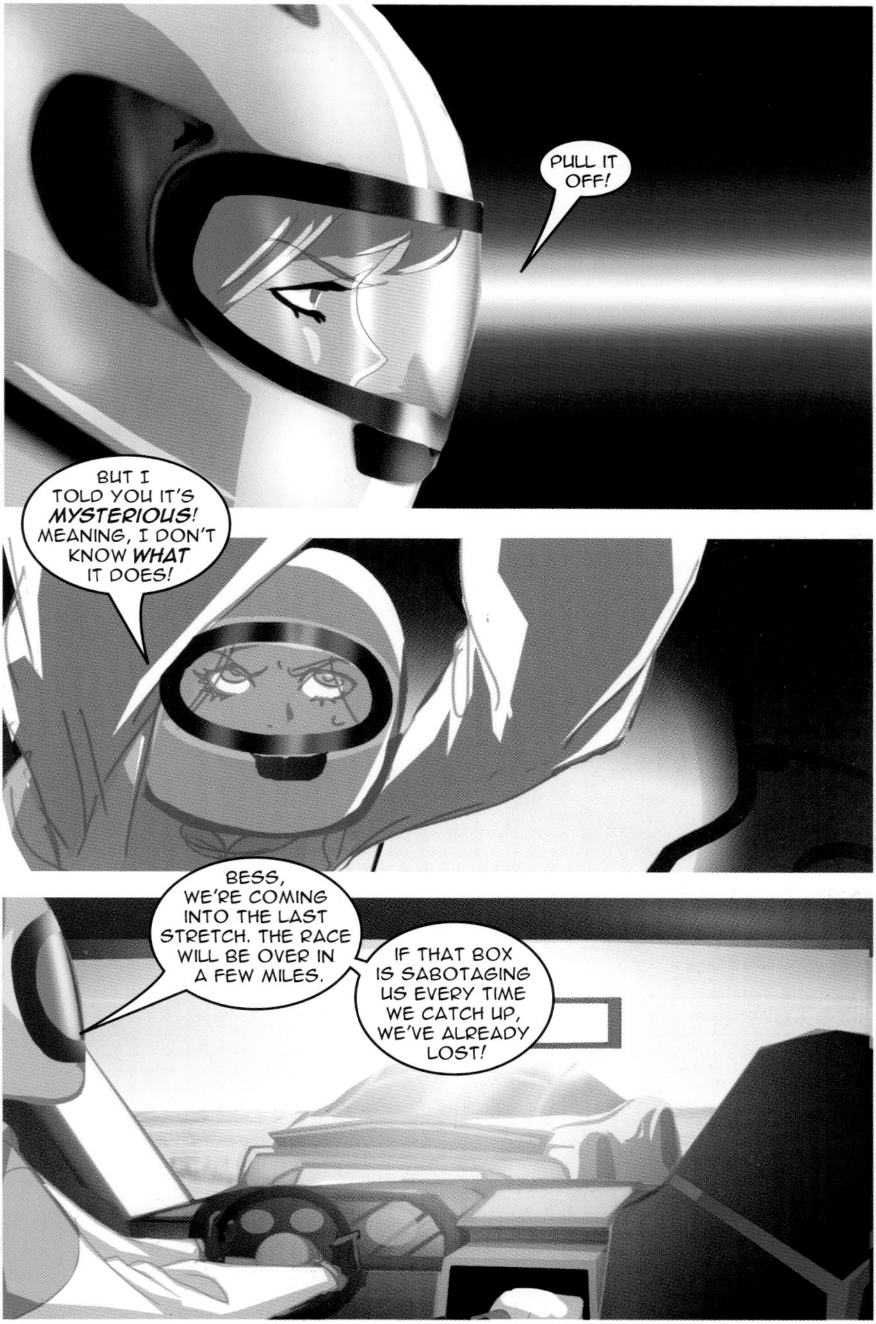
PULL IT OFF!
BUT I TOLD YOU IT'S **MYSTERIOUS**! MEANING, I DON'T KNOW **WHAT** IT DOES!
BESS, WE'RE COMING INTO THE LAST STRETCH. THE RACE WILL BE OVER IN A FEW MILES.
IF THAT BOX IS SABOTAGING US EVERY TIME WE CATCH UP, WE'VE ALREADY LOST!

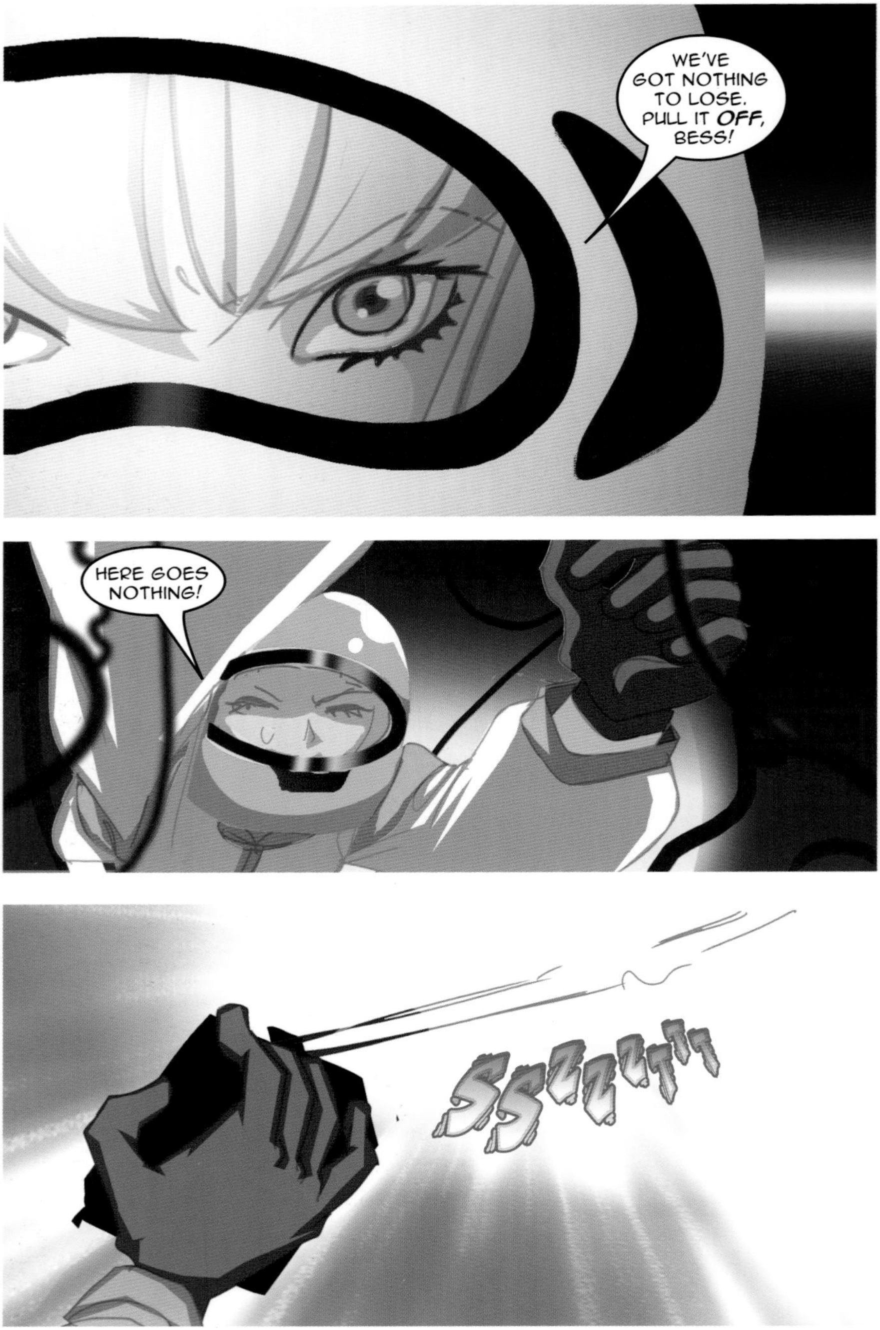
WE'VE GOT NOTHING TO LOSE. PULL IT OFF, BESS!
HERE GOES NOTHING!
SSZZZTTT

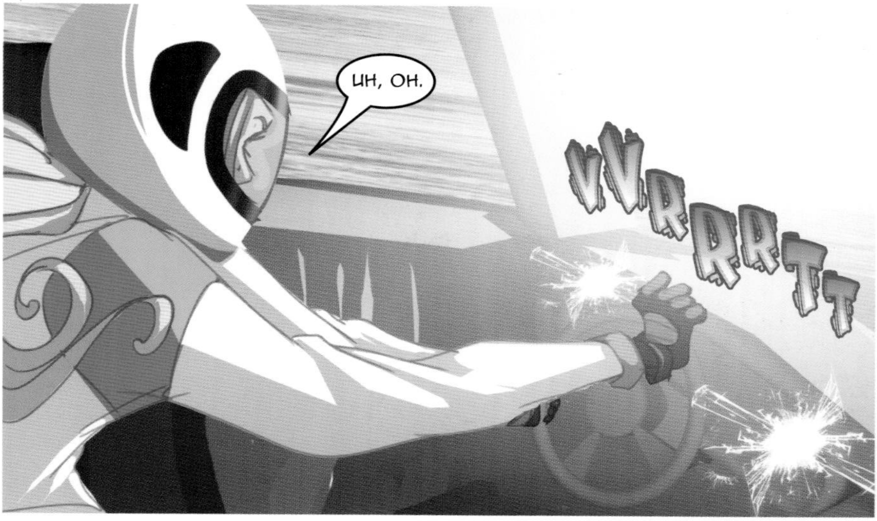
UH, OH.
VVRRRTTT

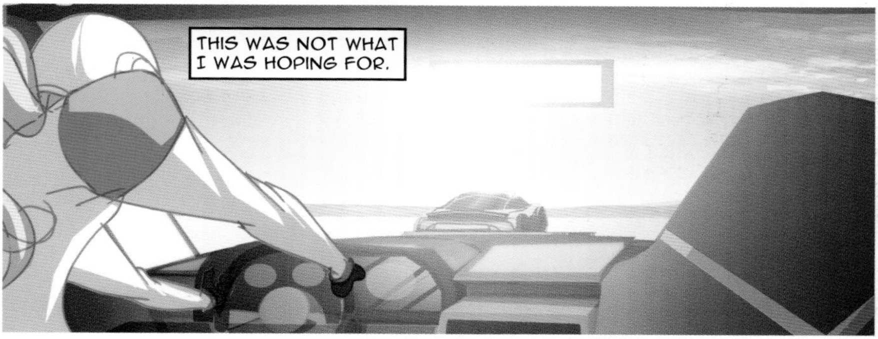
THIS WAS NOT WHAT I WAS HOPING FOR.

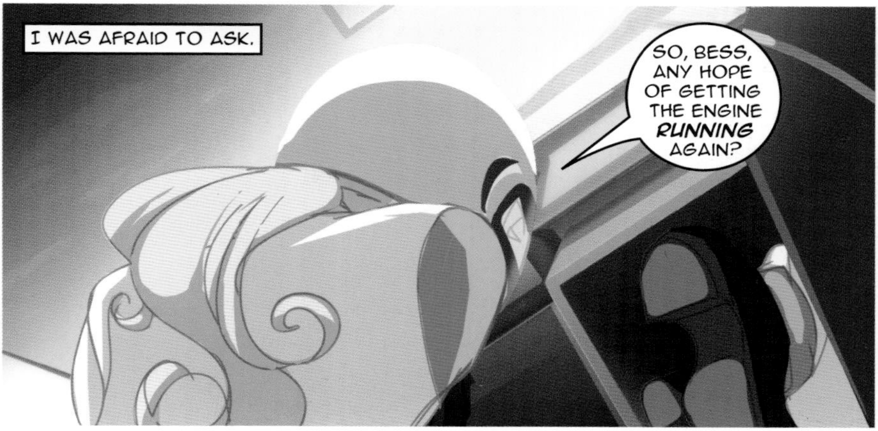
I WAS AFRAID TO ASK.
SO, BESS, ANY HOPE OF GETTING THE ENGINE RUNNING AGAIN?

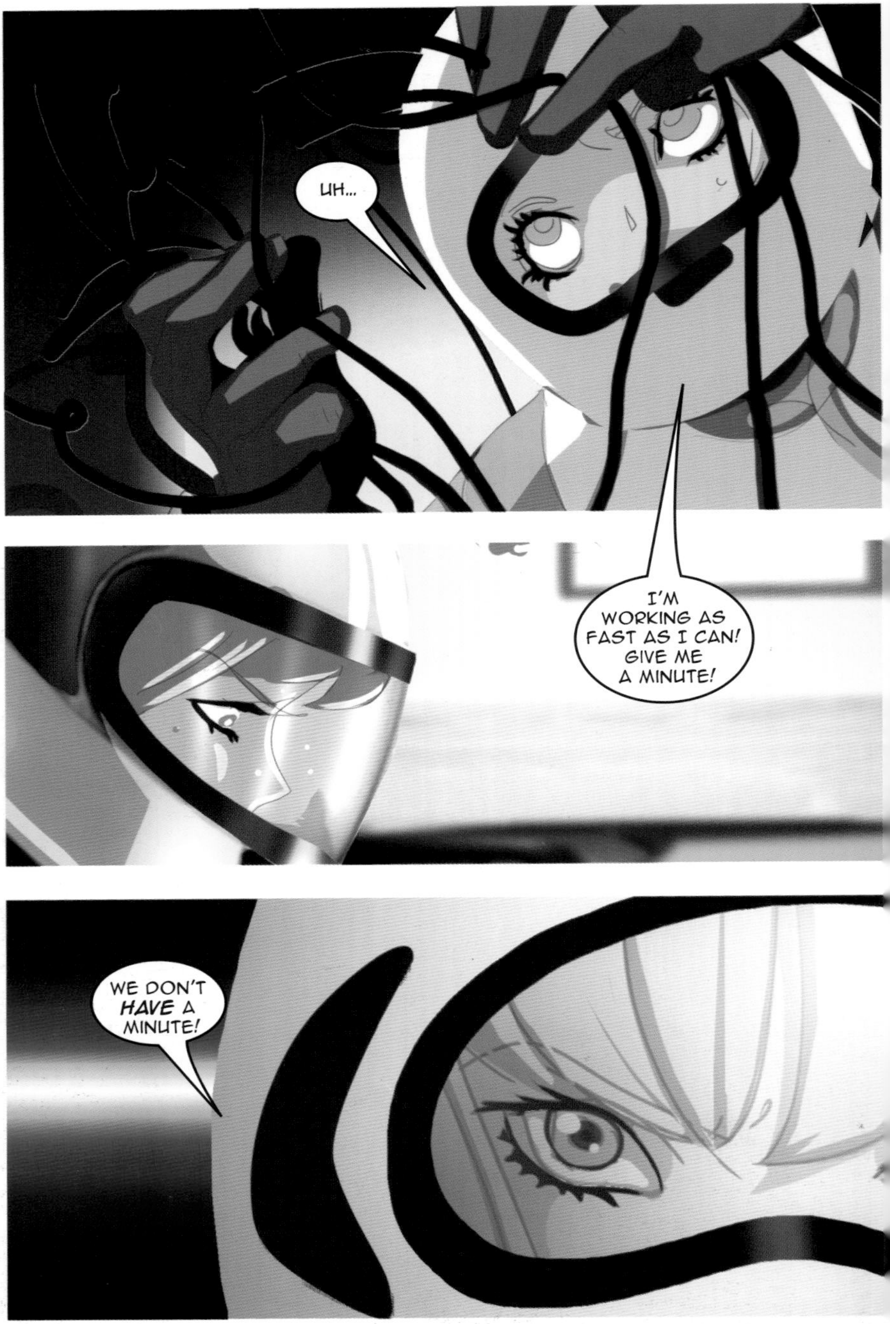
UH...
I'M WORKING AS FAST AS I CAN! GIVE ME A MINUTE!
WE DON'T *HAVE* A MINUTE!

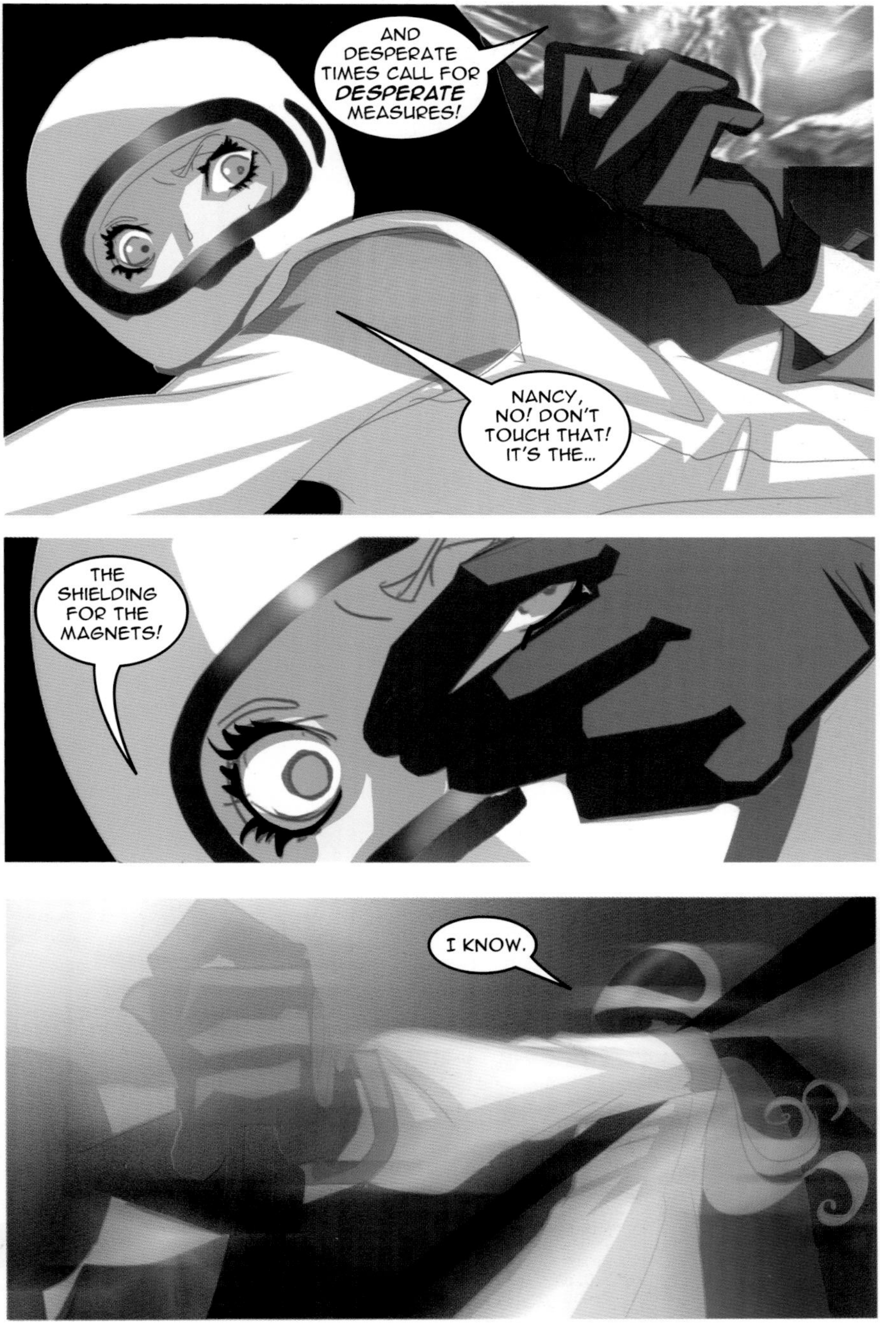
AND DESPERATE TIMES CALL FOR DESPERATE MEASURES!
NANCY, NO! DON'T TOUCH THAT! IT'S THE...
THE SHIELDING FOR THE MAGNETS!
I KNOW.

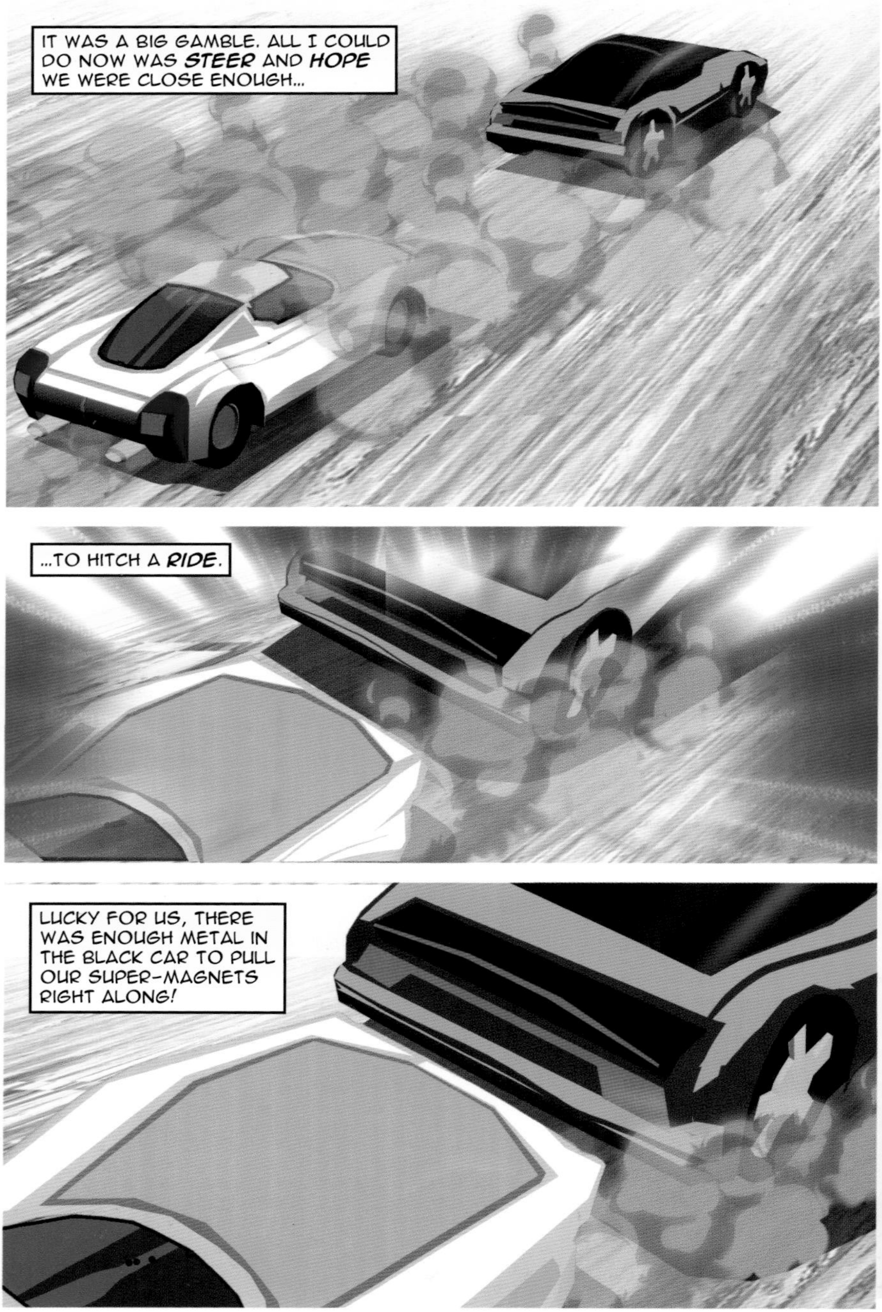
IT WAS A BIG GAMBLE. ALL I COULD DO NOW WAS STEER AND HOPE WE WERE CLOSE ENOUGH...
...TO HITCH A RIDE.
LUCKY FOR US, THERE WAS ENOUGH METAL IN THE BLACK CAR TO PULL OUR SUPER-MAGNETS RIGHT ALONG!

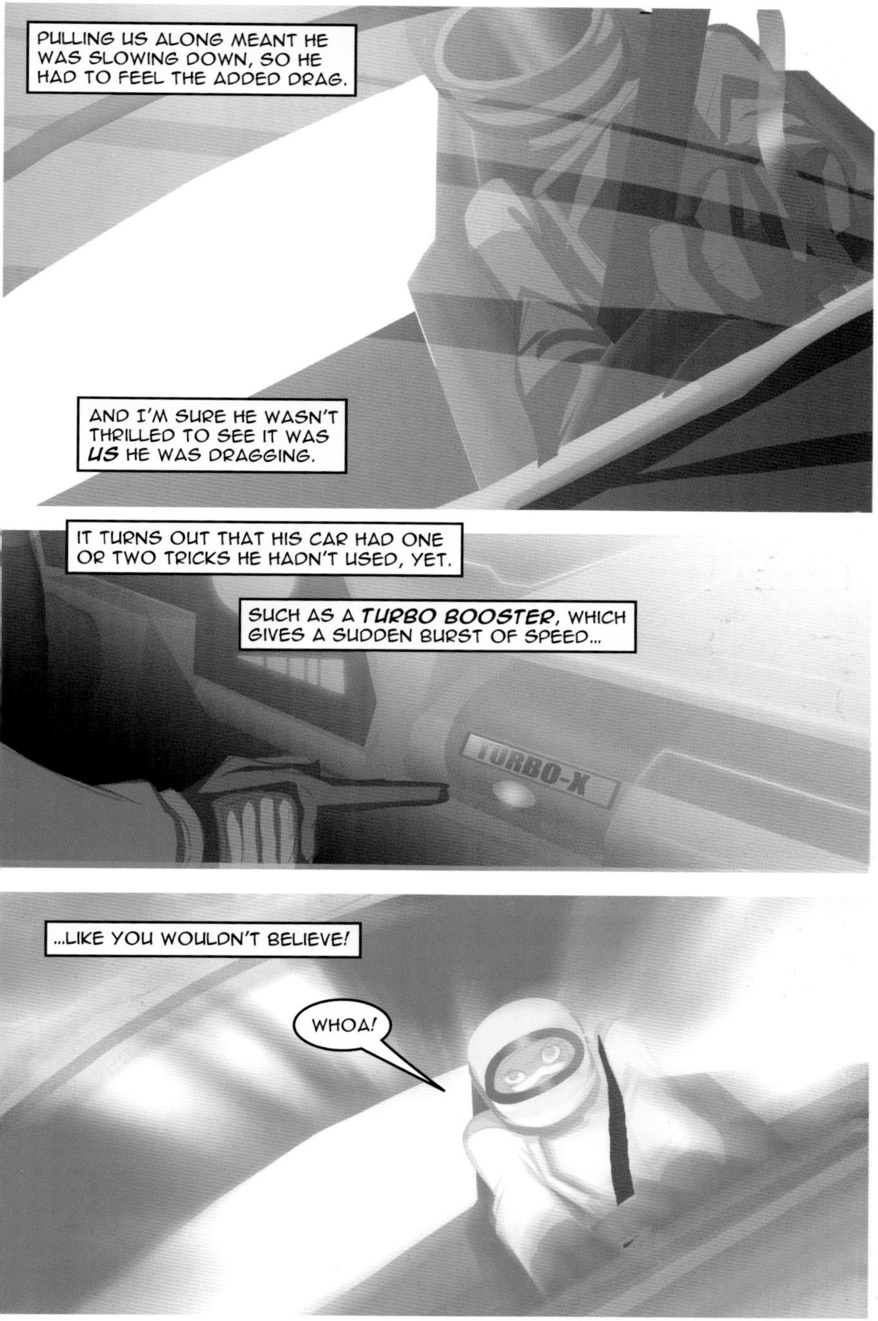
PULLING US ALONG MEANT HE WAS SLOWING DOWN, SO HE HAD TO FEEL THE ADDED DRAG.
AND I'M SURE HE WASN'T THRILLED TO SEE IT WAS ***US*** HE WAS DRAGGING.
IT TURNS OUT THAT HIS CAR HAD ONE OR TWO TRICKS HE HADN'T USED, YET.
SUCH AS A ***TURBO BOOSTER***, WHICH GIVES A SUDDEN BURST OF SPEED...
TURBO-X
...LIKE YOU WOULDN'T BELIEVE!
WHOA!

SO, NANCY, IS GETTING *TOWED* TOWARD THE FINISH LINE, YOU KNOW... *CHEATING?*

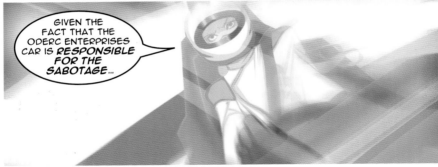

GIVEN THE FACT THAT THE ODERC ENTERPRISES CAR IS *RESPONSIBLE FOR THE SABOTAGE*...

...I DON'T THINK SO.

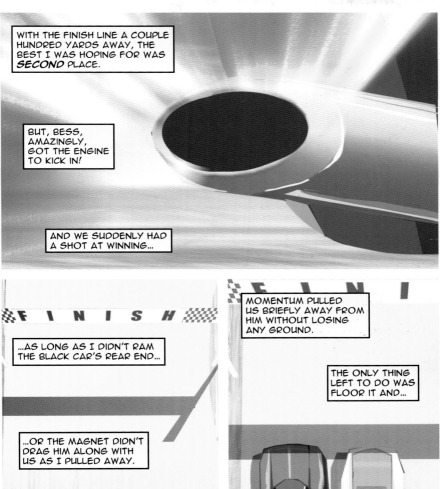

WITH THE FINISH LINE A COUPLE HUNDRED YARDS AWAY, THE BEST I WAS HOPING FOR WAS *SECOND* PLACE.

BUT, BESS, AMAZINGLY, GOT THE ENGINE TO KICK IN!

AND WE SUDDENLY HAD A SHOT AT WINNING...

F I N I S H

...AS LONG AS I DIDN'T RAM THE BLACK CAR'S REAR END...

...OR THE MAGNET DIDN'T DRAG HIM ALONG WITH US AS I PULLED AWAY.

MOMENTUM PULLED US BRIEFLY AWAY FROM HIM WITHOUT LOSING ANY GROUND.

THE ONLY THING LEFT TO DO WAS FLOOR IT AND...

VRROOOM

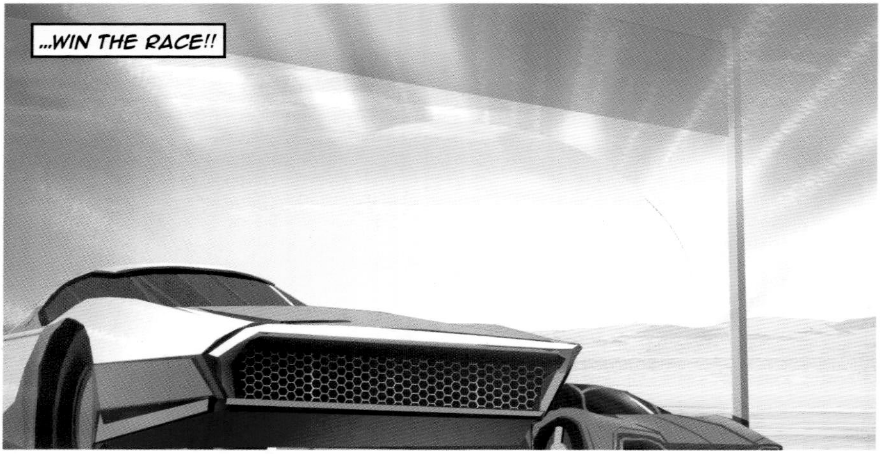
...WIN THE RACE!!

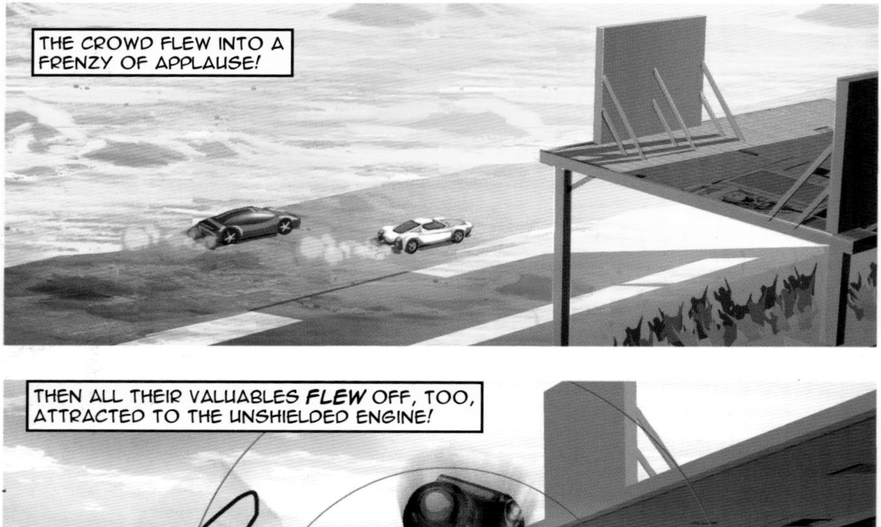
THE CROWD FLEW INTO A FRENZY OF APPLAUSE!

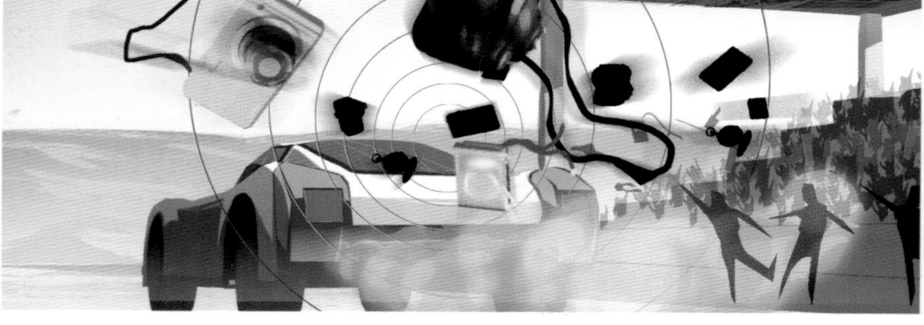
THEN ALL THEIR VALUABLES *FLEW* OFF, TOO, ATTRACTED TO THE UNSHIELDED ENGINE!

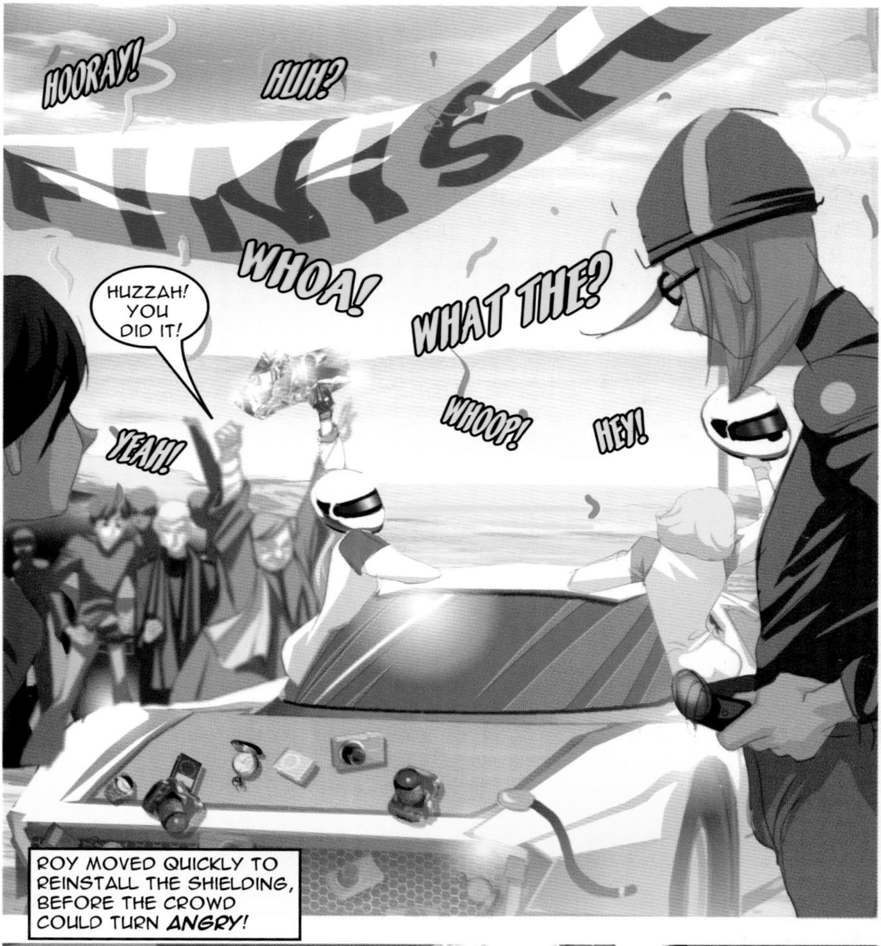
HOORAY!
HUH?
WHOA!
HUZZAH! YOU DID IT!
WHAT THE?
WHOOP!
HEY!
YEAH!
ROY MOVED QUICKLY TO REINSTALL THE SHIELDING, BEFORE THE CROWD COULD TURN ANGRY!

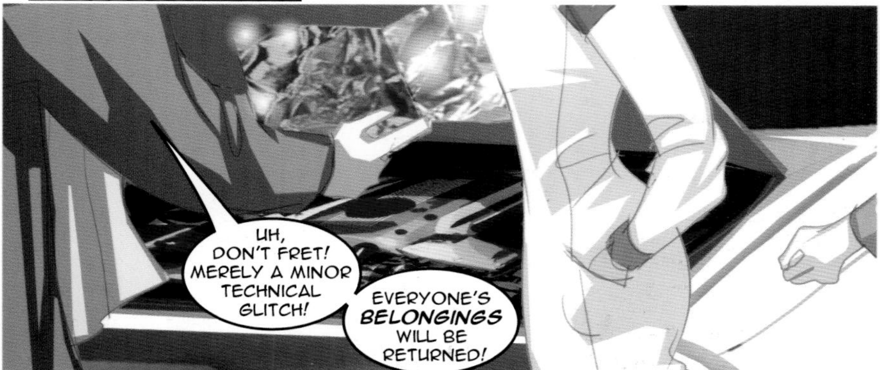
UH, DON'T FRET! MERELY A MINOR TECHNICAL GLITCH!
EVERYONE'S BELONGINGS WILL BE RETURNED!

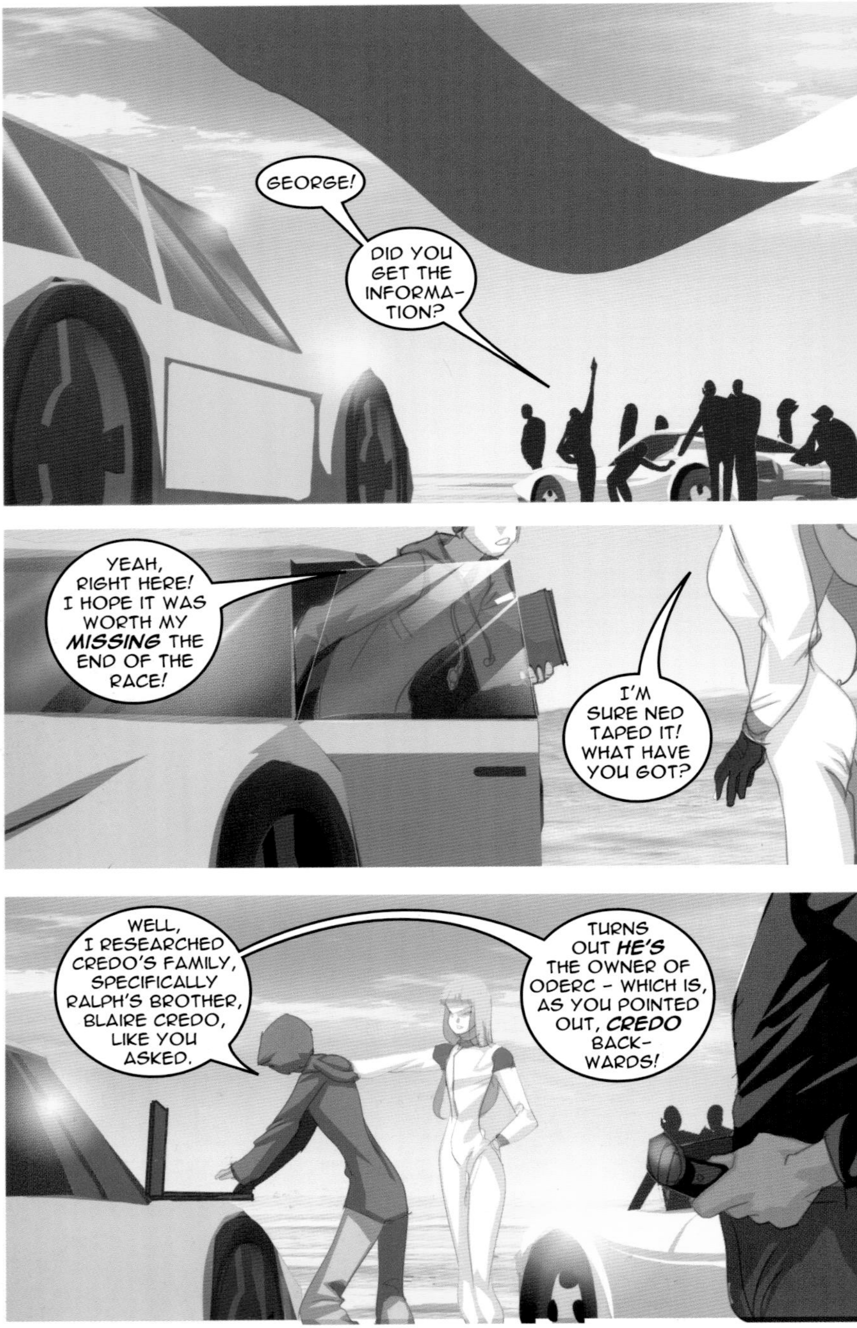
GEORGE!
DID YOU GET THE INFORMA-TION?
YEAH, RIGHT HERE! I HOPE IT WAS WORTH MY *MISSING* THE END OF THE RACE!
I'M SURE NED TAPED IT! WHAT HAVE YOU GOT?
WELL, I RESEARCHED CREDO'S FAMILY, SPECIFICALLY RALPH'S BROTHER, BLAIRE CREDO, LIKE YOU ASKED.
TURNS OUT *HE'S* THE OWNER OF ODERC - WHICH IS, AS YOU POINTED OUT, *CREDO* BACK-WARDS!

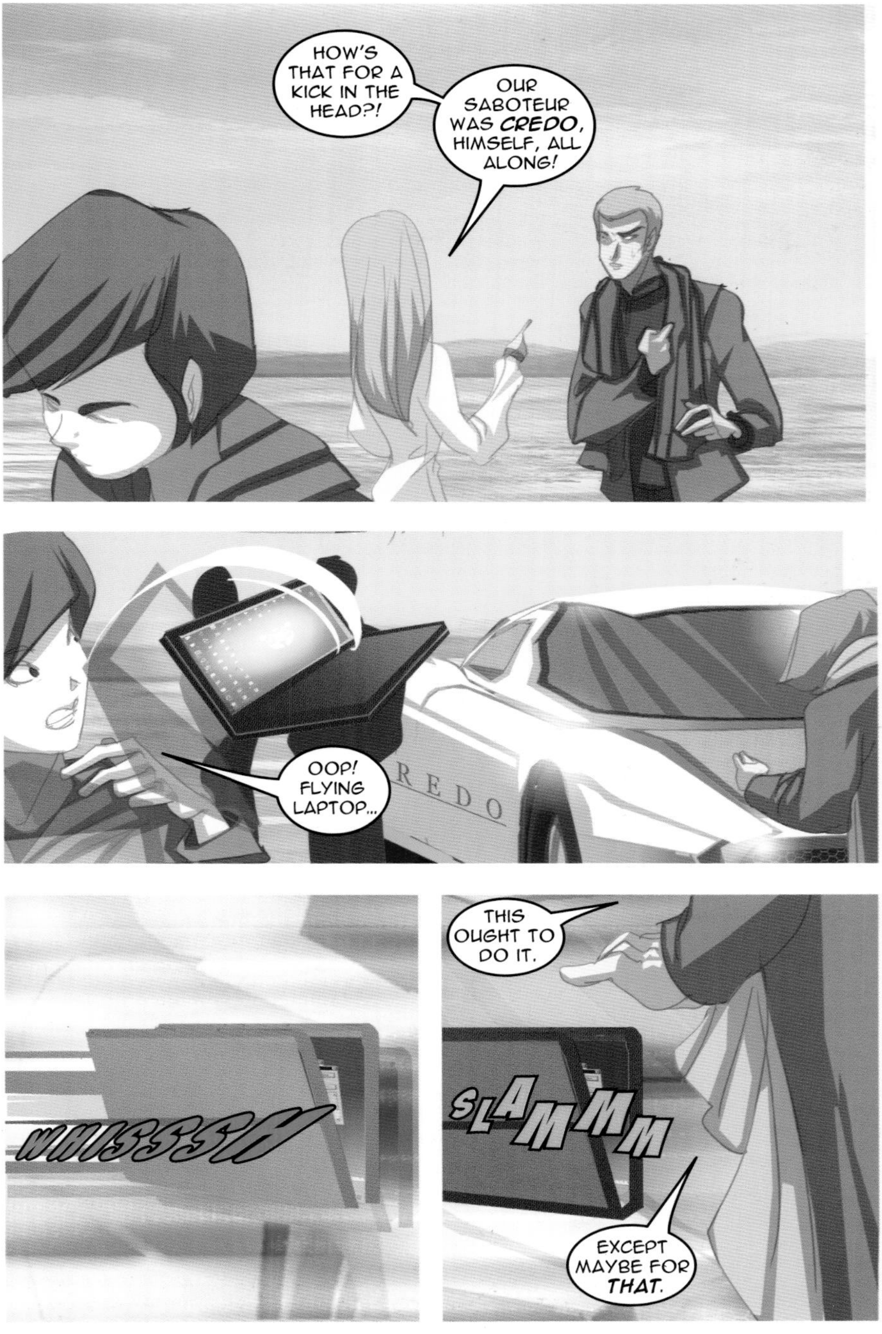
HOW'S THAT FOR A KICK IN THE HEAD?!
OUR SABOTEUR WAS CREDO, HIMSELF, ALL ALONG!
OOP! FLYING LAPTOP...
REDO
WHISSSH
THIS OUGHT TO DO IT.
SLAMMMM
EXCEPT MAYBE FOR THAT.

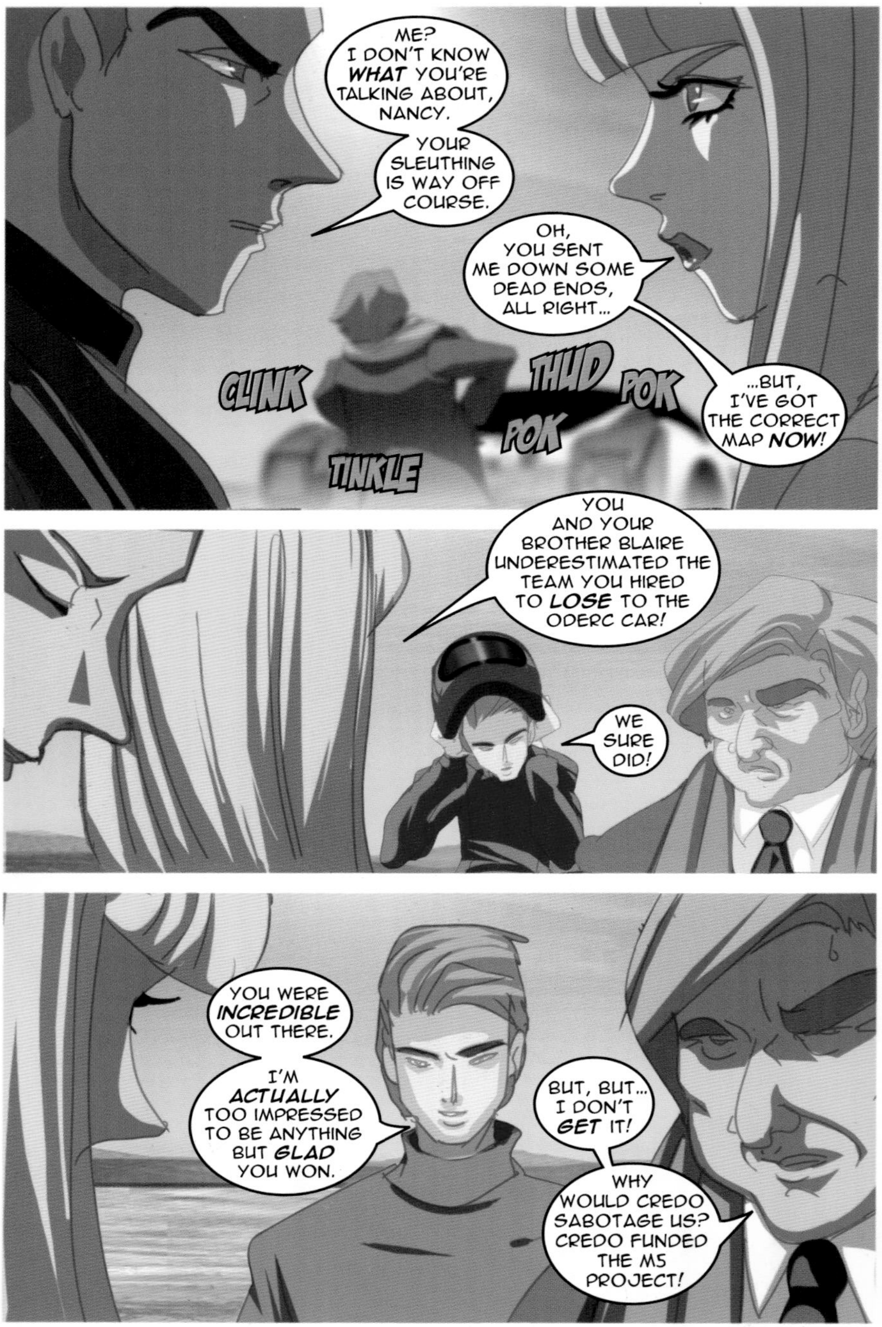
ME? I DON'T KNOW WHAT YOU'RE TALKING ABOUT, NANCY.
YOUR SLEUTHING IS WAY OFF COURSE.
OH, YOU SENT ME DOWN SOME DEAD ENDS, ALL RIGHT...
...BUT, I'VE GOT THE CORRECT MAP NOW!
CLINK
TINKLE
THUD
POK
POK
YOU AND YOUR BROTHER BLAIRE UNDERESTIMATED THE TEAM YOU HIRED TO LOSE TO THE ODERC CAR!
WE SURE DID!
YOU WERE INCREDIBLE OUT THERE.
I'M ACTUALLY TOO IMPRESSED TO BE ANYTHING BUT GLAD YOU WON.
BUT, BUT... I DON'T GET IT!
WHY WOULD CREDO SABOTAGE US? CREDO FUNDED THE M5 PROJECT!

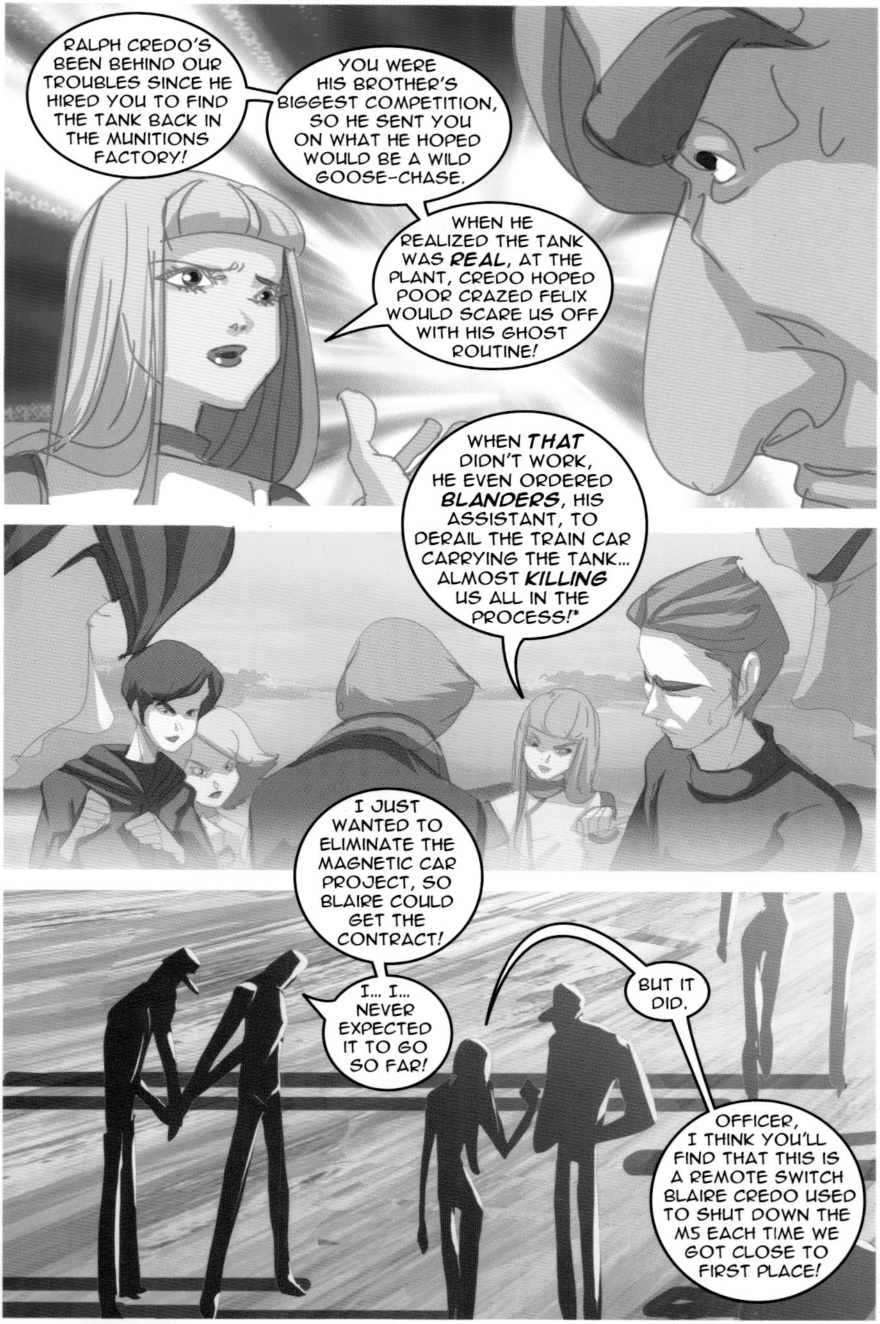
RALPH CREDO'S BEEN BEHIND OUR TROUBLES SINCE HE HIRED YOU TO FIND THE TANK BACK IN THE MUNITIONS FACTORY!
YOU WERE HIS BROTHER'S BIGGEST COMPETITION, SO HE SENT YOU ON WHAT HE HOPED WOULD BE A WILD GOOSE-CHASE.
WHEN HE REALIZED THE TANK WAS REAL, AT THE PLANT, CREDO HOPED POOR CRAZED FELIX WOULD SCARE US OFF WITH HIS GHOST ROUTINE!
WHEN THAT DIDN'T WORK, HE EVEN ORDERED BLANDERS, HIS ASSISTANT, TO DERAIL THE TRAIN CAR CARRYING THE TANK... ALMOST KILLING US ALL IN THE PROCESS!*
I JUST WANTED TO ELIMINATE THE MAGNETIC CAR PROJECT, SO BLAIRE COULD GET THE CONTRACT!
I... I... NEVER EXPECTED IT TO GO SO FAR!
BUT IT DID.
OFFICER, I THINK YOU'LL FIND THAT THIS IS A REMOTE SWITCH BLAIRE CREDO USED TO SHUT DOWN THE M5 EACH TIME WE GOT CLOSE TO FIRST PLACE!

*SEE NANCY DREW GRAPHIC NOVELS #9 AND #10.

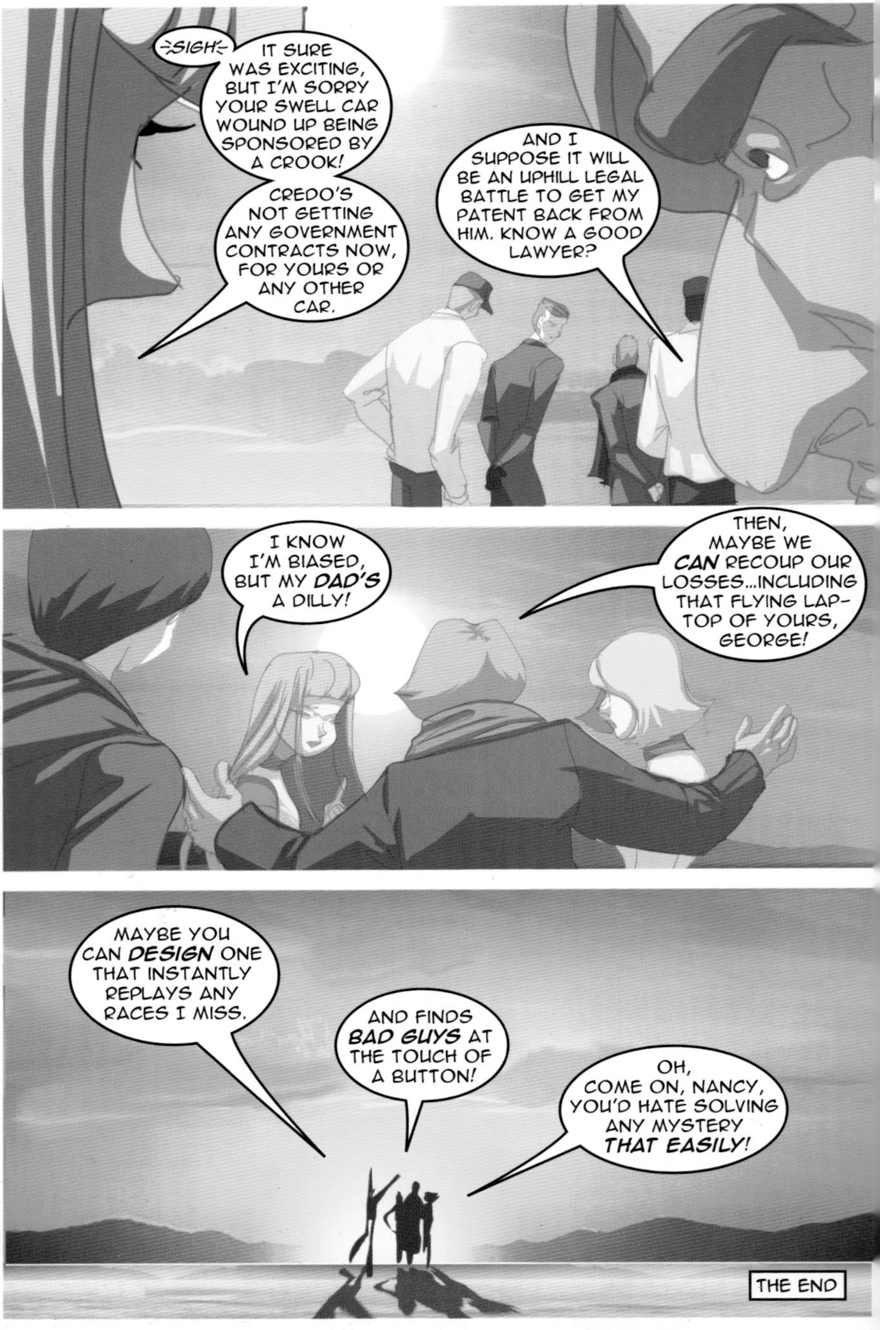
SIGH
IT SURE WAS EXCITING, BUT I'M SORRY YOUR SWELL CAR WOUND UP BEING SPONSORED BY A CROOK!
CREDO'S NOT GETTING ANY GOVERNMENT CONTRACTS NOW, FOR YOURS OR ANY OTHER CAR.
AND I SUPPOSE IT WILL BE AN UPHILL LEGAL BATTLE TO GET MY PATENT BACK FROM HIM. KNOW A GOOD LAWYER?
I KNOW I'M BIASED, BUT MY DAD'S A DILLY!
THEN, MAYBE WE CAN RECOUP OUR LOSSES...INCLUDING THAT FLYING LAP-TOP OF YOURS, GEORGE!
MAYBE YOU CAN DESIGN ONE THAT INSTANTLY REPLAYS ANY RACES I MISS.
AND FINDS BAD GUYS AT THE TOUCH OF A BUTTON!
OH, COME ON, NANCY, YOU'D HATE SOLVING ANY MYSTERY THAT EASILY!
THE END

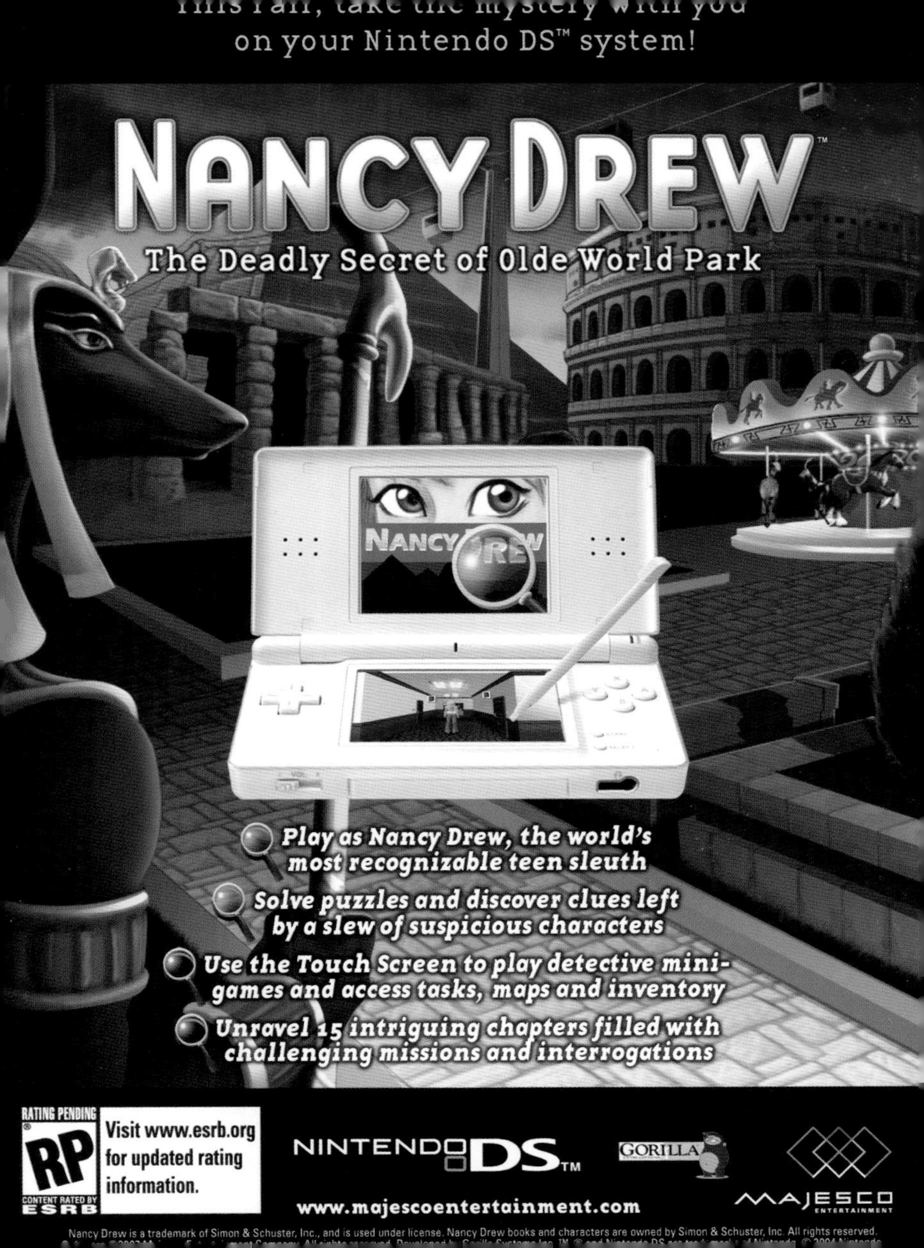
This Fall, take the mystery with you
on your Nintendo DS™ system!
NANCY DREW™
The Deadly Secret of Olde World Park
Play as Nancy Drew, the world's most recognizable teen sleuth
Solve puzzles and discover clues left by a slew of suspicious characters
Use the Touch Screen to play detective mini-games and access tasks, maps and inventory
Unravel 15 intriguing chapters filled with challenging missions and interrogations
RATING PENDING
RP
CONTENT RATED BY ESRB
Visit www.esrb.org for updated rating information.
NINTENDO DS™
GORILLA
MAJESCO ENTERTAINMENT
www.majescoentertainment.com
Nancy Drew is a trademark of Simon & Schuster, Inc., and is used under license. Nancy Drew books and characters are owned by Simon & Schuster, Inc. All rights reserved.

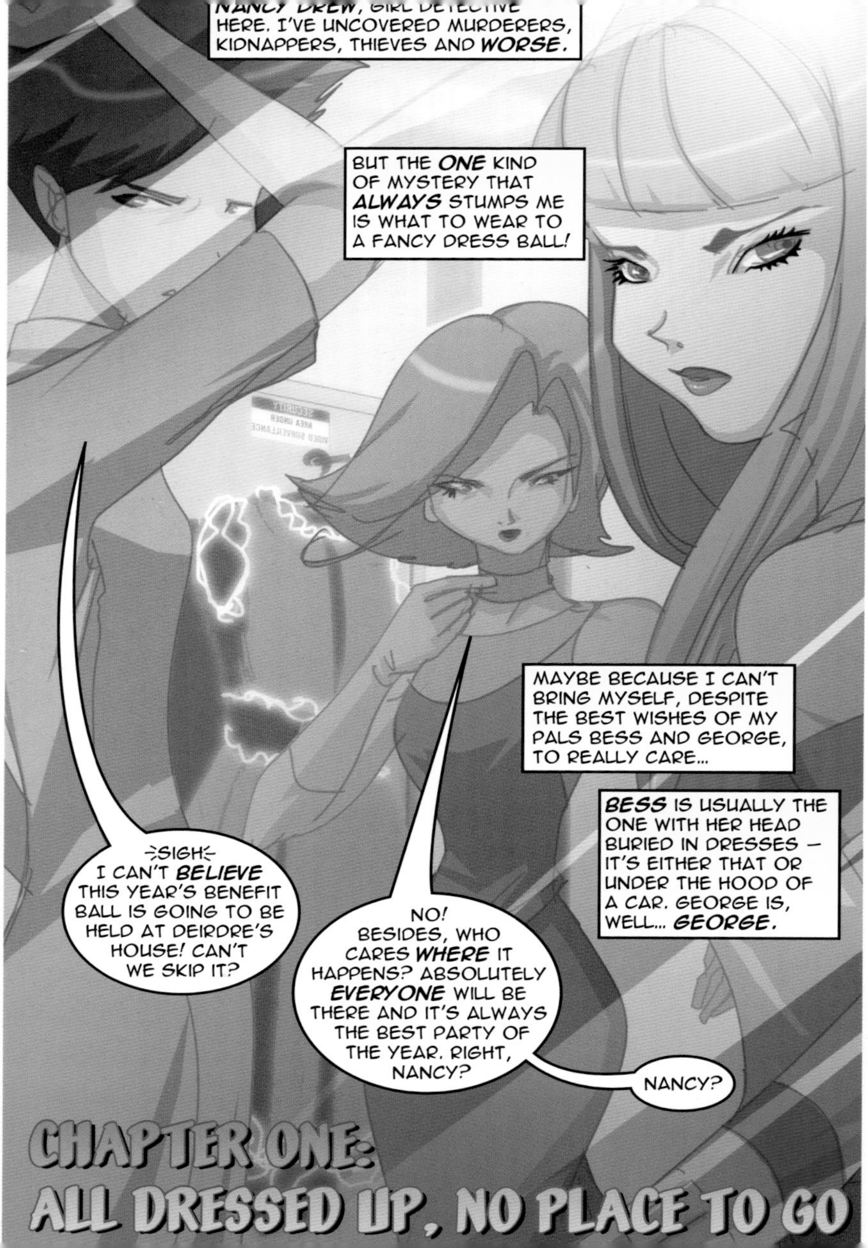
NANCY DREW, GIRL DETECTIVE HERE. I'VE UNCOVERED MURDERERS, KIDNAPPERS, THIEVES AND WORSE.
BUT THE ONE KIND OF MYSTERY THAT ALWAYS STUMPS ME IS WHAT TO WEAR TO A FANCY DRESS BALL!
MAYBE BECAUSE I CAN'T BRING MYSELF, DESPITE THE BEST WISHES OF MY PALS BESS AND GEORGE, TO REALLY CARE...
BESS IS USUALLY THE ONE WITH HER HEAD BURIED IN DRESSES — IT'S EITHER THAT OR UNDER THE HOOD OF A CAR. GEORGE IS, WELL... GEORGE.
SIGH I CAN'T BELIEVE THIS YEAR'S BENEFIT BALL IS GOING TO BE HELD AT DEIRDRE'S HOUSE! CAN'T WE SKIP IT?
NO! BESIDES, WHO CARES WHERE IT HAPPENS? ABSOLUTELY EVERYONE WILL BE THERE AND IT'S ALWAYS THE BEST PARTY OF THE YEAR. RIGHT, NANCY?
NANCY?
CHAPTER ONE: ALL DRESSED UP, NO PLACE TO GO

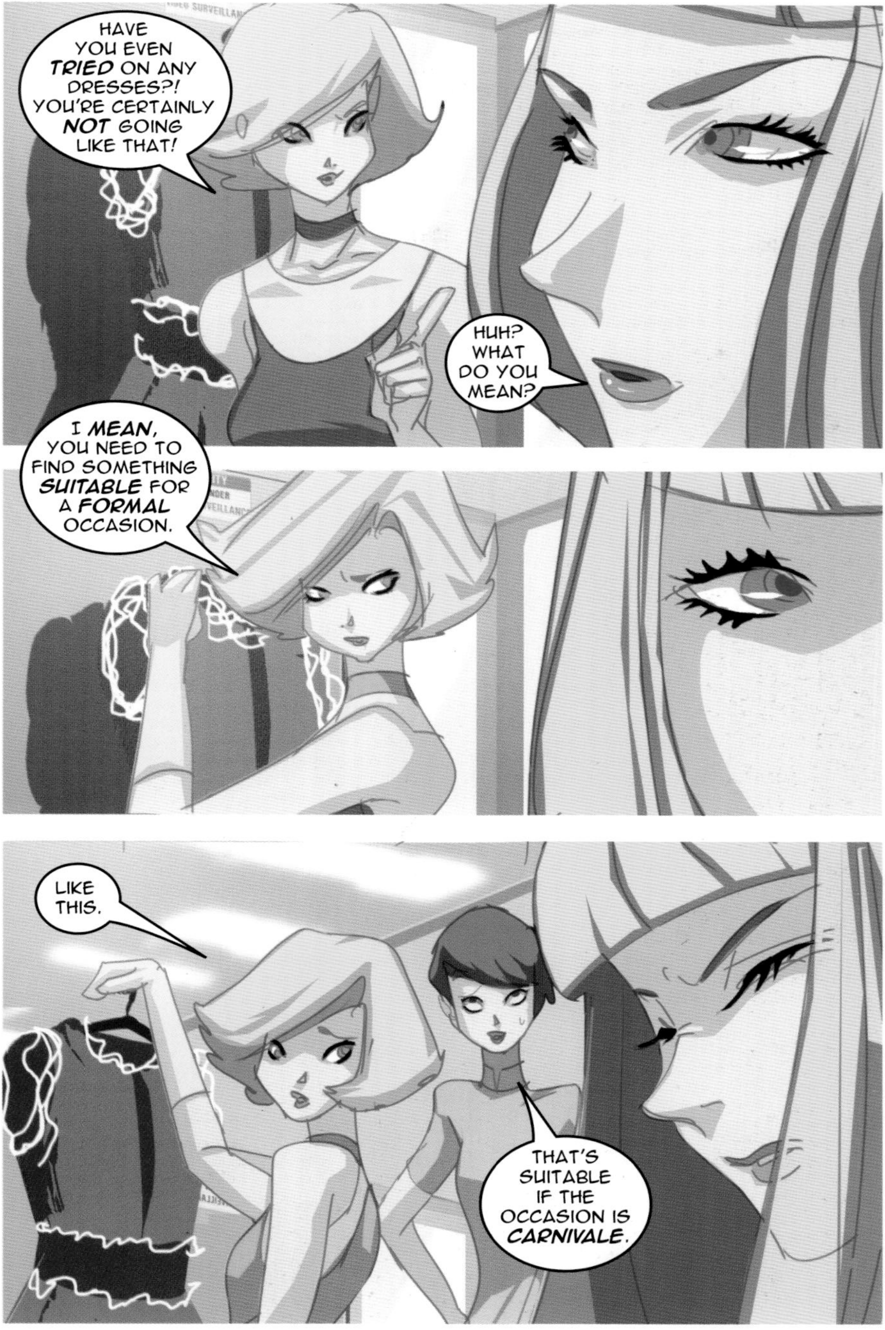
HAVE YOU EVEN TRIED ON ANY DRESSES?! YOU'RE CERTAINLY NOT GOING LIKE THAT!
HUH? WHAT DO YOU MEAN?
I MEAN, YOU NEED TO FIND SOMETHING SUITABLE FOR A FORMAL OCCASION.
LIKE THIS.
THAT'S SUITABLE IF THE OCCASION IS CARNIVALE.

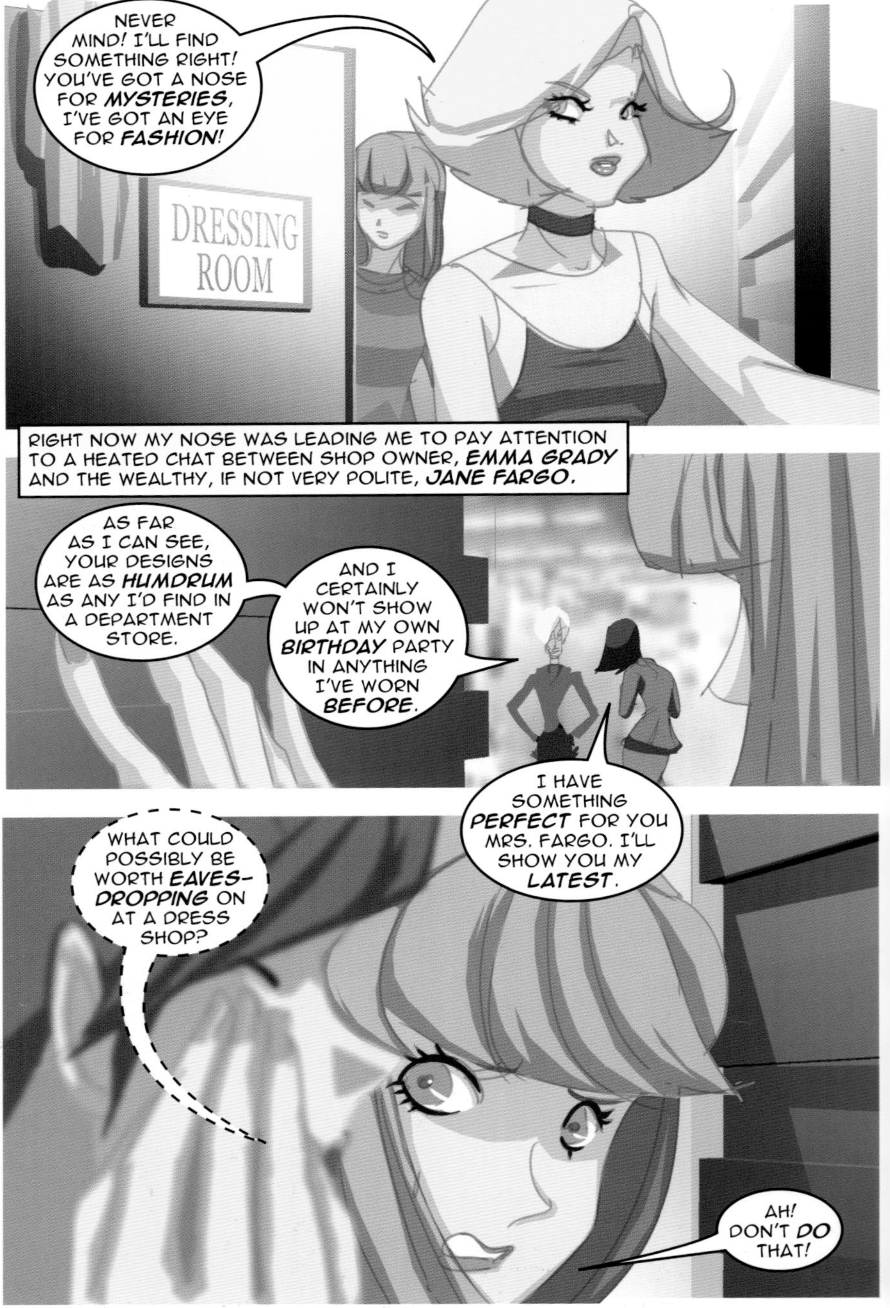
NEVER MIND! I'LL FIND SOMETHING RIGHT! YOU'VE GOT A NOSE FOR MYSTERIES, I'VE GOT AN EYE FOR FASHION!
DRESSING ROOM
RIGHT NOW MY NOSE WAS LEADING ME TO PAY ATTENTION TO A HEATED CHAT BETWEEN SHOP OWNER, EMMA GRADY AND THE WEALTHY, IF NOT VERY POLITE, JANE FARGO.
AS FAR AS I CAN SEE, YOUR DESIGNS ARE AS HUMDRUM AS ANY I'D FIND IN A DEPARTMENT STORE.
AND I CERTAINLY WON'T SHOW UP AT MY OWN BIRTHDAY PARTY IN ANYTHING I'VE WORN BEFORE.
I HAVE SOMETHING PERFECT FOR YOU MRS. FARGO. I'LL SHOW YOU MY LATEST.
WHAT COULD POSSIBLY BE WORTH EAVES-DROPPING ON AT A DRESS SHOP?
AH! DON'T DO THAT!

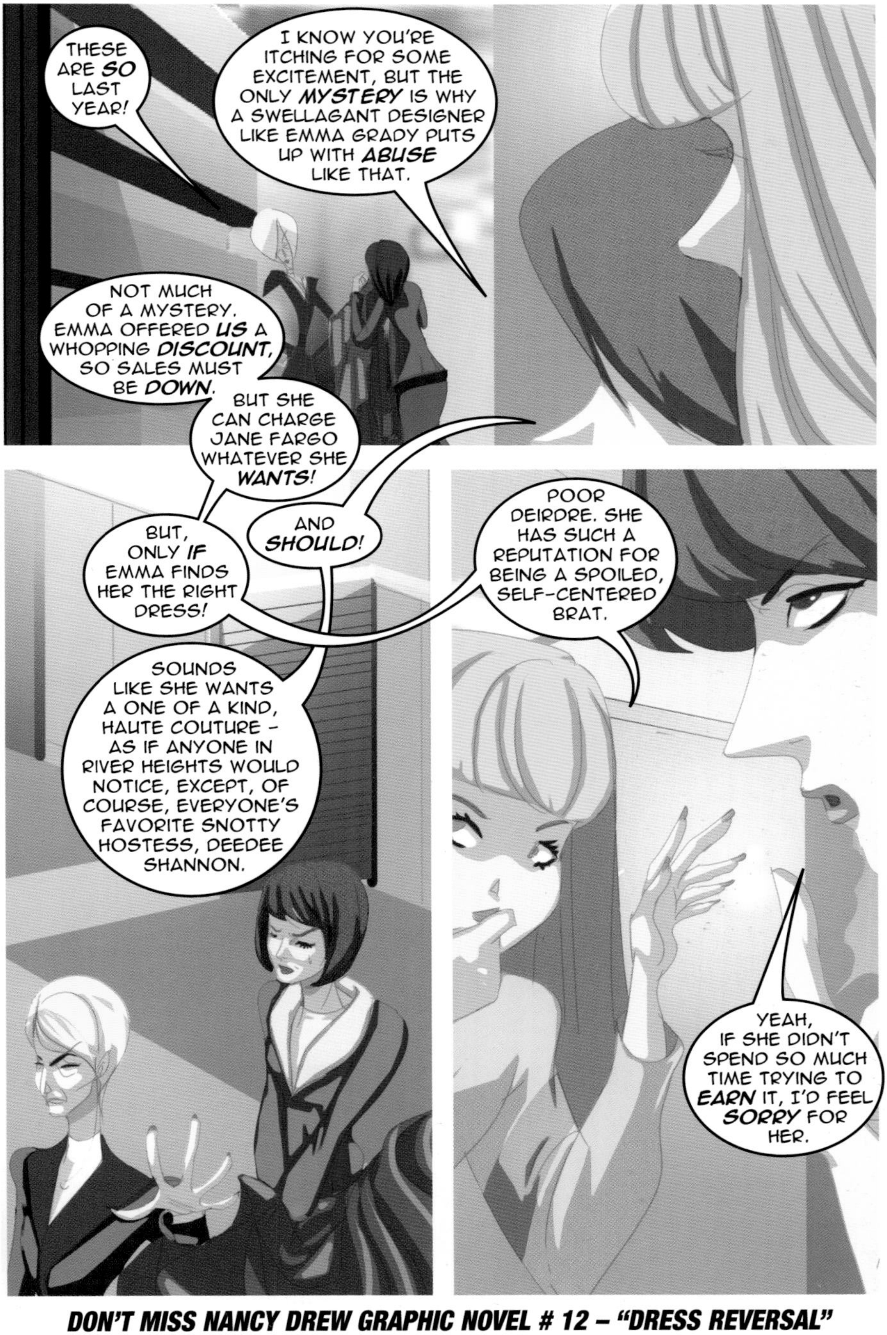
THESE ARE SO LAST YEAR!
I KNOW YOU'RE ITCHING FOR SOME EXCITEMENT, BUT THE ONLY MYSTERY IS WHY A SWELLAGANT DESIGNER LIKE EMMA GRADY PUTS UP WITH ABUSE LIKE THAT.
NOT MUCH OF A MYSTERY. EMMA OFFERED US A WHOPPING DISCOUNT, SO SALES MUST BE DOWN.
BUT SHE CAN CHARGE JANE FARGO WHATEVER SHE WANTS!
BUT, ONLY IF EMMA FINDS HER THE RIGHT DRESS!
AND SHOULD!
SOUNDS LIKE SHE WANTS A ONE OF A KIND, HAUTE COUTURE – AS IF ANYONE IN RIVER HEIGHTS WOULD NOTICE, EXCEPT, OF COURSE, EVERYONE'S FAVORITE SNOTTY HOSTESS, DEEDEE SHANNON.
POOR DEIRDRE. SHE HAS SUCH A REPUTATION FOR BEING A SPOILED, SELF-CENTERED BRAT.
YEAH, IF SHE DIDN'T SPEND SO MUCH TIME TRYING TO EARN IT, I'D FEEL SORRY FOR HER.

DON'T MISS NANCY DREW GRAPHIC NOVEL # 12 – "DRESS REVERSAL"

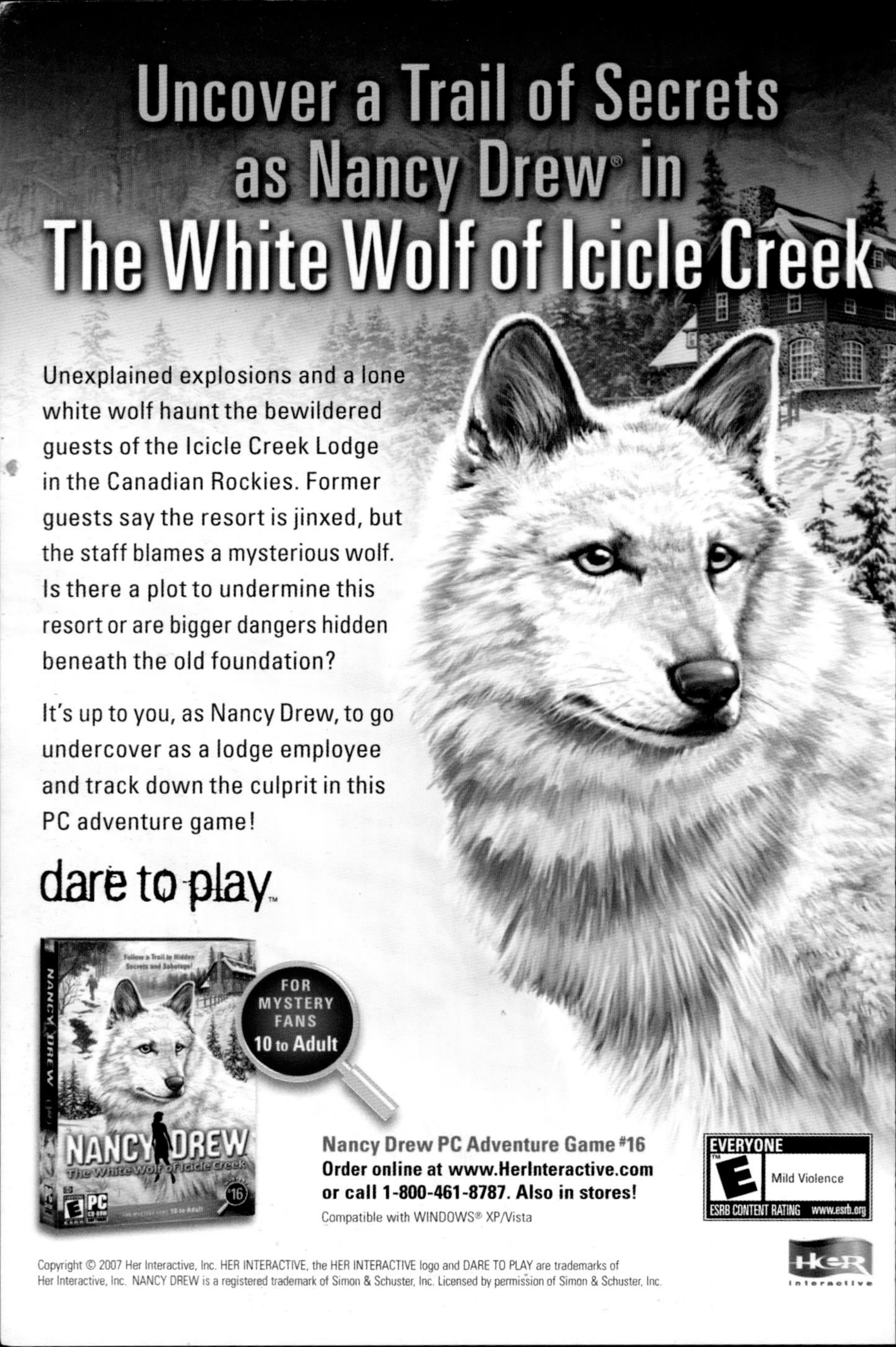
Uncover a Trail of Secrets
as Nancy Drew® in
The White Wolf of Icicle Creek
Unexplained explosions and a lone white wolf haunt the bewildered guests of the Icicle Creek Lodge in the Canadian Rockies. Former guests say the resort is jinxed, but the staff blames a mysterious wolf. Is there a plot to undermine this resort or are bigger dangers hidden beneath the old foundation?
It's up to you, as Nancy Drew, to go undercover as a lodge employee and track down the culprit in this PC adventure game!
dare to play™
NANCY DREW
The White Wolf of Icicle Creek
FOR MYSTERY FANS 10 to Adult
Nancy Drew PC Adventure Game #16
Order online at www.HerInteractive.com
or call 1-800-461-8787. Also in stores!
Compatible with WINDOWS® XP/Vista
EVERYONE
E
Mild Violence
ESRB CONTENT RATING www.esrb.org
Copyright © 2007 Her Interactive, Inc. HER INTERACTIVE, the HER INTERACTIVE logo and DARE TO PLAY are trademarks of Her Interactive, Inc. NANCY DREW is a registered trademark of Simon & Schuster, Inc. Licensed by permission of Simon & Schuster, Inc.
HeR interactive

THE *HARDY BOYS*®

A NEW GRAPHIC NOVEL EVERY 3 MONTHS!

#10 – "A Hardy Day's Night"
ISBN – 978-1-59707-070-6
#11 – "Abracadeath"
ISBN – 978-1-59707-080-5
#12 – "Dude Ranch O' Death!"
ISBN – 978-1-59707-088-1
#13 – "The Deadliest Stunt"
ISBN – 978-1-59707-102-4
NEW! **#14 – "Haley Danelle's Top Eight!"**
ISBN – 978-1-59707-113-0
Also available – Hardy Boys #1-9
All: Pocket sized, 96-112pp., full color, $7.95
Also available in hardcover! $12.95 each.

THE HARDY BOYS

#1-4 Box Set
5x7 1/2, 400 pages, full-color, $29.95
ISBN – 978-1-59707-040-9
#5-8 Box Set
5x7 1/2, 432 pages, full-color, $29.95
ISBN – 978-1-59707-075-1
#9-12 Box Set
5x7 1/2, 448 pages, full-color, $29.95
ISBN – 978-1-59707-125-0

ON SALE NOW!

NEW STORY! FULL-COLOR GRAPHIC NOVEL
THE HARDY BOYS®
#14 HALEY DANELLE'S TOP EIGHT
based on the series by Franklin W. Dixon
UNDERCOVER BROTHERS
Scott LOBDELL
Paulo HENRIQUE
PAPERCUTZ

CLASSICS *Illustrated*®
Featuring Stories by the World's Greatest Authors

#1 "Great Expectations"
ISBN – 978-1-59707-097-3
#2 "The Invisible Man"
ISBN – 978-1-59707-106-2
NEW! **#3 "Through the Looking Glass"**
ISBN – 978-1-59707-115-4

FULL-COLOR GRAPHIC NOVEL ADAPTATION
CLASSICS *Illustrated*®
Featuring Stories by the World's Greatest Authors
THROUGH THE LOOKING-GLASS
By Lewis Carroll
Adapted by KYLE BAKER
PAPERCUTZ

At bookstores or order at Papercutz, 40 Exchange Place, Ste. 1308, New York, NY 10005,
1-800-886-1223 (M-F 9-6 EST) Please add $4.00 postage and handling, $1 each additional item.
Make check payable to NBM publishing. MC, VISA, AMEX accepted, Distributed by Macmillan

PAPERCUTZ™.COM

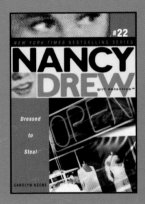

WATCH OUT FOR PAPERCUTZ™

Guess what? If you're reading this, that means you may be a Papercutz person. Don't panic -- that's a good thing. It means you're not only enjoying the latest, greatest Hardy Boys graphic novel, but you're part of a special club that's on the cutting edge of pop culture entertainment.

Let's back up a little. If you're just joining the Papercutz party, allow me to indroduce myself. I'm Jim Salicrup, Papercutz Editor-in-Chief. It's my happy responsibility to produce the best graphic novels for people of all ages. Graphic novels, as I'm sure you're hip enough to know, are simply comicbooks disguised as regular books. Or as some people say "real books."

Graphic novels also happen to be the latest thing to take the publishing world by storm. Just a few years ago, only comicbook publishers produced graphic novels, but now just about every big-time publisher there is wants to get in on the act. And you know, we think that's terrific. The more publishers giving opportunities to writers and artists to create all-new graphic novels, the greater the chances are that we'll get to see some amazing new graphic novels from new writers and artists.

On the other hand, with so many graphic novels being produced at such a rapid rate -- more now than ever before -- it's easy to be completely overwhelmed by it all. How can anyone know which graphic novels to choose, with so many to pick from? Well, we have one helpful suggestion. If you like the graphic novel you're reading now, chances are you may enjoy other Papercutz graphic novels. In the following pages, you'll find some sample pages from TALES FROM THE CRYPT, which features several scary stories within each volume, and CLASSICS ILLUSTRATED, which features comicbook adaptations of many of the world's greatest novels, such as The Wind in the Willows, Great Expectations, The Invisible Man, and many more.

So, check us out. If you like what you see, you may just be a Papercutz person. And, as we said, that's a good thing.

Thanks,

Jim

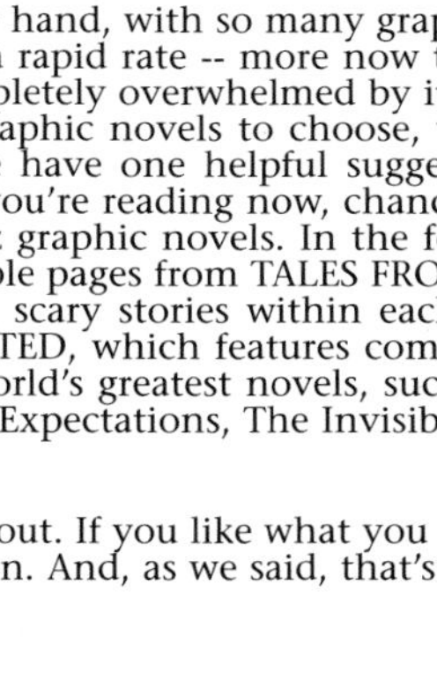

THE OLD EDITOR

Caricature by Rick Parker

Greetings, Fiends!

It's your ol' pal the CRYPT-KEEPER here, giving a guided TERRIFYING TOUR through the SCARIEST GRAPHIC NOVEL ever! It's TALES FROM THE CRYPT #4 "CRYPT-KEEPING IT REAL."

You'll not only find page after page of PULSE-POUNDING CHILLS, but me and my fellow GhouLunatics decided to get all COMPUTER AGE-Y on you! Wait till you see the stories we found on the INTERRED-NET site known as YOU-TOOMB! The SHOCKS and SUS-PENSE come at you FAST and FURIOUS!

But that's not all! Just gaze upon the CREEPY COVER on the next page, if you DARE! That poor guy made the UNFORTUNATE MISTAKE of appearing on a REALITY TV SHOW that was perhaps a little TOO REAL! The show is called "JUMPING THE SHARK" and you can see a quick preview starting right after the next PUTRID PAGE!

THE CRYPT-KEEPER

ALL-NEW STORIES! FULL-COLOR GRAPHIC NOVEL!
TALES FROM THE CRYPT
NO. 4
CRYPT-KEEPING IT REAL
TERROR
AN ENTERTAINING COMIC EC
FEATURING 2 ALL-NEW STORIES BY
JOE R. LANSDALE &
JOHN L. LANSDALE
TODAY'S TOP HORROR WRITERS!
FEATURING...
THE CRYPT-KEEPER
THE OLD WITCH
THE VAULT-KEEPER
PAPERCUTZ

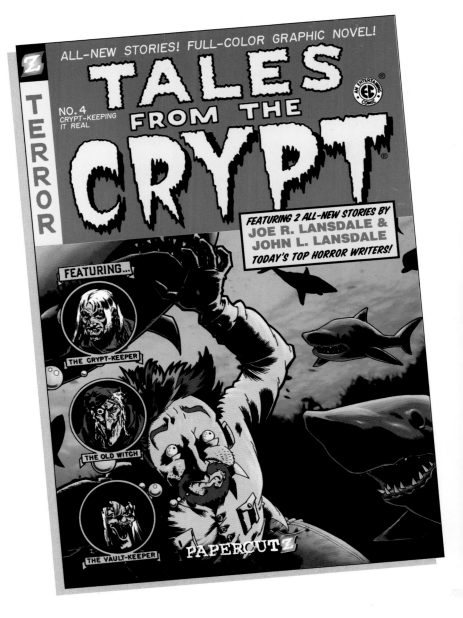

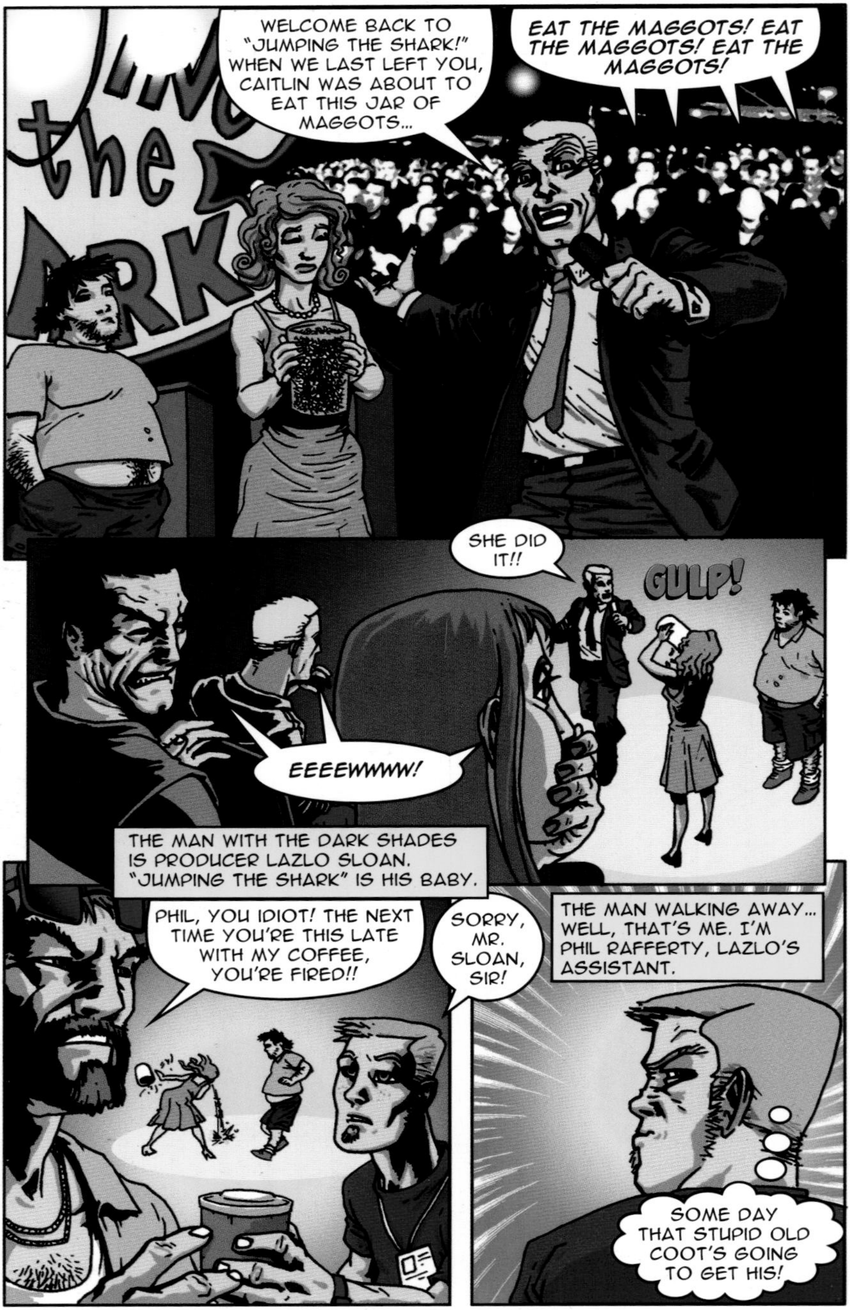

WELCOME BACK TO "JUMPING THE SHARK!" WHEN WE LAST LEFT YOU, CAITLIN WAS ABOUT TO EAT THIS JAR OF MAGGOTS...
EAT THE MAGGOTS! EAT THE MAGGOTS! EAT THE MAGGOTS!
SHE DID IT!!
GULP!
EEEEWWWW!
THE MAN WITH THE DARK SHADES IS PRODUCER LAZLO SLOAN. "JUMPING THE SHARK" IS HIS BABY.
PHIL, YOU IDIOT! THE NEXT TIME YOU'RE THIS LATE WITH MY COFFEE, YOU'RE FIRED!!
SORRY, MR. SLOAN, SIR!
THE MAN WALKING AWAY... WELL, THAT'S ME. I'M PHIL RAFFERTY, LAZLO'S ASSISTANT.
SOME DAY THAT STUPID OLD COOT'S GOING TO GET HIS!

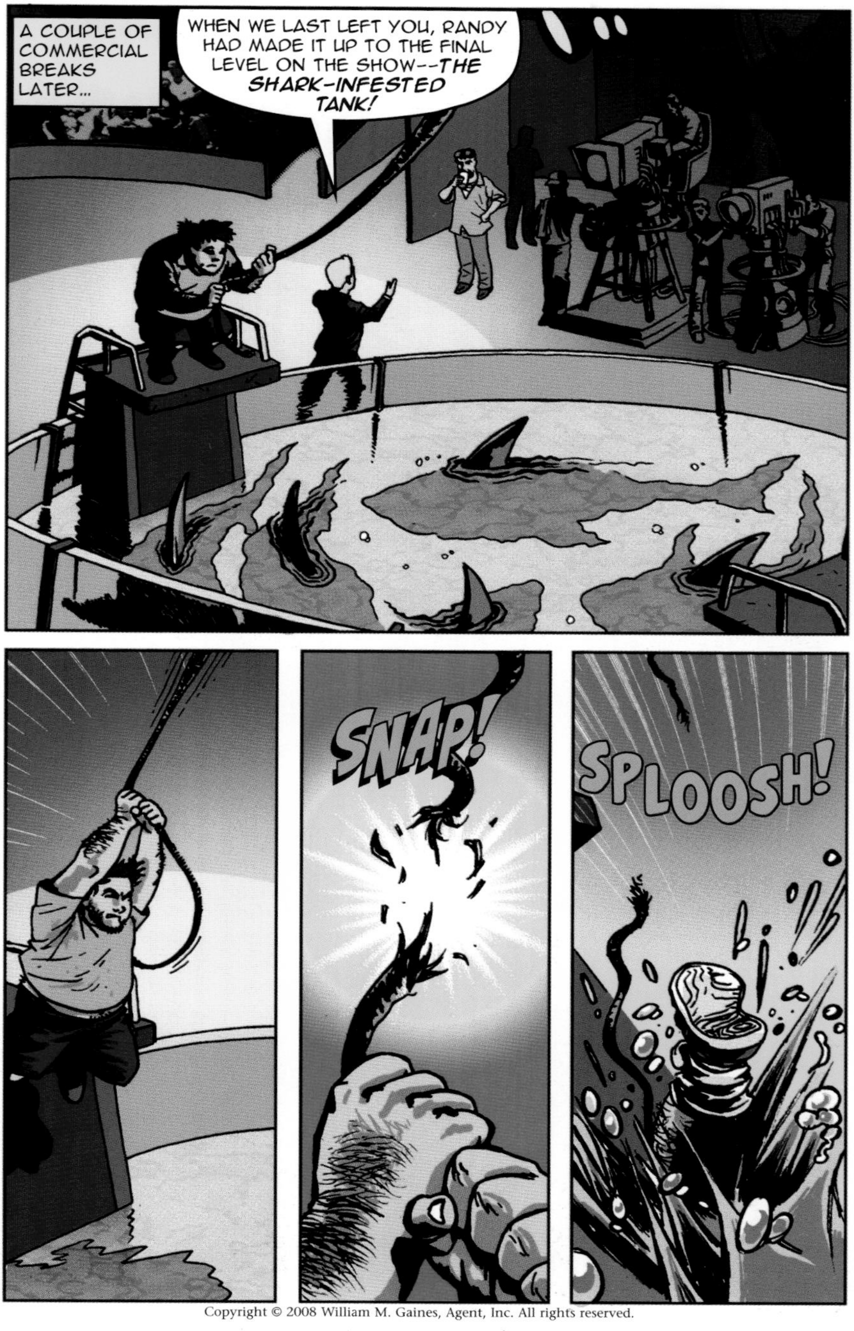
A COUPLE OF COMMERCIAL BREAKS LATER...
WHEN WE LAST LEFT YOU, RANDY HAD MADE IT UP TO THE FINAL LEVEL ON THE SHOW--THE SHARK-INFESTED TANK!
SNAP!
SPLOOSH!

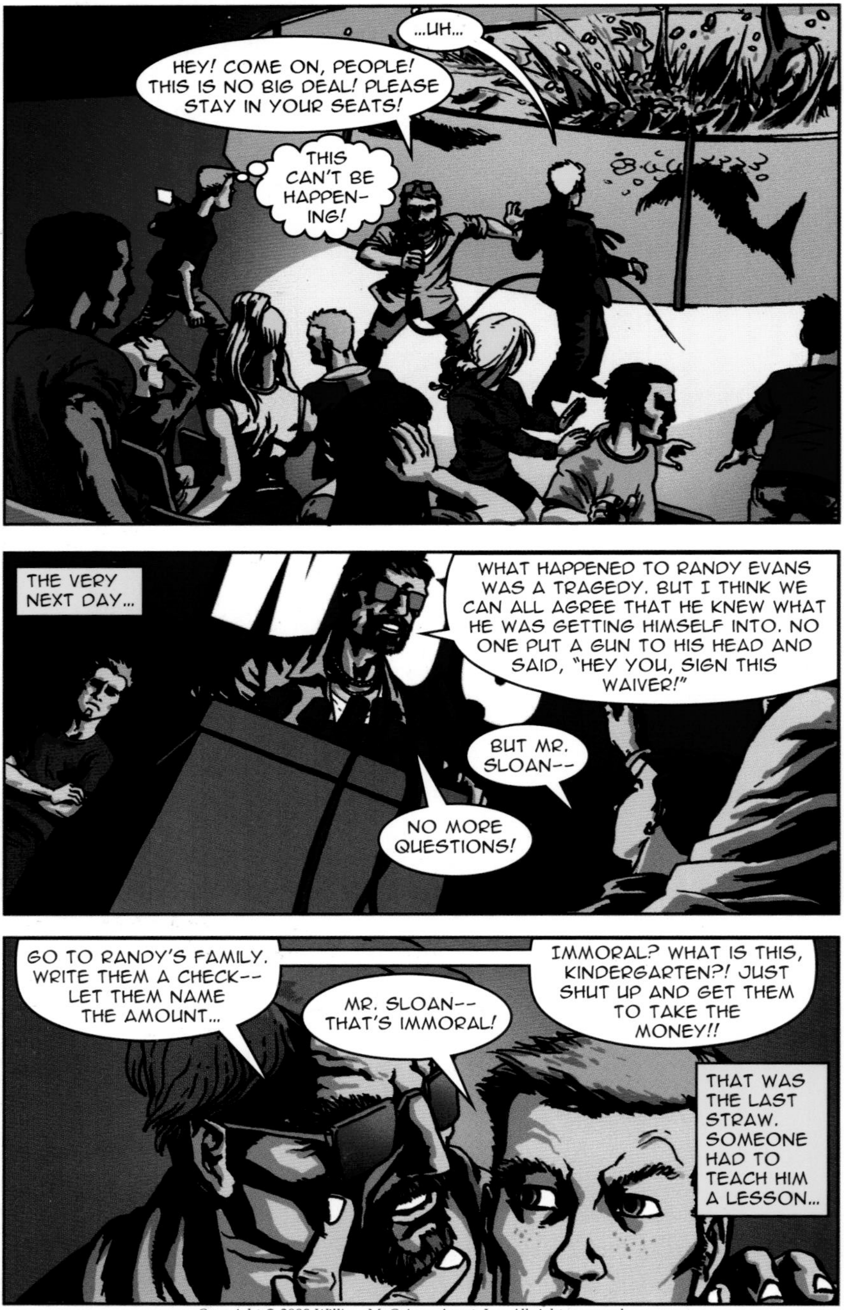
HEY! COME ON, PEOPLE! THIS IS NO BIG DEAL! PLEASE STAY IN YOUR SEATS!
...UH...
THIS CAN'T BE HAPPEN- ING!
THE VERY NEXT DAY...
WHAT HAPPENED TO RANDY EVANS WAS A TRAGEDY. BUT I THINK WE CAN ALL AGREE THAT HE KNEW WHAT HE WAS GETTING HIMSELF INTO. NO ONE PUT A GUN TO HIS HEAD AND SAID, "HEY YOU, SIGN THIS WAIVER!"
BUT MR. SLOAN--
NO MORE QUESTIONS!
GO TO RANDY'S FAMILY. WRITE THEM A CHECK-- LET THEM NAME THE AMOUNT...
MR. SLOAN-- THAT'S IMMORAL!
IMMORAL? WHAT IS THIS, KINDERGARTEN?! JUST SHUT UP AND GET THEM TO TAKE THE MONEY!!
THAT WAS THE LAST STRAW. SOMEONE HAD TO TEACH HIM A LESSON...

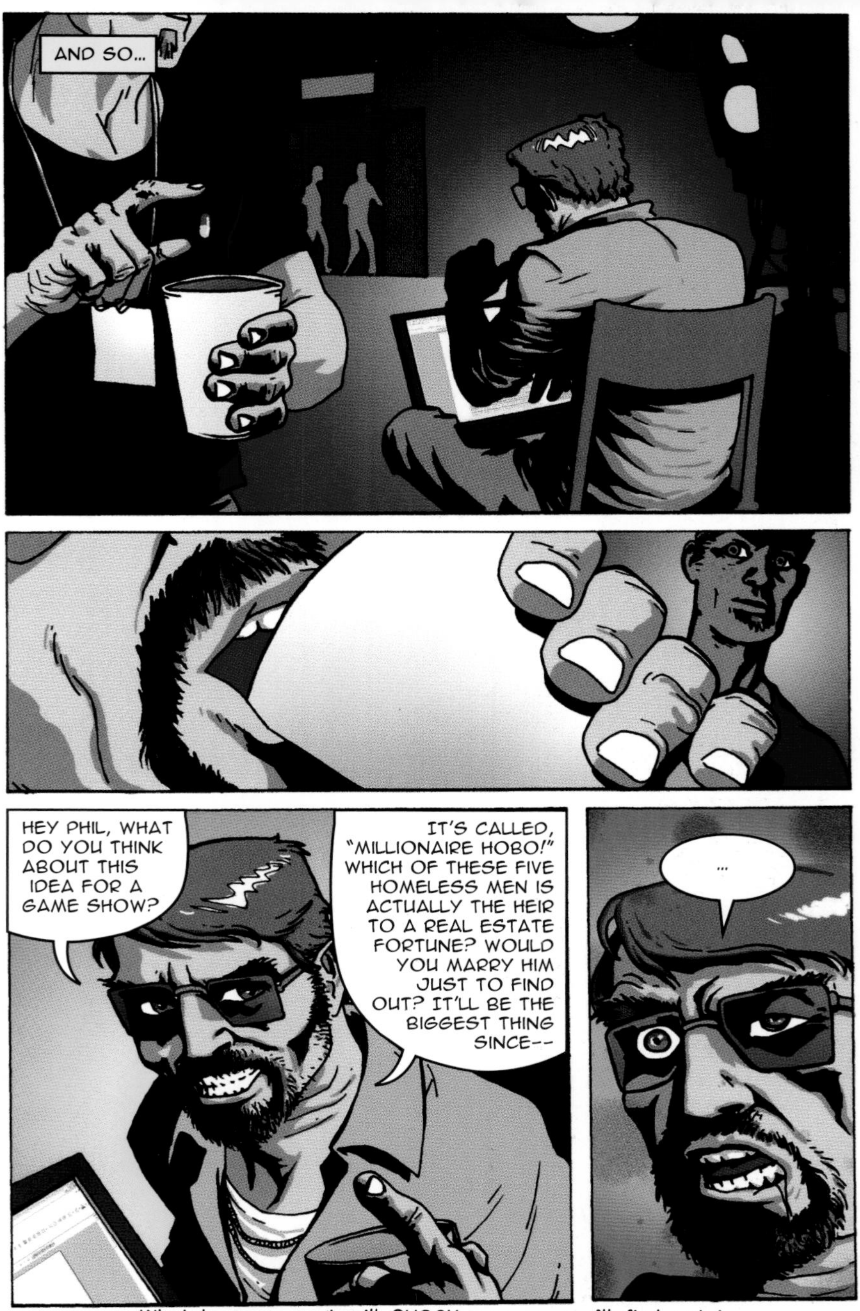
AND SO...
HEY PHIL, WHAT DO YOU THINK ABOUT THIS IDEA FOR A GAME SHOW?
IT'S CALLED, "MILLIONAIRE HOBO!" WHICH OF THESE FIVE HOMELESS MEN IS ACTUALLY THE HEIR TO A REAL ESTATE FORTUNE? WOULD YOU MARRY HIM JUST TO FIND OUT? IT'LL BE THE BIGGEST THING SINCE--
...

What happens next will SHOCK you, as you'll find out in
TALES FROM THE CRYPT Graphic Novel #4 "Crypt-Keeping It Real"!

But in the meantime here's a quick peek at "MOONLIGHT SONATA" also in CRYPT #4...

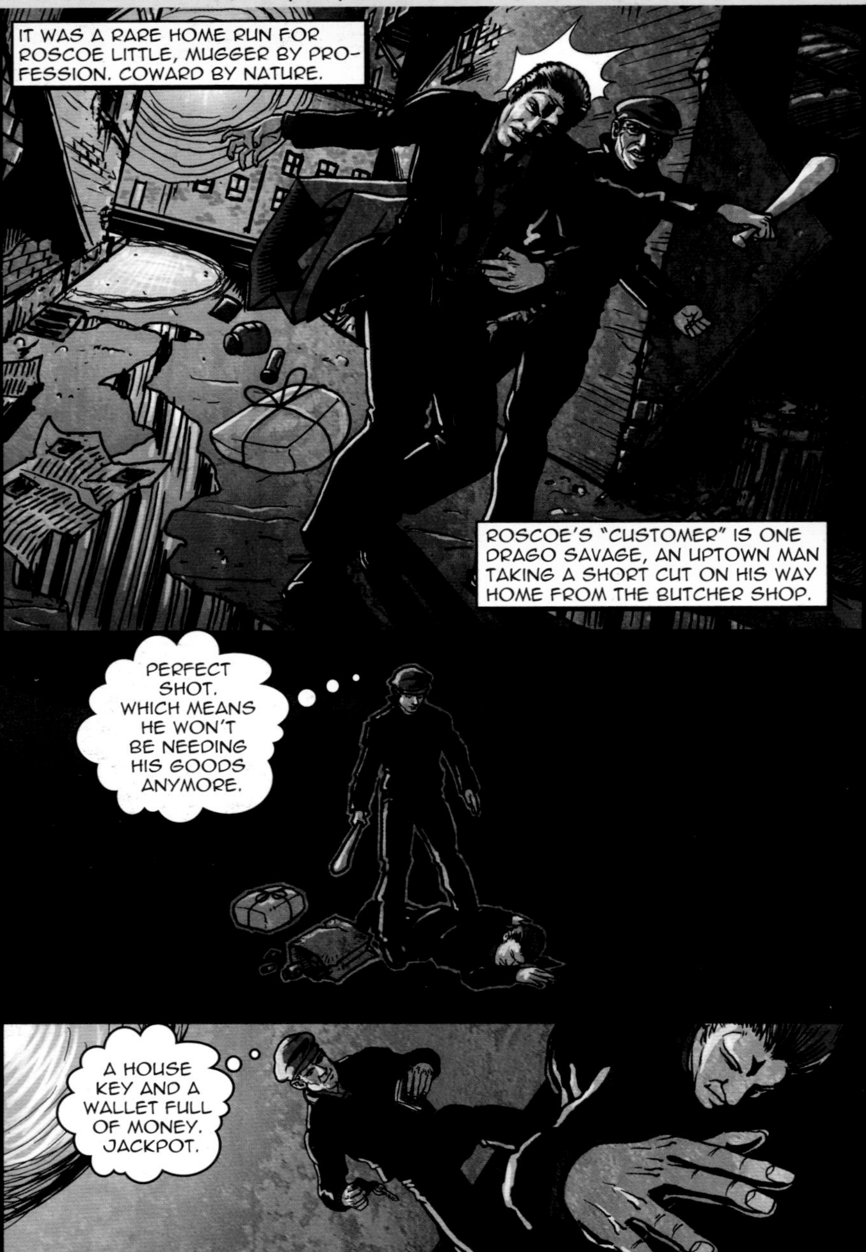
IT WAS A RARE HOME RUN FOR ROSCOE LITTLE, MUGGER BY PROFESSION. COWARD BY NATURE.
ROSCOE'S "CUSTOMER" IS ONE DRAGO SAVAGE, AN UPTOWN MAN TAKING A SHORT CUT ON HIS WAY HOME FROM THE BUTCHER SHOP.
PERFECT SHOT. WHICH MEANS HE WON'T BE NEEDING HIS GOODS ANYMORE.
A HOUSE KEY AND A WALLET FULL OF MONEY. JACKPOT.

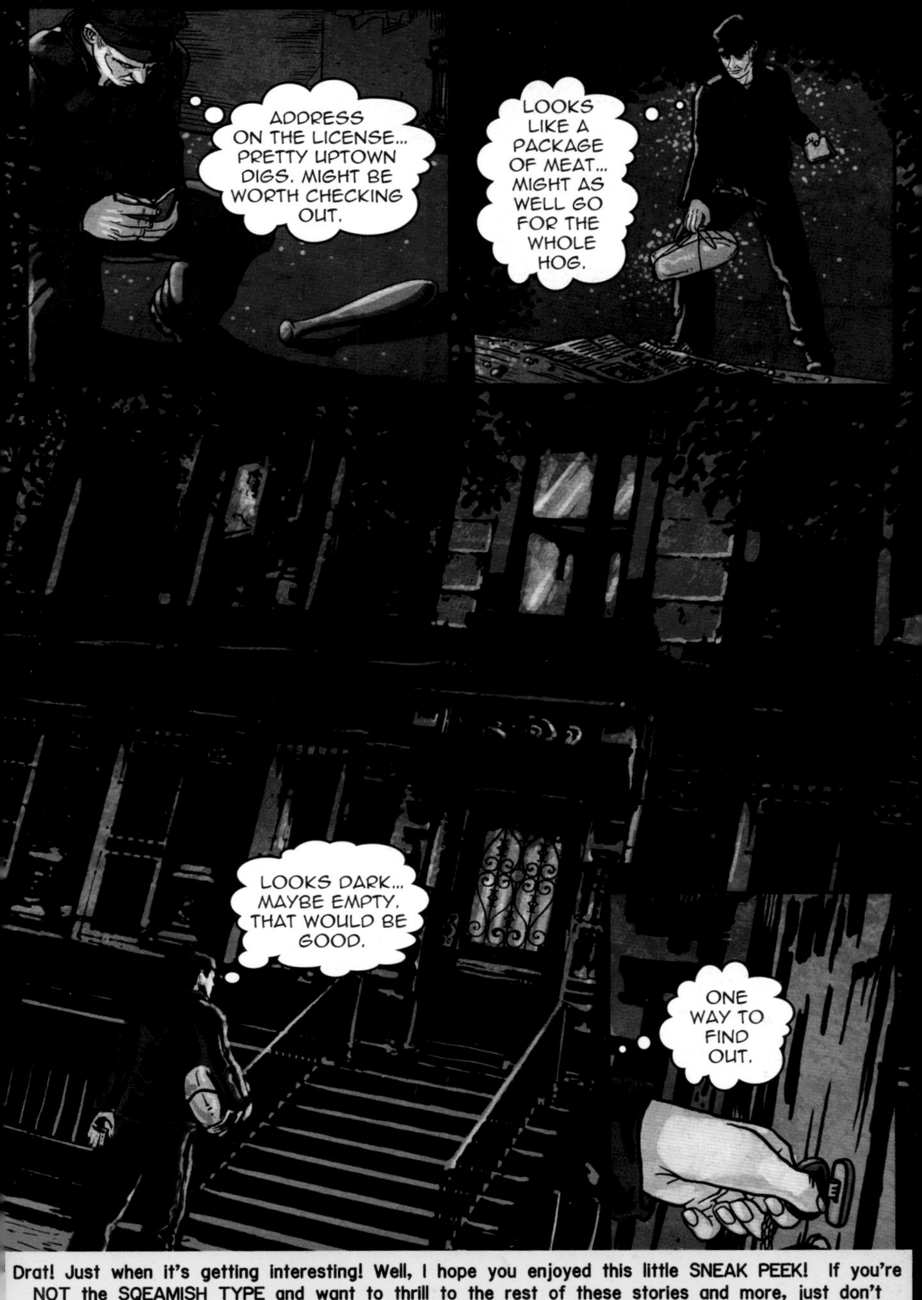
ADDRESS ON THE LICENSE... PRETTY UPTOWN DIGS. MIGHT BE WORTH CHECKING OUT.
LOOKS LIKE A PACKAGE OF MEAT... MIGHT AS WELL GO FOR THE WHOLE HOG.
LOOKS DARK... MAYBE EMPTY. THAT WOULD BE GOOD.
ONE WAY TO FIND OUT.

Drat! Just when it's getting interesting! Well, I hope you enjoyed this little SNEAK PEEK! If you're NOT the SQEAMISH TYPE and want to thrill to the rest of these stories and more, just don't miss TALES FROM THE CRYPT #4 "CRYPT-KEEPING IT REAL"! At BOOkstores everywhere!

CLASSICS Illustrated

Featuring Stories by the World's Greatest Authors

Returns in two new series from Papercutz!

The original, best-selling series of comics adaptations of the world's greatest literature, CLASSICS ILLUSTRATED, returns in two new formats--the original, featuring abridged adaptations of classic novels, and CLASSICS ILLUSTRATED DELUXE, featuring longer, more expansive adaptations-from graphic novel publisher Papercutz. "We're very proud to say that Papercutz has received such an enthusiastic reception from librarians and school teachers for its NANCY DREW and HARDY BOYS graphic novels as well as THE LIFE OF POPE JOHN PAUL II...*IN COMICS!*, that it only seemed logical for us to bring back the original CLASSICS ILLUSTRATED comicbook series beloved by parents, educators, and librarians," explained Papercutz Publisher, Terry Nantier. "We can't thank the enlightened librarians and teachers who have supported Papercutz enough. And we're thrilled that they're so excited about CLASSICS ILLUSTRATED."

Upcoming titles include The Invisible Man, Tales from the Brothers Grimm, and Frankenstein.

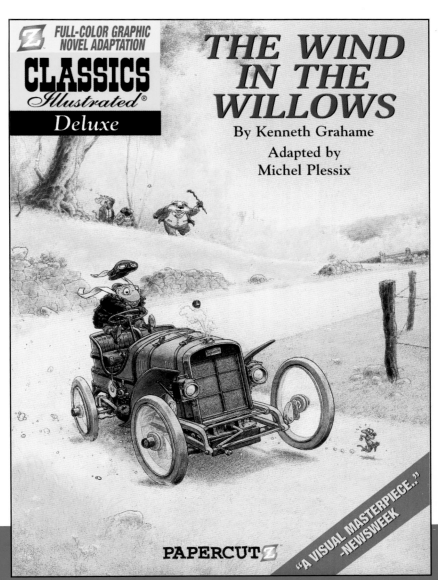

FULL-COLOR GRAPHIC
NOVEL ADAPTATION

CLASSICS
Illustrated
Deluxe

THE WIND
IN THE
WILLOWS
By Kenneth Grahame

Adapted by
Michel Plessix

"A VISUAL MASTERPIECE.."
-NEWSWEEK

PAPERCUTZ

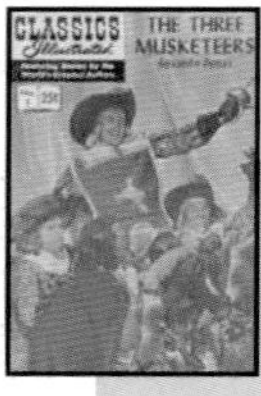
CLASSICS Illustrated
THE THREE MUSKETEERS
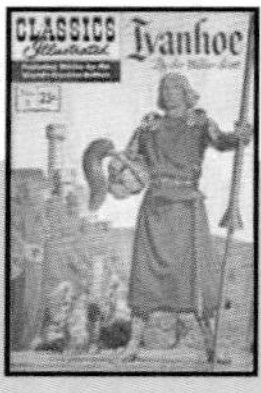
CLASSICS Illustrated
Ivanhoe
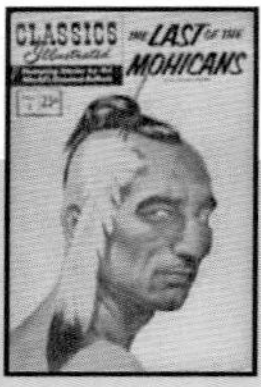
CLASSICS Illustrated
THE LAST OF THE MOHICANS
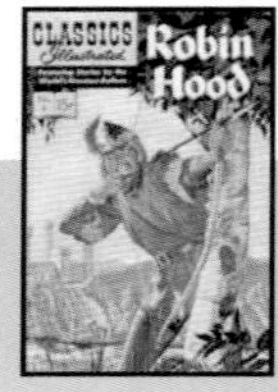
CLASSICS Illustrated
Robin Hood
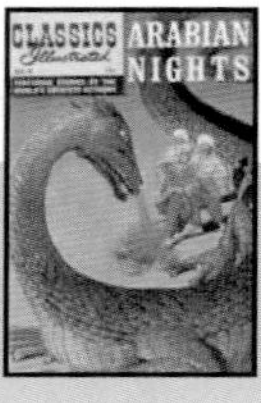
CLASSICS Illustrated
ARABIAN NIGHTS
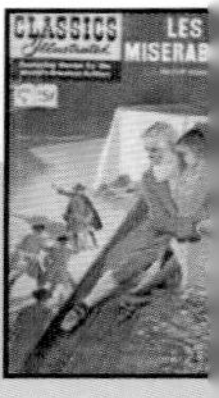
CLASSICS Illustrated

A Short History of CLASSICS ILLUSTRATED...

William B. Jones Jr. is the author of Classics Illustrated: A Cultural History, which offers a comprehensive overview of the original comic-book series and the writers, artists, editors, and publishers behind-the-scenes. With Mr. Jones Jr.'s kind permission, here's a very short overview of the history of CLASSICS ILLUSTRATED adapted from his 2005 essay on Albert Kanter.

CLASSICS ILLUSTRATED was the creation of Albert Lewis Kanter, a visionary publisher, who from 1941 to 1971, introduced young readers worldwide to the realms of literature, history, folklore, mythology, and science in over 200 titles in such comicbook series as CLASSICS ILLUSTRATED and CLASSICS ILLUSTRATED JUNIOR. Kanter, inspired by the success of the first comicbooks published in the early 30s and late 40s, believed he

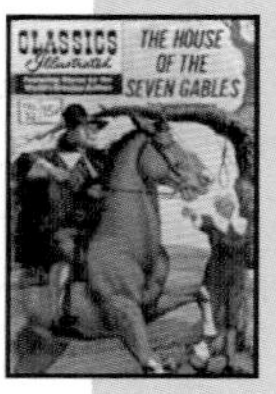
CLASSICS Illustrated
THE HOUSE OF THE SEVEN GABLES
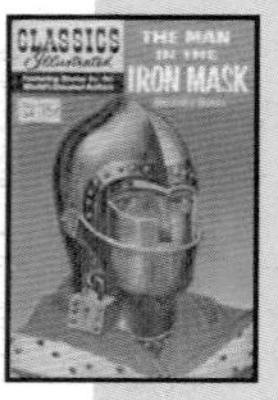
CLASSICS Illustrated
THE MAN IN THE IRON MASK
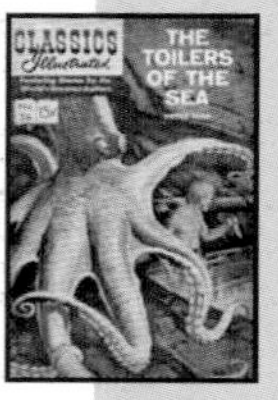
CLASSICS Illustrated
THE TOILERS OF THE SEA
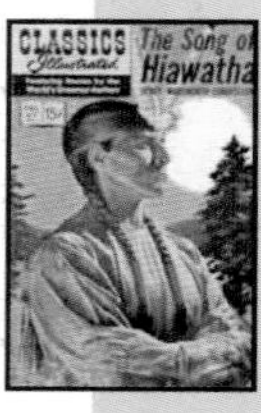
CLASSICS Illustrated
The Song of Hiawatha

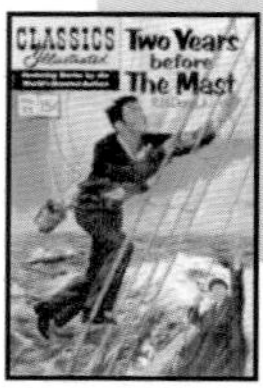
CLASSICS Illustrated
Two Years before The Mast
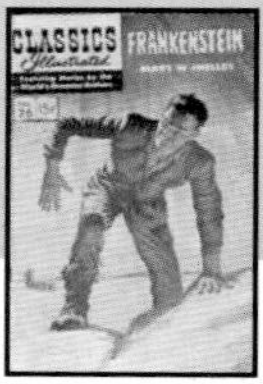
CLASSICS Illustrated
FRANKENSTEIN
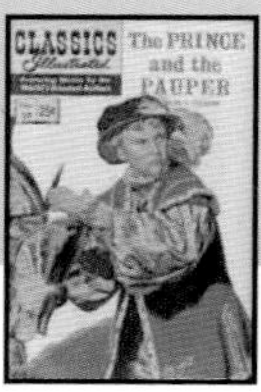
CLASSICS Illustrated
The PRINCE and the PAUPER
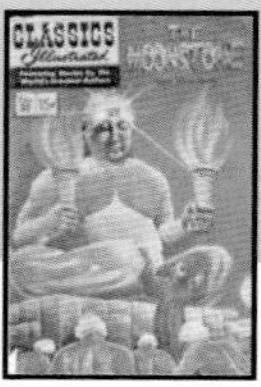
CLASSICS Illustrated
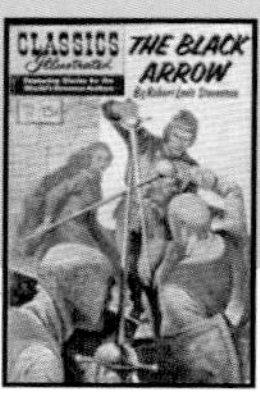
CLASSICS Illustrated
THE BLACK ARROW
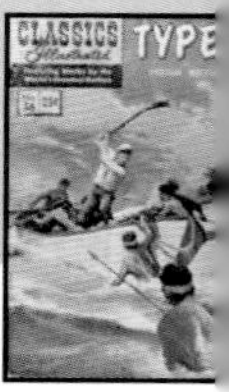
CLASSICS Illustrated

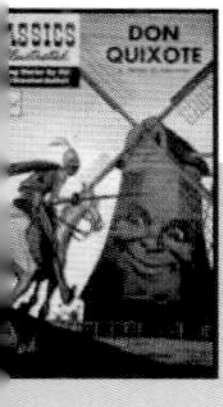
DON
QUIXOTE

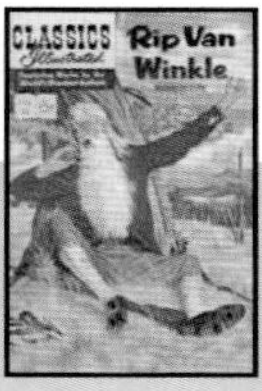
CLASSICS Illustrated
Rip Van
Winkle

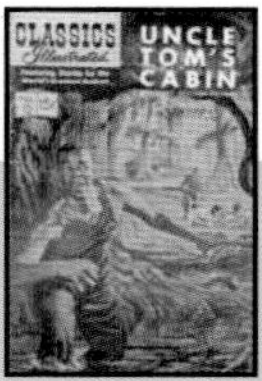
CLASSICS Illustrated
UNCLE
TOM'S
CABIN

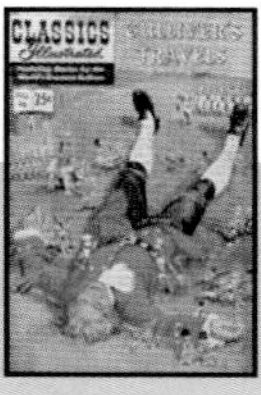
CLASSICS Illustrated

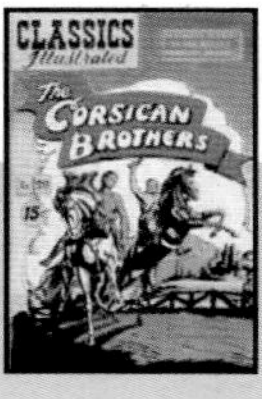
CLASSICS Illustrated
The
CORSICAN
BROTHERS

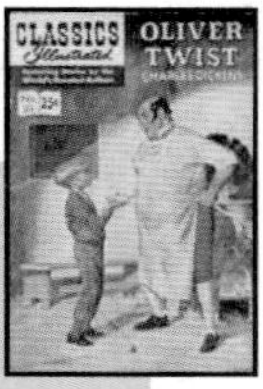
CLASSICS Illustrated
OLIVER
TWIST

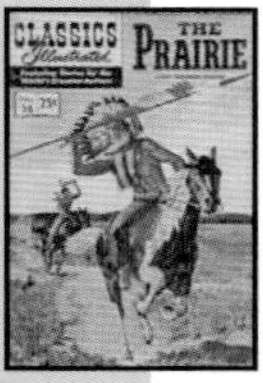
CLASSICS Illustrated
THE
PRAIRIE

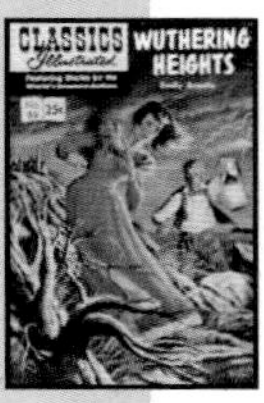
CLASSICS Illustrated
WUTHERING
HEIGHTS

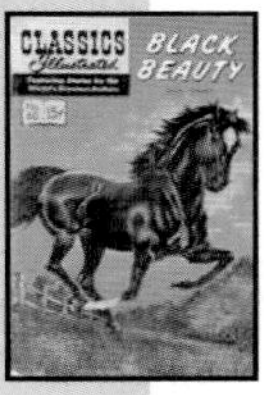
CLASSICS Illustrated
BLACK
BEAUTY

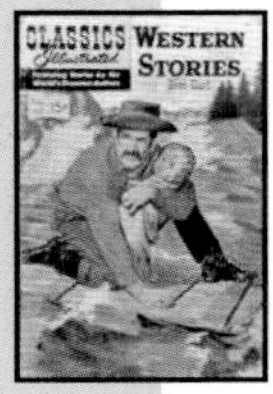
CLASSICS Illustrated
WESTERN
STORIES

could use the same medium to introduce young readers to the world of great literature. CLASSIC COMICS (later changed to CLASSICS ILLUSTRATED in 1947) was launched in 1941, and soon the comicbook adaptations of Shakespeare, Stevenson, Twain, Verne, and other authors, were being used in schools and endorsed by educators.

CLASSICS ILLUSTRATED was translated and distributed in countries such as Canada, Great Britain, the Netherlands, Greece, Brazil, Mexico, and Australia. The genial publisher was hailed abroad as "Papa Klassiker." By the beginning of the 1960s, CLASSICS ILLUSTRATED was the largest childrens publication in the world. The original CLASSICS ILLUSTRATED series adapted into comics 169 titles; among these were Frankenstein, 20,000 Leagues Under the Sea, Treasure Island, Julius Caesar, and Faust.

Albert L. Kanter died, March 17, 1973, leaving behind a rich legacy for the millions of readers whose imaginations were awakened by CLASSICS ILLUSTRATED.

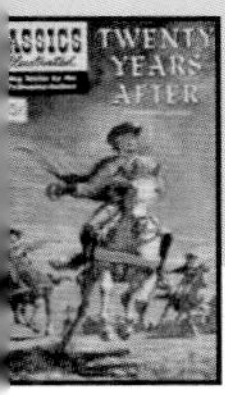
TWENTY
YEARS
AFTER

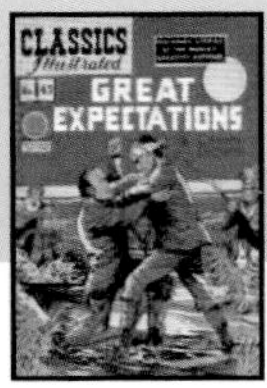
CLASSICS Illustrated
GREAT
EXPECTATIONS

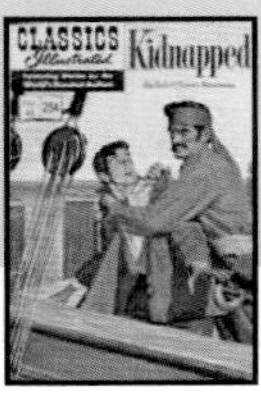
CLASSICS Illustrated
Kidnapped

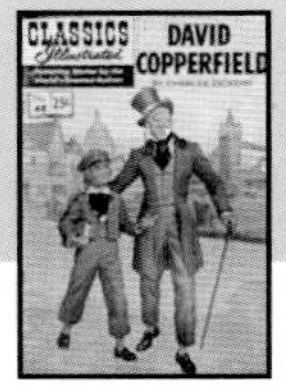
CLASSICS Illustrated
DAVID
COPPERFIELD

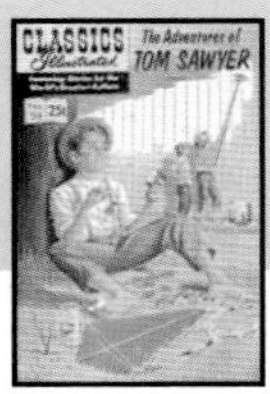
CLASSICS Illustrated
The Adventures of
TOM SAWYER

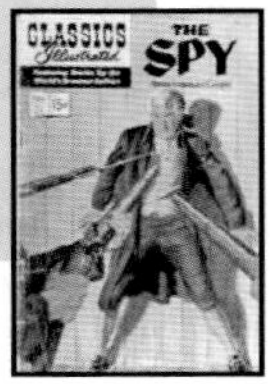
CLASSICS Illustrated
THE
SPY

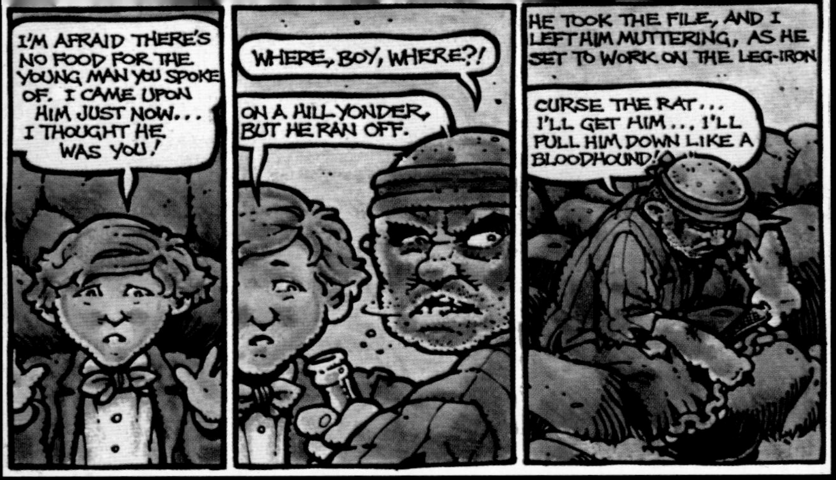
I'M AFRAID THERE'S NO FOOD FOR THE YOUNG MAN YOU SPOKE OF. I CAME UPON HIM JUST NOW... I THOUGHT HE WAS YOU!
WHERE, BOY, WHERE?!
ON A HILL YONDER, BUT HE RAN OFF.
HE TOOK THE FILE, AND I LEFT HIM MUTTERING, AS HE SET TO WORK ON THE LEG-IRON
CURSE THE RAT... I'LL GET HIM..., I'LL PULL HIM DOWN LIKE A BLOODHOUND!

CLASSICS ILLUSTRATED was re-launched in 1990 in graphic novel/book form by the Berkley Publishing Group and First Publishing, Inc. featuring all-new adaptations by such top graphic novelists as Rick Geary, Bill Sienkiewicz, Kyle Baker, Gahan Wilson, and others. "First had the right idea, they just came out about 15 years too soon. Now bookstores are ready for graphic novels such as these," Jim explains. Many of these excellent adaptations have been acquired by Papercutz and will make up the new series of CLASSICS ILLUSTRATED titles.

The first volume of the new CLASSICS ILLUSTRATED series presents graphic novelist Rick Geary's adaptation of "Great Expectations" by Charles Dickens. The bittersweet tale of one boy's adolescence, and of the choices he makes to shape his destiny. Into an engrossing mystery, Dickens weaves a heartfelt inquiry into morals and virtues-as the orphan Pip, the convict Magwitch, the beautiful Estella, the bitter Miss Havisham, the goodhearted Biddy, the kind Joe and other memorable characters entwine in a battle of human nature. Rick Geary's delightful illustrations capture the newfound awe and frustrations of young Pip as he comes of age, and begins to understand the opportunities that life presents.

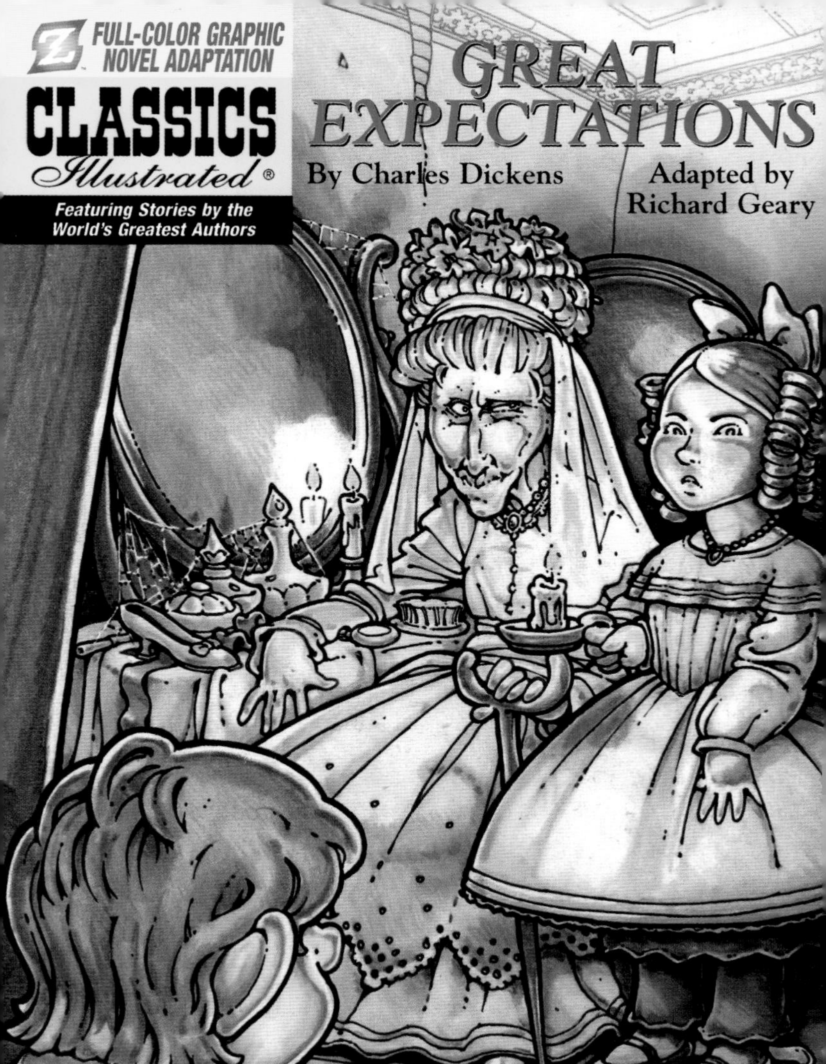
FULL-COLOR GRAPHIC NOVEL ADAPTATION
CLASSICS Illustrated®
Featuring Stories by the World's Greatest Authors
GREAT EXPECTATIONS
By Charles Dickens
Adapted by Richard Geary
PAPERCUTZ

Here is a page of CLASSICS ILLUSTRATED #1 "Great Expectations" by Charles Dickens, as adapted by Rick Geary.

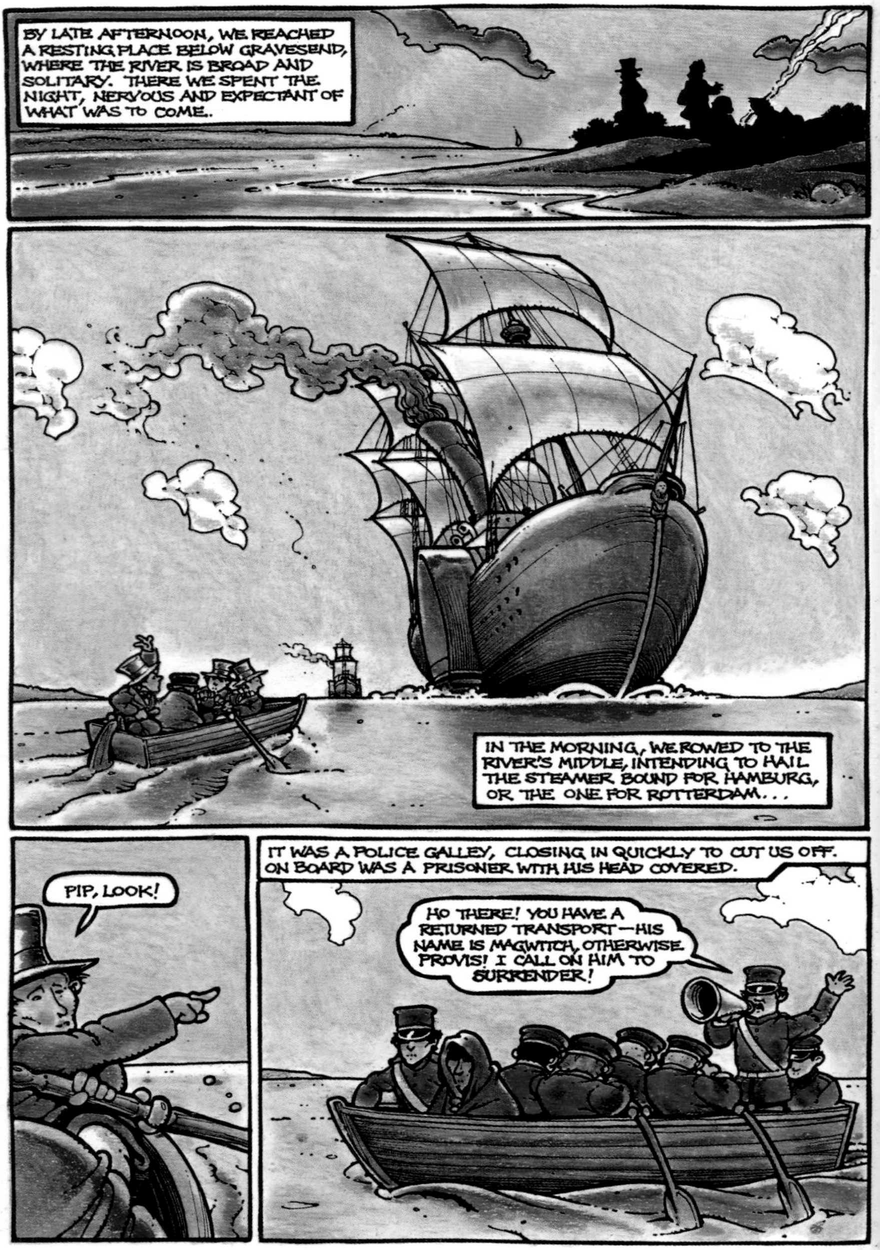

BY LATE AFTERNOON, WE REACHED A RESTING PLACE BELOW GRAVESEND, WHERE THE RIVER IS BROAD AND SOLITARY. THERE WE SPENT THE NIGHT, NERVOUS AND EXPECTANT OF WHAT WAS TO COME.
IN THE MORNING, WE ROWED TO THE RIVER'S MIDDLE, INTENDING TO HAIL THE STEAMER BOUND FOR HAMBURG, OR THE ONE FOR ROTTERDAM...
PIP, LOOK!
IT WAS A POLICE GALLEY, CLOSING IN QUICKLY TO CUT US OFF. ON BOARD WAS A PRISONER WITH HIS HEAD COVERED.
HO THERE! YOU HAVE A RETURNED TRANSPORT—HIS NAME IS MAGWITCH, OTHERWISE PROVIS! I CALL ON HIM TO SURRENDER!